MONSTERS TAKE MANHATTAN

DARREN ARONOFSKY, ARI HANDEL, AND LANCE RUBIN

ART BY RONALD KURNIAWAN

HARPER

An Imprint of HarperCollinsPublishers

Library of Congress Control Number: 2023936920

ISBN 978-0-06-313669-4

Book design by Alison Klapthor

23 24 25 26 27 LBC 5 4 3 2 1

First Edition

Dedicated to all my teachers over the years, especially the ones who I will never forget: Rachell, Mrs. Solomon, Mrs. Lester, Mrs. Bruno, Mrs. Spielman, Mrs. Meiselman, Mrs. Vera Fried, Mr. Franklin, Mr. Manson, Mr. Schneider, Professor Macy Marcy, Professor Will Reiman, Professor John Stilgoe, Professor Alfred Guzzetti, Miklos Jancso, Stuart Rosenberg, and Stuart Cornfeld. Thank you for your patience and for sparking and feeding my curiosity.

—D. A.

PROLOGUE

King Neptune, god of the sea, sits on his throne, ready for his life to change.

He's wearing his toga and crown, gold trident in one hand as the other strokes his white beard. He gazes at the large circular glass tank surrounding him, teeming with aquatic life—manta rays, clown fish, nurse sharks, crabs.

He is trembling with excitement.

Because soon he may finally be able to join them.

"I've made the transfer, boss," his bearded employee says, crossing the marble floor with a tattoo pen and a hand mirror.

"Wonderful." King Neptune takes the pen, feels the weight of the contraption in his hand.

The ink inside it is anything but ordinary.

In fact, it's *extra*ordinary.

And, after a decades-long search, it's finally his.

"Position the mirror. I shall begin."

His employee stands in front of him, angling the large hand mirror toward the right side of King Neptune's neck.

The tattoo pen hums to life in the king's hand, giving off a buzz that hits his ears like a siren song. He stares into the mirror and begins to work, the needle of the pen stabbing again and again into the skin of his neck. It is as painful as ever. Neptune knows this ache well—his body is already covered with art, much of it created by him. But this time is sweeter, because this agony holds so much promise.

As King Neptune shifts the tattoo pen to the left side of his neck, he remembers the first time he saw the power of this ink, back when he still believed he was human. He was a Brooklyn boy, twelve years old. He snuck backstage at King's Sideshow Extraordinaire and watched tattoos of monsters come to life—jumping off the skin of two strongmen and then battling before his eyes.

One of those tattoo monsters was a foot-tall King Neptune, gold trident in hand. Well, he was more like a King Neptune *monster*—god on top, crab legs on bottom.

But whatever he was, he was glorious. And the Boy

Who Became King Neptune was forever changed for having witnessed that greatness.

"Done," King Neptune says, the thrum of the tattoo pen abruptly stopping. "Show me." The employee angles the mirror to give the god a view of his finished work.

The king is so moved, his breath leaves his body. The tattoos are absolutely perfect, just as he'd always dreamed. Simple yet elegant. But before he can bask in the achievement any further, he is in pain again.

There is nothing sweet about this pain.

King Neptune can feel the skin shriveling up on either side of his neck, bunching and stretching just as he'd watched the skin of the Geilio Brothers do a lifetime ago.

The searing pain brings to the surface of his mind everything that happened *after* he first watched those tattoos come to life:

He shrieked in joy, making his presence known to the sideshow performers, including their ringleader, Isaac King.

Since the ritual they were in the midst of was meant to be a secret one, they were not happy to see him.

He ran.

The performers chased.

In the hubbub, he accidentally knocked over a torch that set fire to the sideshow's curtains—along with his left hand—and burned the entire warehouse to the ground.

"Aaaaaaghhhh!" King Neptune hears himself scream.

The pain of the memory is indistinguishable from the blinding agony of the tattooed skin continuing to bunch itself up on his neck.

He tries to redirect his brain, to remember that he is finally completing his transformation into the god he was always meant to be, the god whose likeness he would sit in his bedroom and draw over and over again, thinking, *If only I had King Neptune's power, then Dad couldn't push me around anymore.*

His parents had been angry, so angry, after learning their son had snuck out to the Coney Island sideshow and then burned it down. No amount of apology or explanation on his part seemed to make a difference. Not to his father, anyway.

And he didn't know that he was King Neptune back then—that wouldn't be revealed to him until some years later—so when his father shouted at him, or cursed him out, or smacked him, there was little else the boy could do but run.

He left home at age fifteen.

And he's been searching for a new one ever since.

Now, some seventy years later, King Neptune grips his gold trident and lets out a primal scream that crescendos into two giant *POP!* sounds, which reverberate off the marble floors. There is the feeling of release, and the fiery stabbing in the king's neck dissipates into nothing.

For a moment, he is panicked that the tattoos have leapt off his body to become independent creatures.

There is no need to worry, though. For, as he takes a deep breath, he can feel that his calculations were correct:

Not only can the magical ink bring illustrated monsters to life—

It can turn a being *into* a monster.

Or, in this case, allow a god of the sea to more fully become . . . himself.

"Mirror," the king commands the shocked employee, who again holds it up, this time with trembling hands.

And there they are:

Gills.

Open, fleshy, gloriously real gills.

King Neptune prac- tically bounces off his throne, yelping with glee as he jogs toward the only

spherical tank in the room, this one free of sea life. It's his breathing tank, used for years to strengthen his lung capacity and extend his time underwater. He recently hit three minutes and twelve seconds, but that record is about to seem laughable.

The king climbs the ten-foot ladder—quite quickly, considering his physical body is that of an eighty-seven-year-old man—and steps into the tank, toga and all. He lowers himself down into the water.

At first, instinct takes over, and he can't help but hold his breath.

You no longer need to do that, he reminds himself.

He opens his mouth, lets the water flow in.

It immediately feels like a mistake.

His lungs fill, his head spins, that terrible, crushing feeling.

But then:

His gills open.

Relief.

And joy.

He can breathe down here!

It's real.

He has truly become the god he's always been meant to be.

Which means his new plan can officially happen.

With the ink his at last, and his aquatic form a reality,

6

the god of the sea is going to *create* the home he's been searching for his entire life. Right here in New York City. Soon, very soon, all of lower Manhattan will be transformed into his kingdom.

His Atlantis.

And there's no one who could possibly stop him.

1

CONEY ISLAND IS HISTORY

Eric

It's been a good summer.

No, scratch that.

It's been an *amazing* summer.

And I really don't want it to end.

"Am I the only one who's kinda hyped for school to start tomorrow?" Yvette "Beanie" Ofege asks, standing and holding a remote as she focuses on the rolling robot she's constructed out of wheels and plastic sand toys (pail body, shovel arms).

"One hundred percent yes," my best friend, Alan Yoo, says, in helmet, kneepads, and elbow pads, as he glides past on his skateboard. "You might be the only one on the entire East Coast."

"Yeah, Bean, I'm gonna pretend you didn't say that,"

Ahmed "Hollywood" Wilson says, face in his phone.

Yoo leaps into the air on his board, with an ease he definitely didn't have when the summer started, successfully landing an ollie.

"Perfect form!" Linda "Smash" Cartageña shouts as she skates directly into him, a collision that turns into a hug. "I'm so proud of you, Yooby."

"Thanks, Smashy," Yoo says, and then, as has been their way all summer, they start messily kissing in front of all of us, their helmets awkwardly clacking together. In a weird way, I've gotten used to their PDA. Once fall starts, I might even miss it a little. Okay, maybe not that much. But still.

It's Labor Day, and I'm hanging out with my closest friends at my dad's Coney Island amusement park, which is packed with families trying to wring the last drops of fun out of the summer. Until a few months ago, it was known as King's Wonderland, founded as it was by my great-great-grandfather Isaac King, but then, after everything that went down in the beginning of the summer—you know, finding Isaac's magic ink, bringing our monster drawings to life, accidentally letting things get out of hand, leaving us no choice but to save Coney Island from hundreds of scary Noodle Monsters and their giant Crumple Noodle leader—Dad renamed it after us: Monster Club Wonderland.

All of us—me, Yoo, Smash, Hollywood, and Beanie—had met over the years playing a monster-fighting game that Yoo and I invented in fourth grade. Everyone drew their own monster, with its own specific set of powers and attacks, and we'd have battles, using tetrahedral dice and a spinner and the letter die from Scattergories. It was the best. We were Monster Club, and that game was our whole world.

But now, we've all sort of grown past it. Once your drawings actually come to life, it's hard to go back to the two-dimensional versions. I used to be so scared for us to stop playing, like that would mean we wouldn't be friends anymore, but that's part of why this summer has been so incredible—we've been as close as ever, without a single monster battle.

It helps that we usually meet here to hang, near the side of Dad's toolshed where I spray-painted a detailed mural immortalizing all our monsters—Brickman (mine), BellyBeast (Yoo's), Skelegurl (Smash's), RoboKillz (Hollywood's), and DecaSpyder (Beanie's)—as they fought off Crumple Noodle.

It also helps that together we went through that real-life monster battle of epic proportions. We all became a little famous afterward—me most of all—which has been part awesome, part totally weird. A video some guy took of me on the Parachute Jump facing off against

Crumple Noodle went viral, and I got interviewed by the news, and people I didn't know started saying hi to me on the street, shouting stuff like "Yo, Monster Kid!" or "Whaddup, Parachute Jump!"

It felt really good but also confusing. And I'm pretty sure the rest of Monster Club feels that way too.

Well, everyone except Hollywood, who's been loving it. He's used the attention to grow a massive following on his TikTok account (@RoboKillz, naturally), and it's pretty much all he talks about.

"Awwww yeah," Hollywood says now, right on cue, holding out his phone as he dances around and sings a made-up song we're all sick of: "My latest vid is . . . blowing up! That's right, it's blowing up! And I am glowing up!"

"Congrats, Hollywood," I say, without looking up from my sketch pad, where I'm penciling in Beanie's rolled eyes. I'm trying to draw lifelike depictions of all my friends so I can capture these final moments of summer. I'm still not the best at drawing real people, but I'm less scared to attempt it, which is something.

"You don't sound very sincere, Doodles," Hollywood says, stopping his song but not his dance, sliding one hand along the buzzed swoop on the side of his head as he shimmies toward me.

"Oh, I am the most sincere," I say, looking at him. "I

spend every moment of every day hoping and praying that your videos blow up, Hollywood. That's all I want in life."

"Much better," Hollywood says with a grin. "You know, I've been trying to think bigger than just my account. I want to monetize this thing into an empire, baby! Get my film career going! What do y'all think of this name?" He puts a hand up as if each word is a block he's placing onto an invisible shelf. "Hollywood. Studios."

We all look at him, then each other, then back at him.

"Is that a joke?" Yoo asks.

"A joke? No!" Hollywood says. "It's just a sick name. You don't like it?"

"That's already a thing," Beanie says, steering her beach robot past the line of parents and kids waiting to get on the Twisty Turtles. "Hollywood studios is not an idea you had, it's an already existing thing. There are movie *studios* in *Hollywood*."

"Yeah," Hollywood says. "But I'm turning it into a name!"

"Isn't it already a name? Hollywood Studios is one of the theme parks in Disney World, right?" Yoo asks.

"It definitely is," I say. "We went there when I was in first grade."

And as Hollywood continues to mount his ridiculous defense, I'm stuck thinking about that vacation. When

Mom and Dad were still together. When we were still a family.

I know their separation is for the best—since they made it official, they've both seemed happier than they have in a while. But that doesn't mean I'm used to it. Or all the havoc it's about to wreak on my life.

"Hey." There's a tap on my shoulder, and I look up to see Jenni Balloqui. Until a few months ago, I knew her only as a girl in my grade who was driven and passionate and, well, very pretty. And now she's my girlfriend. It's rad, but it's another thing I'm not totally used to.

"Oh, hey," I say, standing up from where I was leaning against the shed. Even though Jenni's been hanging out with us all summer, I still haven't mastered how to be with her and my friends at the same time. I wish I could be as comfortable as Yoo and Smash, just making out in front of everybody, but I get self-conscious and awkward and end up forgetting how to be a person. Like right now, for example. Should I kiss Jenni hello? Just a hug? High five? Fist bump? Wave?

Thankfully Jenni now knows this about me, so she makes the decision for us, leaning in for a kiss. I happily reciprocate, immediately feeling more chill. "What's up, everybody," Jenni says once our lips pull apart.

"Yo, J," Hollywood says, "weigh in on this. For the name of my new empire: Hollywood Studios."

Jenni narrows her eyes, genuinely contemplating before she comes to a decision. "Way too boring for a company run by you."

Hollywood opens his mouth to fight back but then nods a couple of times. "Okay, okay. Now that's an argument I can respect."

Jenni shrugs. "There's something I need everyone to weigh in on too," she says, using both hands to tighten her already-tight ponytail. "Informal vote: Who thinks Eric should return to Mark Twain tomorrow with us for the first day of school instead of going to this horrible new place?"

And there it is. She's said what I've been trying desperately not to think about all day, the devastating reality I'm hours away from inhabiting.

Yoo looks down at his skateboard. Hollywood looks down at his phone. Smash bites her lower lip. Beanie lets out a huge sigh.

"Oh, I'm sorry," Jenni says sarcastically as she looks around at us. "Was I not supposed to bring that up? Are we just supposed to pretend everything is normal when it isn't? My bad."

"We're not pretending," Smash says. "It's just a bummer to talk about."

"I was definitely pretending," I say.

"Same," Yoo says.

14

Jenni shakes her head and lets out a grunt. "It's not too late for you to change your mind, Eric! Then you won't have to pretend anything because you'll still be where you belong. With all of us!"

I close my eyes and try to breathe, letting my brain fill with nothing but the dings, shrieks, and repetitive melodies coming from the rides. I hate all this so much.

"Jenni," I say quietly. "You know I . . . I don't have a choice."

"But tell your parents that—"

"Nothing I say will make a difference!" I shout. "It's happening, Jenni!"

Jenni looks like I've slapped her, eyes blinking in shock.

My friends look pretty shocked too.

I instantly feel terrible. But, hard as I've tried to avoid it, what I said is the truth.

Tonight, I will be headed back to the Manhattan home I moved into a week ago, living with Mom on the seventy-seventh floor of a luxury condo building in Battery Park.

And tomorrow, rather than returning to my school— Mark Twain Middle School for the Gifted and Talented—I will start seventh grade at Tinsdale, one of the fanciest private schools in all of New York City.

Gross.

After Mom and Dad officially separated, Mom accepted a job offer from a high-powered corporate law firm that had been pursuing her for a while. Fresh start, new chapter of life, all that. It turns out this firm wooed Mom not only with the promise of an incredible salary but also with an offer to fully pay for me to go to Tinsdale.

"Uh, no thanks" was of course my response when Mom first mentioned it. "I want to stay at Mark Twain. With all my friends."

Dad agreed with me initially, said that staying in Brooklyn was never a wrong decision. He's now living in our Sea Gate house by himself—well, him and all his ancient Coney junk—and he wanted me to spend most of my time there. But then Mom broke him down with her lawyer superpowers.

"I don't think you understand what a gift this is, Eric," she said one summer night as we sat outside with Dad eating Nathan's hot dogs. "This is a *very* expensive school that you could go to for *free*. The education you'll get there will be unparalleled."

"I get that," I said, "but—"

"Your mom's right, kid," Dad interrupted. "When you get handed a winning lottery ticket, you don't throw it away." That's when I realized this wasn't a fun night out for our broken family. It was an ambush.

"Why not?" I spat back at them. "Money can't buy

happiness, you know!"

"Maybe not," Dad said, "but it can buy more opportunities. It can put you in the best possible position to succeed in life."

I gave him a cold stare that screamed *YOU BETRAYED ME.*

"Look, Eric, we get that this is hard," Mom said, wiping a fleck of mustard away from her mouth. "How about this: You try Tinsdale for a year. If you don't like it, we can discuss you returning to Mark Twain for eighth grade."

"And in the meantime," Dad said, "you'll come back to Brooklyn to stay with me every weekend. Hang out with all your friends."

It was barely a better deal, but it was something, and I knew fighting them was hopeless.

And now, here I am, having to listen to Jenni make the same argument I made and then try to lift her and my friends' spirits with the same useless compromise from my parents.

"I'm sorry," I say, taking her hand in mine. "I didn't mean to shout. But the good news is, this is only for one year. If Tinsdale sucks—which it obviously will—then I'll be back at Mark Twain. And I'll be in Coney every weekend till then."

Jenni nods and wipes her face. "You're right," she

says, her voice still shaky. "It is what it is. We'll make it work long distance." Even though that's kind of a funny thing to say, considering we'll still technically be in the same city, I get what Jenni means: Brooklyn and Manhattan feel like entirely separate worlds.

Yoo catches my attention, making a gesture with his arms that I find completely bewildering until I see he's mouthing the words *HUG HER*. I give him a quick nod and then wrap Jenni in my arms, feeling her holding on tight.

This is all a huge downer.

"We should meet every weekend," Beanie says out of nowhere. "Monster Club."

"Like . . . to battle?" Smash asks, a note of concern in her voice.

"No, just to chill," Beanie says. "A way to make sure we can see Doodles every week." (Reminder: Doodles is my nickname. Because of my constant doodling.)

"I would love that," I say.

"Word," Hollywood says. "I'm in."

"Me too," Smash says.

"Definitely," Yoo agrees.

"I'm down too," Jenni says. "If that's all right."

"Of course it's all right," Beanie says with a matter-of-factness that almost makes her seem angry. "You're part of Monster Club now."

18

"Excellent." Jenni finally smiles again, showing off her very adorable dimples.

We're all quiet again for like five seconds, which is a lot for us, but instead of feeling tense and sad, this pause feels more, like, hopeful.

Yoo breaks the silence.

"This feels like a school year with a lot of potential," he says.

"You say that every year," I say, laughing.

"Dude says that every *day*," Hollywood says, and all of us laugh.

"Just speaking my truth!" Yoo says, throwing his arms in the air.

As much as I didn't want to talk about my leaving, I'm really glad Jenni did.

Because it's actually happening, and it's probably better if I start to accept that.

Everyone eases back into normal hangout mode: Yoo and Hollywood shoot some goofy TikTok video, Smash gets on her skateboard and tries to beat Beanie's robot in a race, and Jenni sits next to me against the mural wall, looking at my in-progress portrait of my friends.

"You've gotten so much better," she says.

I feel myself blush a little. "Thanks. Well, so have you. Your writing is sharper than ever."

"Yeah, I know," Jenni says with a grin. "So, look, I

can accept you going to this new school and everything, but you have to admit: it's pretty messed up that we did all this work on our seventh-grade project, and now you won't even get the credit for it."

"Uh, yeah," I say, "it's beyond messed up. It's totally heinous." Jenni and I worked all summer on our graphic novel about the history of Coney Island—her writing, me drawing—and it came out really, really well. "But that project was about more for me than just the credit, you know? I loved working on that with you."

Now it's Jenni's turn to blush. I wasn't even trying to be ooey-gooey romantic or anything, it's just how I feel. "Yeah, okay," she says, glancing away. "I agree with you there."

And it suddenly occurs to me that Coney Island is about to become part of my history. It's an obvious thought, yet it devastates me all the same. I pick up my pencil and sketch pad.

"Keep looking that way," I say to Jenni, and I add her into my picture, starting with her dimples.

2

A BROOKLYN KID

Eric

I'm still sketching the next morning, adding detail and shading to my friends' faces as a way to calm my nerves.

It's the first day of school—*blech*—and I'm in my new bedroom in Mom's luxury condo on the seventy-fricking-seventh floor, sitting at my fancy new desk purchased from some store called West Elm. The condo building is in a lower Manhattan neighborhood called Battery Park, which sits right next to the Hudson River. I have an incredible view of the water through the huge floor-to-ceiling window my desk is up against. I can also see past it, to the beautiful Brooklyn that I left behind. Including, in the distance, the Parachute Jump, which is visible on clear days.

I wish I were in Brooklyn right now.

I imagine Yoo throwing on his Kylo Ren bike helmet

before heading to school on his own, and it nearly wrecks me. He and I have been commuting to school together almost every day since he moved to my neighborhood in first grade.

And today that tradition comes to a definitive halt, with me walking by myself to my new stupid school where I know exactly zero people.

My dog, Dr Pepper, a golden cocker spaniel and a very good girl, nuzzles her head into my thigh. I bet she senses my anxiety.

"Hey there, girl," I say, rubbing behind her ears. "Maybe I just won't go today, right? That's an option." Pepper gives an encouraging bark, followed by a whimper. I don't think she's fully adjusted to condo life either.

There's a knock on my bedroom door. "How's it going in there, sweetie?"

"Fine," I say to Mom. "You can come in."

"Hi," she says, leaning up against the door frame, already dressed and put together in lawyer clothes. "You okay?"

It's clear from how she asks that I look every bit as nervous as I feel.

"I'm thinking of missing the first day."

"Oh, Eric," Mom says, crouching down next to my desk chair to meet my eye level. "I know this is rough, and I'm sorry I've put you in this position, but I think you're actually going to like this school a lot. You sure you don't want me to walk you over there, just today?"

"Beyond sure," I say, which makes Mom laugh. "Manhattan doesn't feel like me, you know? I'm a Brooklyn kid."

"Right now you are, that's true." Mom runs a hand down the back of my head. "But maybe you can be a Manhattan kid too. Eventually."

BUT WHAT IF I DON'T WANT TO BE THAT? is what I'm tempted to shout. Instead I just nod.

"You should head out in ten, okay?" Mom stands and walks out the door, ruffling Pepper's fur as she passes. "I won't leave until after you do, so I can see you on your way. Remember: the first day is always the hardest."

"Okay." I love my mom, but that pep talk did nothing for me. If anything, it made me more anxious.

I know what I have to do.

I open my desk drawer and rip off a blank sheet of paper from one of my pads.

I grab a pen and get to work.

Expressive eyes.

Sharply defined rectangular muscles.

Torso of tightly packed bricks.

And there he is, my first time drawing him since I spray-painted him on the side of Dad's shed months ago:

Brickman.

"Hey, old buddy."

I imagine him grunting and giving me a thumbs-up.

Weirdly, drawing him does make me feel better. It reminds me of everything I've been through. I mean, if I can climb a two-hundred-seventy-foot-tall structure and face off against a terrifying monster, I can definitely handle some dinky new high school.

"Eric," Mom shouts from down the hall. "You really need to get going!"

"Here I come," I say, grabbing my backpack.

I glance down at my drawing once more, and I swear there's a look in Brickman's eyes that's like: *You got this.*

Whatever confidence I've summoned quickly ebbs away once I hit the street. Everyone in Manhattan seems like they're in such a fricking rush. It's a little terrifying. There's some of that in Brooklyn, but there's also, like, people strolling on the boardwalk, or chilling on the beach, or generally moving toward their destination without seeming like they're on a treadmill.

I tried to memorize the route to Tinsdale before I left so I wouldn't look like a tourist, but clearly not well enough, so I'm using my phone to navigate the fifteen-minute walk there, well-dressed people flowing past me on both sides like a raging river.

As I'm trying to figure out the next turn, a call comes in.

"Whaddup!" Yoo says as his face fills my screen. He's got his helmet on, the background blurring past as he journeys to school.

"Hey hey!" I say. "I was just thinking about you! Probably shouldn't be talking to me while you ride."

"I know, I know," Yoo says, swerving past a construction site. "But I wanted to check in. Seventh grade, baby!"

"Excuse me," a professional-looking woman says with intensity as she shoves past me.

"You're excused," I mutter. "Geez."

"Man!" Yoo says. "People are rude in Manhattan!"

"They kind of are," I say, shifting away from the middle of the sidewalk.

"This ride isn't the same without you! I was—" There's a loud honk on Yoo's end, and his image jostles around a bit before stabilizing. "You stink, stinky!" Yoo shouts at someone off camera. "Learn how to drive better!"

"Are you okay?" I ask.

"Guess we got some rudies in Brooklyn too," Yoo says. "I'm fine. But you're right, I probably shouldn't be talking to you when I'm on this thing. Go crush your first day, Doodles! And remember: you are a freaking rock star."

"Thanks, Yoo. You are too. Say hey to everybody, okay? Except Darren Nuggio. You can ignore him."

Yoo laughs, then swerves and says "Whoa!" as he hangs up.

I laugh to myself as I keep walking.

3

SKETCH

Eric

When I arrive outside Tinsdale six minutes later, it's even more intimidating than I was expecting. There are these big stone steps that lead to the middle school entrance, with tons of kids hanging out, laughing, sitting on the ornate stone banisters on either side. They all look super confident and disturbingly well-dressed.

I quickly walk past them into the school, where it only gets worse.

The more kids I see, the more self-conscious I am about what I'm wearing: one of my favorite worn-out white T-shirts and raggedy blue shorts. Mom kept telling me I should pick out some new clothes for school, and I kept saying no. I am such a dingus.

After a few wrong turns, I finally find my homeroom and slink down into one of the gleaming empty desks in the middle of the room, trying not to attract attention to myself. Everything in the room looks so new and shiny, it's almost confusing. Like, do they buy completely new stuff for every school year? Is that how it works in private school?

The teacher's not here yet, so everyone's yakking away. In spite of my best efforts not to, I overhear two girls behind me talking about their summer vacations. One of them says she spent a month in a villa in Tuscany, and the other one says her family used to do that when she was younger, but then it "got a little old" so this year they were in Croatia and it was "dope beyond belief."

All I can think is: *WHAT AM I DOING HERE???*

I'm so angry at my parents.

I take out my phone. Jenni's texted:

Have a good first day. Thinking of you ♥

Thinking of you too, I text back. *So far I hate it he—*

"Yo," a voice says from next to me, and there's a kid

with shaggy black hair leaning toward me. He's wearing a T-shirt that says The 1975, which I'm pretty sure is a band, but it's one of those expensive T-shirts made of really nice fabric. "You're new, right?"

"Uh, yeah," I say.

"Cool. What's your deal?"

"My deal?"

"Yeah," the kid says. "Like, where are you from? What do you do? Who do you roll with?"

"Oh. I'm from Brooklyn," I say. "Coney Island."

"Whoa, for real? That's sick. I love Coney. Never met anyone who actually lives there."

"Yeah," I say, shifting in my seat. "It's the best."

"So you're probably, like, pretty tough if you grew up down there."

I'm not sure where the kid's going with this, and I wish the teacher would show up already, but instead I'm saved by those girls behind me.

"Wait," the Croatia girl says. "Did you say you're from Coney Island?"

I nod. She pushes on the shoulder of Tuscany girl. "He's that kid from that video! You are, right? The kid who fought that giant animal thing on the Parachute Jump?"

"I am, yeah," I say. "But it was actually a monster, not a—"

"I knew it!" Croatia girl says. "Right when you walked in, I was like, *that kid looks mad familiar.*"

"You didn't say that," Tuscany girl says.

"No, I didn't *say* it, but I was *thinking* it."

"Aw man," the shaggy-haired kid says, staring at me like I'm a museum exhibit. "I can't believe that was you. You really *are* tough."

I shrug and nod, unsure how to respond to any of this. They haven't even asked me what my name is, or told me theirs. Thankfully, the teacher—a short man named Mr. Stillgoe—walks in wearing an orange suit and all eyes go toward him.

"Good morning!" he says in a surprisingly loud voice.

By the time I've made it through three classes, I'm feeling slightly less disdainful of Tinsdale. Emphasis on *slightly.* I haven't exactly made any friends yet, though a few other people have asked about the viral video of me and Crumple Noodle, looking at me with the same awed expression that shaggy-haired kid and the vacation girls had. It's not my favorite, but it's definitely better than being made fun of. Or totally ignored.

Fourth period is here, and it's the one moment of my day I've actually been looking forward to:

Art class.

This was the part of Mom and Dad's argument for

going here that actually had some sway on me. "You'll see, Eric," Mom said. "The resources they have are going to blow your mind."

As I step into the art room, it's instantly clear that she was right.

The room looks like a professional art studio, with tables and easels and all kinds of ridiculous technology. There's a darkroom and giant poster printers and a 3D CAD printer, whatever that is, and a sign on the far side of the room that says Glass Blower. I feel way out of my depth. Thankfully there are also items I understand, stuff like pencils and watercolor paints and pens and tempera paints and charcoals and oil paints, more high-end art supplies than I've ever seen in one place.

"Welcome, welcome," the art teacher, Ms. Reiman, says as kids walk in. She's in her fifties, wearing a flowing green dress and seeming infinitely chill. "After you put your things down, pick a medium and begin creating. This is about process, not product, so don't think too hard. Just choose a medium that makes you comfortable and go."

I'm impressed to see some people have already started. As I go to put my backpack down, I pass this tall kid at a table who's working with an X-ACTO knife on a sheet of paper, cutting out an intricate pattern of swirls that looks like a whirlpool as he gives off intense brooding artist vibes.

"That's really good," I say. When he doesn't respond, I for some reason decide to speak more. "What you're making, I mean. That's what's really good."

The kid slowly turns his head toward me and blinks. "I'm working right now, man." Then he turns back and keeps cutting.

I skitter away like a mouse.

Not wanting to be shot down by anyone else, I beeline for one of the tables, where I sit and pick up a pencil, my current medium of choice.

I start to draw. Before I can consciously decide, I realize I'm sketching our house in Sea Gate: the two steps in front; the roof, complete with missing shingles; my small bedroom window on the second floor.

"Wow, dude." As I look up, I'm hopeful that it's the cool artist kid, but it's actually the shaggy-haired kid from homeroom. He's sat down next to me at the table, working on something with fine-tipped pens. "That looks real. You got serious skills, Sketch."

"Oh, hey," I say. "Thanks."

"I'm Pete, by the way."

"I'm Eric."

"Not anymore, you're not," he says with a grin. "Now you're Sketch."

"Oh, I—" I'm about to tell him that my nickname is actually Doodles before it occurs to me that Sketch is maybe cooler. And more fitting for the kind of art I'm currently into. I point at his art. "I like what you're making."

With the fine-tipped pens, Pete is drawing a logo for Lil Nas X. The lettering looks ancient in a really cool way, like it was written in medieval times.

"You think so?" Pete asks. "Word. Hopefully my dad agrees. He represents Lil Nas X, so I'm hoping he'll show this to him as a potential new merch design."

"Wait, really?" I say. "Your dad represents Lil Nas X?"

"One hunny percent. He's a manager, represents some of the dopest artists working today. Lil Nas X. Phoebe Bridgers. The 1975." He points to his shirt for the last one.

"That's amazing. Did you design that logo? The one on your shirt?"

"This? Nah, I wish. This was made by Fuller Hopkins. He's a famous artist. You probably know him."

I do not. "For sure, yeah."

"He and my dad are, like, best friends. He even came over for Thanksgiving last year."

"Wow. That's rad."

Even though I thought Pete was kind of annoying when I met him in homeroom, he's definitely growing on me. And I can't believe his dad works with so many famous people. That level of celebrity makes my tiny Brooklyn Parachute Jump fame seem like nothing. He and I sit next to each other through the rest of class, Pete cracking jokes as Ms. Reiman teaches us about tapping into the deep recesses of our subconscious or something like that. It feels good to have a friend.

When class ends, Pete tells me to walk with him in the hall and then he's introducing me to a girl wearing all silver—an expensive-looking skirt, tank top, and high-top sneakers—and a tall, beefy blond guy practically busting out of his short-sleeve button-down. He's chewing on some kind of candy.

"Yo, this is the guy I was telling you about," Pete says. "Meet Sketch."

I'm thrown to hear that: A. he was telling other people about me and B. he's straight-up introducing me by the nickname he came up with.

"Well," I say, "my real name is Eri—"

"Oh wow, so you're the Brooklyn boy," the girl in silver says, sizing me up without a smile. She's really pretty. "Welcome to our world. I'm Bobo."

"Bobo?" I ask. It's an odd name. I'm assuming a nickname or something.

"Yeah. Bobo." It's clear she's not open to any more follow-up questions at this time.

"And I'm Knapp," the tall guy says. "Good to meet-cha. Want a piece of this?" He holds out a bag of the candy he's eating, which looks like licorice.

It doesn't look amazing, but Knapp seems very set on me trying it, so I take a piece.

"You'll love it," he says. "It's from Sweden. Like me. I'm from Sweden."

"Oh wow," I say. I've never met anybody from Sweden. But I do like Swedish Fish. "Okay." I bring the licorice up to my mouth, noticing that Knapp, Pete, and Bobo are all watching to see my reaction.

I take a bite and immediately wince. "Oh my god, it's salty."

All three of them crack up, like it's the funniest thing in the world.

"Isn't it narsty?" Pete says, through giggles. "Knapp actually likes that stuff!"

"It's an acquired taste," Knapp says with a huge grin on his face. "I don't understand why none of you have acquired it yet."

"Because we're not Swedish weirdos like you," Bobo says, reaching up to flick Knapp's ear. "You have lunch now, Sketch?"

I'm still trying to get the taste of salty licorice off my tongue, but I nod. I guess I'm Sketch now.

"Good. So do we. Come." She links her arm with mine and starts walking us toward the cafeteria, Pete and Knapp following behind. As we move down the hallway, people stare and whisper and move to the side, and it occurs to me that I may have just accidentally fallen in with the popular kids.

I think I'm okay with that.

4

SORTING THROUGH THE PAST

Eric

"Sketch? Seriously?" Yoo asks, looking up from an old box he's pawing through.

"Yeah," I say. "I kinda like it."

"But you're Doodles. Not Sketch."

It's Saturday morning, and Yoo and I are at my dad's house in the dining room, sorting through his Coney Island junk for ten bucks an hour. Dad's more passionate than ever about opening a museum to show off all this stuff and preserve history, and thanks to a lucrative summer at Monster Club Wonderland, his junk stash has grown exponentially—he's been buying up all the neighbors' nasty mildewed boxes that were ruined a year ago by Hurricane Zadie, in the hopes of digging up some historical treasures. Dad says some of these boxes have been "absolute gold mines." I say that absolutely depends on one's definition of gold.

"Ahem," I say to Yoo as I kick aside the box I just went through, "may I remind you that we had this exact same conversation about a certain nickname you no longer wanted to go by."

I'm speaking, of course, about the moment a few months ago when Yoo told me he no longer wanted to go by Yoo-hoo, the nickname he'd had since the end of first grade. Much like he's doing now, I refused to entertain the idea. I did come around eventually, though!

"Oh wow," Yoo says, as if I've just blown his mind. "That is a good point. That is a very good point. If you want to be Sketch now, then Sketch it is."

"Thanks, dude."

"You're welcome, Sketch. Sketch Sketchy Sketch-erson. Oh baby, look at this!" Yoo reaches into a box, pushing aside an old rotting wooden picture frame, and pulls out a moldy strongman outfit with red-and-white stripes that looks like it's from the 1940s. He holds the ancient leotard up to his body. "I would totally wear this!" Yoo says. "Show off my guns."

"You'd probably want to grow a mustache for the full effect," I say. "One of those ones that twirls up at the ends."

"Oh yeah!" Yoo says. "Glad you mention that, because

I noticed this morning that I have TWO NEW HAIRS coming in. Look!" He leans toward me and points to his upper lip. I don't see anything. "Good stuff, right? I'll be shaving in no time!"

We both crack up.

"All jokes aside," Yoo says, throwing the strongman outfit into his *keep* pile, "Buzzy Hoffman grew a little goatee over the summer. It's very intimidating."

"That should be illegal," I say. "No facial hair till high school."

"Definitely."

"But, like . . ." It's almost too hard to ask, but my curiosity wins in the end. "How is everything at Mark Twain going?"

"Oh," Yoo says. "It's good, it's good." I can tell he's trying to play it down so I don't feel bad. "I mean, not amazing, obviously, without you there, but it's good."

"Nice," I say.

"One thing, though, that I wanted to talk to you about." Yoo leans toward me again over his stack of boxes. "Now that we're back at school, Smashy—I mean, Smash—has been kind of weird. Like, she's embarrassed to hug me in the hall or even, like, hold hands."

"That *is* weird," I say, considering they were making out in front of us all summer.

"Yeah, right?" Yoo says. "She says she feels

uncomfortable doing that because teachers might see."

"Smash *has* always been really shy in front of people she doesn't know well. Remember when we first met her?"

"Another very good point!" Yoo says. "Smash *was* really shy when we met her. Man, she's so adorable, isn't she?"

I don't really know how to answer that, so I sort of nod and shrug as Yoo stares straight ahead, thinking about Smash.

"Anyway!" he says, snapping out of his daze. "How's school for you?"

"Actually, pretty good." I probably would have said that even if it wasn't true, but I really mean it. Once Pete, Bobo, and Knapp folded me into their little group, the week got better and better. They're not replacements for my Brooklyn friends or anything, but they're funny and cool, and they seem to think I'm funny and cool too. And they all have really important parents: like, Pete's dad is that music manager, Bobo's dad teaches at Columbia University and used to be the minister of finance in Nigeria, and Knapp's dad is an ambassador from Sweden or something. Because they're some of the most popular kids in our grade, now everyone else knows me too—random kids wave at me in the hallway and shout "Hey, Sketch!" It's kind of unsettling but also maybe a little . . . amazing?

"That's great!" Yoo says, looking up from some yellowed newspaper clippings. "Glad you made those new friends already. I gotta meet them sometime."

"Definitely. You'll like them." As the words come out of my mouth, I'm not entirely sure they're true, but I want them to be.

"You know," Yoo says, "Jenni was asking me yesterday how I thought you were doing. Have you been, like, in touch with her?"

"Oh shoot!" I say. "I was supposed to call her back last night. I totally forgot."

"Yikes."

"No, no, it'll be all good. It's just been a wild first week, so I . . . Yeah, I'll text her now." I take out my phone, my thumb rapidly bouncing around to form an apology. I meant to call her but then I got distracted by a group thread with Bobo, Pete, and Knapp.

"Relationships, am I right?" Yoo says, shaking his head as he tries on a ratty old fedora.

"Monster Club assemble!" Hollywood shouts as Yoo and I roll up to Nathan's on a skateboard and bike respectively "What what!"

He's sitting at one of the outdoor tables next to a girl with neon-blue hair who doesn't look up from her phone

as we approach. I'm kind of annoyed that he brought someone new to our first Saturday Monster Club meeting, but I try not to show it. "Yo!" I shout as I give Hollywood a hug.

"This is Keiko," Hollywood says, gesturing to the girl, who still doesn't look up. "She's media talent at Mark Twain. But you may also know her as EmptyMirror. She's huge on TikTok. Like, ridiculous. Keiko, these are my boys, Yoo and Doodles."

"Hi," Keiko says, looking up for just a split second.

"I'm actually going by Sketch now," I say.

"Sketch," Hollywood says, like it's a new food and he's trying to figure out if he likes the taste. "All right, yeah. There's a certain dope quality to that that I can embrace. Keiko, forget what I just said. These are my boys, Yoo and Sketch."

"Okay," Keiko says without looking up.

Out of my Brooklyn crew, Hollywood is the one most likely to get along with my new Tinsdale friends. Because, like them, he's very cool. I've never been very cool. But maybe that's changing.

"Who's Sketch?" Smash says as she skates up so quickly she collides with a bench and just barely stops herself from tumbling to the ground.

"I am," I say. "It's not a big deal. Just what I go by now."

"Hmm," Smash says, narrowing her eyes as she takes her helmet off. "I thought I had the lock on one-syllable nicknames that start with S, but I guess I'll allow it."

I see Yoo hovering nearby, waiting for Smash to initiate the hello, since he's unsure if they're back to summer rules or not.

"Hey, Yooby," she says, throwing her arms around him.

"Hey, Smashy," he says, hugging her back. They seem awkward in a way they didn't a week ago, like they're both trying to figure out how to be with each other.

Hollywood introduces Smash to Keiko, who's no more enthusiastic than she was meeting us, as Beanie shows up on her scooter. She's brought someone new too, a girl with glasses, also riding a scooter and somehow just as tall as Beanie. Maybe even an inch taller.

"Good afternoon, friends," Beanie says. "This is Lynsey."

"Hey," Lynsey says, stepping off her scooter and waving. She's wearing a red hooded sweatshirt and black track pants.

"We're both prepping for the NYC Teen Science Competition in October," Beanie says. "Even though she's athletics talent." Everyone at Mark Twain Middle School gets in based on a specific area of focus. I was art talent. "She's on the all-city swim team. But she's also super chill."

Lynsey nods four times in a row, as if to emphasize her chillness.

"I'm here with Monster Club, baby!" Hollywood says, standing up on the table, and it takes me a moment to realize he's filming. "Gang's all here, ready to cause some mayhem!" He aims his phone at each of us before turning it back on himself and roaring into the screen. He ends the video and steps off the table.

"Not my best," Hollywood says, "but it'll probably get some attention. My followers like it when we're all together."

"What mayhem are we about to cause?" Smash asks.

"Aren't we just hanging out?"

"Yeah, no doubt," Hollywood says, focusing on his phone as he posts the video. "I was trying to, like, you know— I was trying to make good content. Get people hyped. Keiko knows what's up."

"Yeah," Keiko says. "People will be into it. Tag me so I can reshare."

"Sweet!" Hollywood says.

I'm waiting in the Nathan's line with Smash and Yoo to get hot dogs and fries when Jenni shows up. She always comes a little late to Monster Club hangs, I think because she wants to give me some time alone with my friends. It's unnecessary but a sweet gesture, and it makes me feel that much worse that I've totally dropped the ball on being in touch with her.

"I'm so sorry, Jenni," I say. "This week has been nuts, and I—"

"Eric," she interrupts. "It's okay, I get it. I just want to know how you are. I miss talking with you."

"Yeah," I say. "I miss talking with you too."

We hug, and I'm so relieved that I didn't mess things up as much as I thought I did. Once our food comes, the four of us go back to the tables to rejoin the others, and all of us hang for a while.

It's really nice, even though there's something . . . different about it. I guess it's that all of us are kind of paired off: Beanie and Lynsey are deep in some conversation about catalytic converters, Hollywood and Keiko are deep in their phones, Smash and Yoo are deep in some flirty back-and-forth, and Jenni and I are deep in catching up. Like, it's all fun and good, but it's not like the group hangs we had all summer.

I tell Jenni about Tinsdale—what I like, what I despise, who my new friends are (I don't say too much because I don't want her to feel left out). She tells me about her week—how school felt weird, how one section of Mark Twain is still closed off for renovation after the Noodle Monsters ran amok last May, how she thinks she's found a new brilliant artist named Tasha to replace me for the seventh-grade creative project (I try not to show how jealous this makes me feel). But something is different here too. With us. It's less like we're talking to each other and more like we're just reporting information.

And then suddenly everyone is leaving. It starts with Beanie and Lynsey saying they're gonna head to C&D Hardware to shop for gear, and then Smash and Yoo say they're gonna head out too (probably to go messily kiss each other in private), and Hollywood and Keiko say they're gonna go produce some video content from the top of the Wonder Wheel. We all say goodbyes, and I'm not exactly mad at everyone for the way the afternoon's unfolded—because no one's done anything wrong—I'm just a little sad.

It feels like we're a knitted blanket, and the stitches are suddenly loosening.

Jenni and I walk along the boardwalk holding hands, the weather still sunny and summery in mid-September. As we pass the spot on the beach where we'd sat together during the Mermaid Parade in June, I remember how Jenni and I had our first kiss there. It was only a little awkward. Mostly it was electric.

"Hey, you okay?" Jenni asks me.

"Oh, yeah, totally." I smile and lean in to kiss her, hoping for that same feeling, the sparks, the excitement. It's not there, though. All I can think about is how dry both our lips are.

"Can you hang out longer?" Jenni asks.

"Ugh, I wish," I say, even though a small part of me (that I'm not proud of) is glad I have an out. "I have to go with my dad to visit my great-aunt Betty."

"Oh," Jenni says, clearly disappointed. "All right."

I kiss her again, trying to ignore that after just one week at a new school, I'm already feeling like a different person.

5

GREAT-AUNT BETTY AND NOT-SO-GREAT TERRY

Eric

Our visit starts, as it always does, with my least favorite part: a sloppy wet kiss on the cheek from my great-aunt Betty. It's almost like the universe saying, "You thought your kiss with Jenni was too dry, huh? Well here, ENJOY THIS INSTEAD!"

"So good to see you, my love," Aunt Betty says as I discreetly wipe my face with the back of my hand.

"You too, Aunt Betty." She's seventy-nine, and she's been living at this nursing home in Gravesend since she had a stroke almost a year ago. Dad had wanted her to come live with us in Sea Gate, moving me down to the basement so she could take my room, but then Hurricane Zadie flooded said basement and made that impossible. Hate to admit it, but I was glad. Little did I know, I'd soon be making a much bigger move than that.

Aunt Betty walks slower than she used to, but otherwise she seems pretty much herself, and I know this because Dad forces me to visit her at least once a month. She's surprisingly feisty for someone who's had a stroke.

"Hey, Tante Betty," Dad says, leaning down to hug her before handing her a bouquet of flowers, another regular part of this monthly ritual.

"Tulips!" Aunt Betty says. "I love tulips! Much more character than roses."

After Dad's mom died when he was seven, Aunt Betty helped raise him and his younger brother, Harry. So they think of her as a mom, and I think of her as a grandmother. She is, as Mom has always said, "a small lady with a giant personality."

"Renee!" Aunt Betty shouts as she swings the tulips in the air. "Get in here, my dear! Can we vase these? Let's vase 'em up!"

"No problem, Mrs. Grossman," Renee says, laughing as she walks in from the hall. We just met Renee last month; she's a newer caregiver at the nursing home—in her late forties, moved here from Haiti like twenty years ago, has a really amazing accent—who's already been deemed by Aunt Betty as her favorite. She takes the tulips and grabs an empty vase off the windowsill.

"I think there's some plant food attached to the, uh, to the bottom there," Dad says, pointing at the stems.

"Perfect, thanks," Renee says with a smile as she takes the vase to the sink.

"If you can't find it," Dad continues, "I hear tulips also like cheeseburgers and fries. So that's another option."

Oh geez. I can't believe I'm related to this guy. Renee is very good at her job, though, because she laughs in a way that seems completely genuine. Which, come on, is an impossible reaction to a joke that terrible.

"So, tell me what's going on," Aunt Betty says, sitting down on the sad little couch in the corner of the room and gesturing for me to join her. I have to say, I never want to live in a nursing home when I get older. Aunt Betty makes the most of it, but it's kind of depressing. And smelly. Not so much this room—since Betty has counteractive fragrances like tulips and her aggressive perfume to mask it—but the halls, the lobby, everywhere else. They smell like farts and death.

"Is business still booming at Wonderland," Aunt Betty asks Dad, "or have things tanked again?"

As Dad has explained to me in the past, these types of questions—taking a positive situation and finding a way to make it negative—are an integral part of being Jewish.

"That seems kind of insulting, Aunt Betty," I say.

"What? I'm just asking a question!" she says, defensively throwing her hands in the air.

"She's not trying to insult me," Dad says. "She's trying to protect me in case things do go bad again."

"How does that protect you?" I ask.

"Well, it doesn't," Dad says, laughing. "But I understand the impulse."

"Good news makes me nervous!" Aunt Betty says. "Like you're just sitting around waiting for the other shoe to drop. But what about you, my sweet Eric? How's this new school? And what's this I hear about you having a little girlfriend? Is this true? My baby Eric?"

I'm not sure which of her thirty-five questions to answer first. "School's good," I say. "Already made some new friends. And yeah, I have a girlfriend now. Jenni. But . . ."

"But what?"

I regret saying the word *but* as soon as it leaves my mouth. Not sure why I've opened myself up to this. Maybe part of me thinks Aunt Betty might have some wisdom on the topic.

"Well, I don't know," I say, squirming in my seat. "Since I started at this new school, it's gotten kind of weird between us."

"Oh, there's always bumps in relationships," Aunt Betty says, clapping her hands together. "That's what makes them interesting! But especially with your first love."

"Was it . . . Was it like that with you and Uncle Paul?" I never met my great-uncle Paul. He died from lung cancer before I was even born, but Dad says he was a wonderful human.

"Well, sure, Paulie and I had our share of bumps! No question. But I was thinking about Oscar."

"Oscar?" I ask. "Who's that?"

"Yeah, seriously, Tante," Dad says. "I've never heard you mention being with any Oscar. Who is this guy?" It's like he's ready to go fight him or something.

"You schmendricks think just because I married your uncle that means he was the first man I ever loved? Give me some credit here."

"I never heard you mention this guy before," Dad says. "Oscar." He drenches each syllable with sarcasm.

"Well," Aunt Betty says, "maybe it's because I knew you'd react like *this*. And also I don't think about Oscar all that much. He's still meaningful to me, sure, but I was so young when I knew him. I went on to have a very full life. Full of schmendricks like you two who I love so much."

"Yeah, all right," Dad says, a small grin on his face. "But I don't need to hear any more about this guy, thank you very much."

"Fine, fine," Aunt Betty says. "Hold on to your limited, myopic vantage point on my life, that's okay with me, my dear."

I definitely wouldn't have minded hearing more, but clearly Dad is sensitive about this stuff, so I'll have to wait till I can talk to Aunt Betty on my own sometime.

The conversation shifts to usual terrain: Dad and Aunt Betty trading gossip about older people in the neighborhood, most of whom I barely know, talking about which restaurants and shops have closed down and which obnoxious artisanal cafés have replaced them, and complaining about the useless city council members who still haven't done anything about the potholes on Coney Island Avenue. This is usually the moment when I pull out my phone to text Yoo or look at TikTok, but instead I take a closer look at the framed photographs on the windowsill, the kitchen counter, the walls.

It's mainly pictures of Aunt Betty and Uncle Paul, twenty and thirty and forty years ago. Smiling, laughing. So much of her life happened before I existed. It's silly, but it never occurred to me that there was even *more* life that happened before the events of these photos. For example, life with this Oscar dude.

And then my eye lands on a black-and-white photo I've never noticed. It features a young girl, maybe five years old, holding on to the leg of an older man in a black top hat. It quickly becomes clear that this tiny adorable person is Aunt Betty, back when she was less than half my age. And the man is her grandfather—my great-great-grandfather—Isaac King. In the background, there's a sign that reads King's Sideshow Extraordinaire. Wow. It hadn't even become King's Wonderland yet.

It's weird to think that my aunt Betty, the woman in this room with me right now, interacted with this man who was alive over one hundred years ago. It's like the generations linking each other from the past to the future. He was a grandfather to her just like she's pretty much a grandmother to me. It makes my head spin a little bit.

"Hey, Isaac," I say quietly, tapping on his face. "That nutty ink of yours is going to cause a lot of chaos in the future. But it's also gonna be pretty awesome." I imagine him winking back at me and nodding, like he knows exactly what I'm talking about.

"It's gone for good now," I say. "Which is for the best, even though it's a bummer. Anyway. Thanks for leaving it for me to find."

Imaginary Isaac bows his head to me. It makes me smile.

I'm still thinking about my family's past—Betty and Paul and Isaac and Oscar and everyone else—when I get back to Mom's condo Sunday late afternoon and my family's present smacks me in the face.

Mom's laughter rings out from the kitchen nook as soon as I walk in, so I assume she's watching some YouTube video.

But then I hear another voice laughing with her.

A man's voice.

I turn the corner and there they are: Mom and a man I don't know sitting at the table with mugs, having a good ol' time together.

"Oh, Eric," Mom says, a sheepish look on her face. "Hi! I didn't think you'd be back for another hour or so."

"Nope," I say. "I'm here now."

We stare at each other for a few seconds before Mom speaks again. "Well, great! This is my friend Terry."

Terry looks about fifty. He's bald, wearing glasses and a fancy-looking cream-colored button-down shirt, and I can immediately sense that he's more than a friend.

"Hi, Eric," Terry says, cupping his mug tightly in a way that reveals he's not as calm as his voice sounds. "I'm Terry Ortega. Very nice to meet you. Your mom's told me a ton about you."

"Uh," I say. "Okay . . . ?"

"Terry and I actually went to law school together," Mom says. "A long time ago."

"Eons ago," Terry says. "Back when dinosaurs roamed the earth."

Mom laughs, and Terry chuckles, until they see that I am not finding any of it humorous, and they stop.

"We, um, bumped into each other in July at this salad place," Mom continues. I can tell she feels bad and is panicking a little bit, and I like that. Because she should. "Terry works near me, near the Woolworth Building, so we . . . Um, yeah. Ran into each other at the salad . . . place."

"Great," I say, still standing about ten feet away, giving them absolutely nothing. "Salad. Cool."

"Oh geez, Eric," Mom says. "I meant to tell you about this beforehand, but then I realized the timing would work out today for you to potentially meet Terry for a minute, so I thought that could be nice. But of course that was a ridiculous idea, and I'm really sorry."

I'm frustrated, even infuriated, by this whole situation, but I'm also embarrassed to be so caught off guard. It makes me cringe to think that a few minutes ago when I walked in, I was excited to talk to Mom about what I'd learned from Aunt Betty, to ask if *she'd* ever heard about Oscar. But then the universe is all like, "Hey, Eric, guess what? It's not only your great-aunt you don't know everything about. Your *own mother* who you live with has secret relationships too! And one of them is happening RIGHT NOW!!!"

I can't get out any more words, and I suddenly feel

a lump in my throat, so I just give Mom and Terry an aggressive shrug and walk straight to my bedroom. I slam the door. There's a reason it's an angsty teenager cliché; it feels really good.

Lying facedown on my bed, I can hear Terry telling Mom he should go, and her agreeing that's probably for the best, and then the sound of her walking him to the door and saying goodbye, and I wonder if they're going to kiss, and that feels like the most impossible thing in the world, my mom kissing someone who's not my dad, and I want to scream.

The front door of the apartment closes. I know Mom's going to want to come in here and talk all this out, and that's pretty much the last thing in the world I want to do, so when I hear her footsteps coming toward the door, I quickly wipe the tears off my face and pretend I'm sleeping.

Within seconds, I'm asleep for real.

6

TAG, I'M IT

Eric

"Do you tag?" Pete asks me in between bites of his empanada. I'm eating one too, and it's genuinely delicious in a way I've never experienced from school lunch. Cafeteria food at Tinsdale, much like everything else here, is next level.

"Um, what?" I'm sitting with Pete, Bobo, and Knapp at our usual table. (It's never been stated aloud, but based on the way other kids eavesdrop and stare at us the whole meal, it's definitely the cool kids table.) I assume Pete is talking about graffiti, like what Smash does, but it's surprising to think these rich kids would be into that kind of thing.

"Oh!" Bobo shouts. "Mr. Coney Island Tough Guy doesn't know about tagging." Even when she looks like she's about to burst into laughter because she thinks I'm an idiot, she still looks super pretty. "It's when you use spray paint to *tag* the—"

"Of course I know what tagging is," I say. "I do it all the time." That might be an exaggeration, but I did spray-paint that mural on the side of Dad's shed. So that counts. "I just assumed that might not be your style. Don't you all have hired help to go out and tag things for you?"

"Ooh!" Pete says, dipping his empanada into fresh salsa. "Sick burn!"

"Yes, truly!" Knapp says, chomping down on a piece of salty licorice. "Sketch, you deliver honesty that is refreshing."

In the week that I've known my new friends, I've learned that, for them, my being from Coney Island holds a certain power and mystique, that my wisdom from "the streets" makes me cool and gives them something they don't have access to in their wealthy, privileged bubble. When they learned my dad runs an amusement park, and that he actually fixes the rides himself, they couldn't believe it. It was like I'd told them I had the ability to fly.

"Yeah, well, I think he's a little punk," Bobo says, punching me in the shoulder, but she obviously loves being ribbed by a Coney Island kid as much as Pete and

Knapp do. I love it too. These people have become my friends.

"For real, though," Pete says. "We *do* tag, so you want to come with us after school to partake in some? We have a mission. We'll provide the supplies."

Here's how uncool the real me is: my first thought is *But isn't that illegal?*

That's why the only thing I've done even close to tagging was on property my father owns. Smash does it in Brooklyn, though, which makes me feel better about it. And, two days after the whole Terry Incident, I'm still avoiding Mom, which I'd like to keep going for as long as possible. So.

"I'm in," I say.

As Bobo leads us east from Tinsdale after school, a brisk fall wind on our cheeks, I assume we're going to some secluded brick wall or side street where we can tag freely.

But no.

"This probably will be no big for you, Sketch," Pete says, bouncing down the streets of Chinatown like an excited puppy, "but we've never tagged on a major landmark before. This is gonna be *sick*."

A major landmark? Oh boy. We better not be taking a subway to the Empire State Building or something.

"Don't say it so loud, you dingleweed," Bobo says, shoving Pete with a smile, almost knocking him into a sidewalk table of purses for sale. "Don't want the fuzz to overhear."

"Maybe I want them to hear," Pete says, shoving Bobo back. I'm pretty sure he has a crush on her.

And now may be a good time to mention: I might also.

I know. I'm a terrible person.

But Bobo is very cool and very pretty and very confident and very fun to be around. Of course I still like Jenni, and I'm not going to act on this crush because that would be a total jerk move. But still . . . no denying the feeling is there.

"Here," Knapp says, passing each of us a piece of salty licorice that he takes out of his huge and expensive-looking black leather backpack, currently stuffed to the brim with high-quality cans of spray paint.

"Knapp, man," Pete says. "How many times we gotta tell you? None of us like this stuff except you!"

"That's *why* you need to eat it," Knapp says, nodding and smiling, his blue eyes looking eternally optimistic. "We are about to do something challenging, yeah? So you put yourself in the right headspace by eating something that makes you have less comfort."

"Uh, that's not a thing," Bobo says, her eyebrows skeptically arched. "So, no."

"Nah, man," Pete says, waving Knapp off.

"Then, Sketch, you will do this for me," Knapp says, eagerly holding out the licorice. "Yes?"

"Sure, dude," I sigh. "I'll eat your crappy Swedish snack." I take a bite of the hideous excuse for candy, and Knapp cheers.

"Do you like it yet?" he asks.

"Absolutely not," I say, sliding the rest of the licorice into the pocket of my hoodie, where it joins a piece I begrudgingly accepted a couple of days ago.

"You will, my friend," Knapp says. "One day, things will change in a snap! And you won't be able to stop eating it."

"Can't wait." I stop focusing on the blast of salt coating my tongue long enough to see that we're approaching the ramp to the Manhattan Bridge.

A major landmark.

This seems like a bold move.

"What do you think, Sketch?" Pete says, nudging me with his

elbow. "Gotta dream big, right?"

"Sure. Yeah," I say. "Guess so."

"You're not backing out, are you?" Pete asks. "Come on, dawg, you climbed the fricking Parachute Jump! Putting a little paint on a bridge is nothing compared to that!"

Can't argue with him there.

"I'm not concerned at all," I say. "Just scoping it out."

"Word," Pete says. "That's what I'm talking about!"

"Sketch wouldn't back out," Bobo says, poking a flirty finger into my chest. "If anything, he's probably thinking this is way too tame, right?"

"Heh," I say, nodding. "Pretty much."

The four of us follow the walking path onto the bridge, joining a small stream of people, mostly runners and tourists. The walkway goes along the bridge's south edge, bordered by a ten-foot-tall chain-link fence on either side—one to keep the walkers from falling into the water, the other to keep them from stepping onto the subway tracks that run over the bridge. I'm staring up at the structure as we walk, noticing all the graffiti that already exists, when I realize I'm by myself.

"Back here, idiot!" Bobo says. She and Pete are about ten steps behind, huddled around Knapp, who's kneeling as he rifles through his backpack, discreetly organizing the spray paints in front of him.

"It's go time," Pete says with a grin, rubbing his hands together.

I look up toward the fence on the subway side; just above it are lightly rusted steel pylons already dotted with various tags and artwork.

"There's enough blank space up there for all of us to make our mark," Bobo says. "And we're less likely to be seen in the middle of the bridge."

"Smart," I say.

"The big question now," Knapp says as he holds out one of the cans, "is who will be going first?"

No one responds right away, all of us gazing up at the ten feet of fence we're going to have to scale. But then Bobo and Knapp shift their attention to Pete.

"What? Me?" he says.

"Coming here was your idea," Bobo says.

"Yes, this makes some sense," Knapp says. "He who thinks it, brings it."

"That's not a real phrase," Pete says. He looks toward me, his eyes panicked. "And I'm totally down, but shouldn't—"

"I'll go," I say, grabbing the can from Knapp's hand. I couldn't watch Pete squirm anymore.

"Thanks, man," he says, looking both surprised and grateful that I had his back.

Bobo shrieks and gives me a giant hug that makes my decision even more worth it. "You're such a badass," she whispers into my ear.

Pete takes the moment in, a flash of disappointment crossing his face.

"What color is this?" I ask Knapp, gesturing with the spray paint.

"Black," he says.

"I want red."

Knapp nods, impressed by my conviction, and trades out the can in my hand for another by his feet. I flick the top off and let it tumble to the ground as I shake the can and stare up at the bridge pylons. People are still walking by, so we all try to act nonchalant. Then there's a gap when no one is coming, and I take a deep breath.

Pete is right. This is not a big deal for me. I *am* a badass.

I start my ascent.

I'm about three feet off the ground when I realize it's very hard to climb a fence and hold a can of spray paint at the same time. I slip the can into my hoodie pocket with Knapp's nasty licorice.

I'm about eight feet off the ground when I realize that, though the fence is ten feet high, the Manhattan Bridge is way, way higher. I get a glimpse in my peripheral vision of the water far below us, and I get light-headed for a minute.

I grip the fence tighter and lean in close to the links.

And suddenly my heart's beating about eight million

times a minute. I'm right back there on the Parachute Jump, taking it one rung at a time, Crumple Noodle screaming above me, holding my best friend hostage.

I can't do this. I can't.

"Yo, Sketch, you okay?" Pete shouts from below.

It snaps me out of it. "All good!" I shout before taking another deep breath and continuing to climb.

Soon I'm at the top of the fence, so I take the spray paint out of my pocket and try to angle my arm toward a bare patch of steel. I'm momentarily distracted by this incredible graffiti done with stencils, these detailed orange and yellow silhouettes of kids running and jumping. They're oddly beautiful.

"Hey!" Bobo calls out. "Maybe you could do it this century?"

Her voice startles me and I lose my balance. One of my feet slides off the fence, then the other, and suddenly I'm dangling, hanging on for dear life with my left hand to a few chain links.

"Whoa, whoa!" Knapp shouts.

"You need help, son?" some random man wearing a fanny pack asks.

"I'm okay," I say, hoping none of them can hear the terror in my voice. Do I really have to relive *every* moment of my confrontation with Crumple, including the part where I fell? I swing my legs back and forth a few times to gain momentum and then propel myself back onto the fence. Thank god.

"Dude!" Pete says. "That's like some Cirque du Soleil magic right there."

"Sketch is no joke," Bobo says.

"Shouldn't be up there in the first place!" the fanny pack man says as he continues on his way.

I reposition myself on the fence and give the can of spray paint one last shake, which is when I realize I have no clue what my tag should look like. I wanted red as an homage to Brickman, thinking I might include him in my handle, but now that feels kind of cheesy, like something Doodles would do, not Sketch. Without over-thinking it, I spray a big S, then connect the k, e, t, c, and h in cursive, almost like I'm sketching it.

It looks messy. But also rad.

I quickly climb down the fence, jumping at around the five-foot mark and landing in a position not unlike Spider-Man. Which is how I feel. As Bobo, Knapp, and Pete surround me, cheering and patting my back and saying how sick that was, my heart is beating like wild again.

But now it's in the good way.

7

TITANIUM SPECIAL EDITION

Eric

I'm at my desk in my room on Saturday morning, playing around in pen with variations on my *SKETCH* tag when I hear the front door's intercom ring. "Sure, Frank," Mom says after she picks up the receiver. "Send him up."

Frank is one of the building's doormen, and *him* can only be Terry.

Ugh.

I'm heading to Brooklyn in a little bit for my weekend with Dad, and I was hoping I wouldn't have to hear or see this dude before I left.

"Eric," Mom says through my door in a gentle voice. "Terry's coming up, and we're going to brunch. I know you obviously won't come with us since you're headed to Dad's, but . . . do you think you might consider coming out to say hi?"

I've continued avoiding Mom all week. I mean, we've said hello to each other and asked how each other's days were, but I've made sure it never goes beyond that. It's sort of a jerk move, but I hate that she's dating a dork named Terry, and I hate the way she put me on the spot with an ambush introduction. And she needs to understand that. Also I've been hanging out with my Tinsdale crew after school every day, and when I get home I do homework, so even if I wasn't super angry, we wouldn't be seeing each other that much.

"Please, Eric," Mom says, and I can hear how desperate she's getting. "I miss you."

I might be a jerk, but I'm not a complete tool. I sigh and open up my bedroom door just as the buzzer rings.

"Fine, yeah, whatever," I say. "I can say hi."

"Thank you, my love," Mom says, wrapping me up in a hug and kissing my head. She's wearing this, like, stylish jean jacket I've never seen before along with some new perfume that smells like basil. "I know how hard this is, really I do."

"You totally ambushed me with this guy. You get that, right?"

"Ugh." Mom puts a hand over her face. "Eric, I'm so sorry. I don't really know what I'm doing. This is new for me too. And I do like Terry, but I hate this part of it, that it has to disrupt this life you and I are building. It feels weird and stupid."

"I agree."

"Here's what you need to know: Terry and I are having a nice time together, but you're always my number one. Okay? And it's not like I'm marrying Terry any time soon, or anything like that. We're just getting to know each other. So we'll all just . . . take it one step at a time. Does that work?"

I mull over what she said for a moment. She's really trying to make this right. I give her a sigh and a nod.

"Thank you, Eric," she says, giving me another kiss on the head. "This means a lot to me."

I nod and follow her to the front door. I can tell how excited she is, even though she's trying to play it down for my sake, and part of me—a very small part—does feel happy for her. But the other part feels resentful that I can't remember a single time she was this excited to see Dad.

"Hey there," Terry says, giving Mom a hug and a respectable kiss on the cheek, rubbing Pepper's head as she comes up to greet him. She seems every bit as excited to see him as Mom is, way more excited even than she is when she sees me, which is confusing. And annoying. Terry is dressed pretty much the same as last weekend, except this time his fancy button-down shirt is light blue instead of cream. I do not trust this man. "Hey, Eric."

"Hi," I say. Mustering that one syllable takes everything I have.

"You think you might join us for brunch?" he asks, still standing in the doorway. "I would love that."

"Nope." I can't even make eye contact. "I'm going to my dad's."

"Yeah," Mom says, a nervous smile plastered to her face, "Eric is with his dad on the weekends, so . . ."

"Ah, of course," Terry says, and I'm pretty sure he's relieved. "Well, look . . . Your mom mentioned that you and your friends like to play role-playing games, so I . . ." Terry reaches into a leather messenger bag and pulls out a pair of shiny silver multisided dice, one in each hand. "Was thinking maybe you'd be able to find a use for these. Used to be my prized possession. Twenty-sided Dungeons & Dragons die. Titanium special edition."

"We don't play stuff like that anymore," I say, even though I have to admit these dice are incredibly sick.

"Oh," Terry says. "Well—"

"Eric, just take the dice," Mom says. "They're a gift." There's an urgency in her voice I know from experience it's best not to ignore.

I take the dice. Mom arches her eyebrows at me.

"Thanks," I say.

"Sure," Terry says. "No point in them collecting dust at my place."

We stand there awkwardly for a few seconds before they say goodbye and head off to their stupid brunch.

"I don't like that guy," I say to Pepper as she follows

me back into my room and jumps up onto my bed. She cocks her head at me and gives a couple of happy barks, as if to say she disagrees, that I should give Terry a shot. "No way," I say, placing his annoying but undeniably cool gift on my desk.

I'm packing my weekend bag so I can go catch the subway to Brooklyn when my phone vibrates. I'm thinking it's probably Dad asking for my ETA, but it's actually Pete.

What u doing today? Wanna get in some trouble

I'm about to write *Nah I'm in Brooklyn today* but then for some reason I decide not to. *What kind of trouble*

We're tryin for the 5 borough challenge. Mark territory in all of NYC. U game?

Always, I text back. *Tell me when/where*

It's like I'm literally not thinking because as soon as it's sent, I wonder: WHAT DID I JUST DO? It's my weekend with Dad! And my meetup with Monster Club!

But the reality is I'm just starting to get close with Bobo and Pete and Knapp, and it feels good, and Manhattan is where I live now, so putting my attention on these new relationships is actually smart. And yes, I also have this crush on Bobo, but it's not even about that! Plus, do I really want another day sorting through Dad's junk? Or meeting up with Monster Club so that everyone can do their own thing and not even really interact with each other?

Hey Dad, I text. *Woke up with a cold and cough so I think I should lie low here for the day and come tonight. Sorry* ☹

I did have a stuffy nose when I first woke up today, so it's not a total lie.

I text Jenni a version of the same thing.

No prob bud, Dad texts back. *Will see you later*

Wow, that was easier than I thought. *Thanks*, I write back.

Oh no! Jenni texts. *Huge bummer but I get it. Drink a lot of water.*

I'm about to hit up Yoo when Pete texts back that we'll meet in an hour near his place in the West Village. It occurs to me—maybe this is an opportunity: my old best friend can meet my new best friends.

Change of plans, I write to Yoo. *Wanna come here and hang with me and the new crew?*

Mos def! Yoo writes. *Should we invite all of Monster Club?*

I wasn't expecting that. He's probably mainly talking about Smash. Either way, it seems overwhelming.

Not yet, I say. *Just want you to meet them first if that's cool.*

There are three dots in Yoo's word bubble for what seems like a full minute, and I'm wondering if I've said the wrong thing. Finally, though, he responds:

Let's do this

8

WE'RE THE NOODLE MONSTERS

Eric

I'm standing with Bobo, Pete, and Knapp in the West Village outside one of those fancy bodegas with tons of gluten-free snacks when Yoo turns the corner toward us, the usual bounce in his step. As the sun shines down, I'm filled with the same joy I always am upon seeing my best friend, this guy who's been there for me through it all, who I've known practically my entire life.

But that all fades as soon as Bobo opens her mouth.

"Is that him?" she asks. It's clear she's not asking in a neutral way. Her tone is more like: *That couldn't possibly be him, could it?*

I don't respond, but I'm already waving and smiling at Yoo as he approaches, so the answer is obvious.

"Yo, for real?" Pete mutters before taking a swig from his large energy drink.

My heart sinks as I see Yoo through their eyes: this fat kid in cargo shorts, a Kiss T-shirt, and a bulky red backpack. Definitely NOT a cool person. At least not by their standards. In that moment, I want them to know everything about the hero who is Alan Yoo: how hilarious he is, how bighearted, how smart, how supportive. I want to upload all this info directly into their brains, so they can see him the way I do.

"Whaddup, Doodles!" Yoo says as we hug, and he must feel my full-body flinch because he quickly corrects himself. "I mean Sketch. Sketch! My bad."

"All good," I say, and I hate myself, but I hear that my voice has gone cold.

"What did he call you?" Pete asks, a barely suppressed smile on his face. "Doody? Was your old nickname Doody?"

"Yo, mind your own business," I say like a tough Brooklyn guy, trying to turn this potentially embarrassing moment into a joke.

"Doody is poop, yes?" Knapp asks, eyes bright. "Were you the king of poop in Coney Island?"

"This is upsetting," Bobo says, in a way that's half joke and half dead serious.

"Look," I say as I feel everything I've built over the first few weeks of the school year crumbling to dust beneath my feet. "You all need to shut your mouths and meet one of the greatest people I've ever known. Everybody, this is Yoo. Yoo, this is Bobo, Pete, and Knapp."

"Howdy, y'all," Yoo says, and I try not to cringe. "Amazing to meet you. Sketch has said great stuff about you three."

"Sweet," Pete says. "Same." He points to Yoo's Kiss shirt. "You like the oldies, huh?"

"Yeah," Yoo says, understanding that Pete's not giving him a compliment. "I mean, have you ever heard them? They're a pretty sick band."

"Sick as in, like, on life support," Pete says, getting laughs from Bobo and Knapp.

"I like the way you talk," Bobo tells Yoo. "It's interesting. Very Brooklyn."

"It is?" Yoo asks, understandably self-conscious.

"Yeah. Like the way you said *ever* without hitting the *R* too hard at the end."

"Um. Okay."

"I probably talk that way too," I say, a weak attempt at defending him.

"Anyway," Pete says, gulping down the last of his energy drink and then crushing the can. "Should we hit it?"

"Please," Bobo says, already walking down the block, Pete and Knapp immediately falling into step on either side of her.

"That was a little awkward, huh?" Yoo says as we trail behind.

"It's all good," I say again, navigating us past strollers and packs of adults heading to brunch. "I'm glad you came." It doesn't sound as warm as I wanted it to, so I add on a "For real."

"Where are we going anyway?" Yoo asks.

"Tagging mission. Gonna put our mark all over the city. Probably starting with somewhere nearby."

"Wait, tagging like graffiti? Like what Smash does?"

"Pretty much, yeah."

"You didn't tell me you started doing that." I can tell he's annoyed.

"Yeah. I mean, like, *very* recently. So."

"Also, if you knew this is what we were doing, why couldn't Smash have come? She's the expert."

"I know, but . . ." I hadn't really thought about it that much, is the honest answer. I can feel things getting tense between us, and I don't like that at all, so I try to smooth it over. "I'm sorry, Yoo. It's totally my bad. I thought it would be cool to have time with just you, and I know these guys can be a little tough at first, but they're really fun, and we're gonna have a great time today, okay? I promise." It's like I'm trying to convince myself as much as him.

"All right, yeah," Yoo says, smiling. "It's all good, bud."

Bobo, Pete, and Knapp have stopped walking, and I realize we've arrived at a playground. It's bustling with kids. Their adults line the perimeter with coffees in hand, some talking to each other, most looking at their phones.

"First stop on the five-borough tour," Pete says. "Bleecker Playground. Get the gear ready, Knappy."

"On it," Knapp says, swinging his expensive backpack off his shoulders and down to the ground.

"So what's the play?" Pete asks Bobo.

"Thinking," she says, hands in her jean jacket (which I realize is uncomfortably similar to the one Mom was wearing this morning, and yet somehow Bobo's is five hundred times cooler) as she quietly scans the playground equipment.

"Wait, we're starting *here*?" Yoo says to me, eyes wide.

"Guess so," I say.

"There a problem?" Pete asks.

"Well," Yoo says, "it's, like, a nice playground."

"And?" Knapp says, arranging a few cans of spray paint at his feet.

"Let's do the swings," Bobo says. "We can tag those huge poles on either side of the structure."

"Perfect," Pete says. Knapp passes him a can of spray paint, then hands one to Bobo, and they confidently head to the other side of the playground. "You and Doody can sit this one out if you need to," Pete calls back to Yoo.

"We're not," I shout back, giving Yoo a look like *please, just go with it.*

"This is messed up," he says. "Smash wouldn't deface a perfectly good playground. Especially not while *kids are playing on it.*"

"Dude," I say, "I hear you. But it's just gonna be small tags on two poles, it's not a big deal. Start thinking about what your tag might be." I put my arm around Yoo, and he reluctantly crosses toward the swings with me. All six are currently in use, kids giggling and shouting, one of them swinging with her belly on the seat, extending her arms forward like she's flying.

With little fanfare, Pete sprays one of the poles with his handle, a *P* with a lightning bolt through it.

Bobo goes seconds later, using green paint to make her mark, one *Bo* on top of the other, outlined in a square. She passes her can to me.

"What are you doing?" the flying kid asks as she swoops upward.

"Expressing ourselves," Bobo says. "Do it, Sketch."

"Done!" Knapp calls from the pole on the other side of the swings where he's just sprayed his trademark *JK* (his first name is Josef).

I can feel all my friends' eyes on me. Especially Yoo's disapproving ones. I know he doesn't want me to do this. But I don't see what choice I have.

I start spraying my *S.*

"Oh, come on, man!" a short dad in a cap shouts at me

from a spot over by the monkey bars. "That's not cool!"

"See?" Yoo says.

I stop spraying.

"You kids were probably *on* this playground a year or two ago!" the dad continues. "Don't do this."

"Let's get out of here," Yoo says.

"Finish it," Bobo says.

My hand holding the spray paint is frozen in midair.

"I'm very happy to call the cops," the dad says, "if that'll help convince you to stop."

"Finish it!" Bobo shouts.

I pick up where I left off in the *S*, finishing the second loop and speedily scribbling the rest of my handle down the pole.

"Eric!" Yoo shouts.

"Let's roll, come on!" Pete leads a sprint out of the playground, him followed by Knapp, then Bobo, then me and Yoo.

"Sorry!" I say to the dad, and I really mean it, even though I'm also laughing, feeling that same euphoric exhilaration I've gotten accustomed to since I started tagging last week.

We run for at least five blocks, weaving in and out of people, probably the most running I've done through the city since the Noodle Monsters chased us from Mark Twain to Surf Avenue. Except, in this case, I guess we're

the ones creating chaos. We're the Noodle Monsters.

Running is also good because it means Yoo can't let me know how disappointed he is yet. He's keeping up with our pace, but he's totally pissed, I can tell.

Finally, Pete stops at the stairs leading down to the Christopher Street subway stop. "Nice work, team," he says, catching his breath.

"One borough down," Knapp says, similarly breathless.

"That was so dope," Bobo says, putting a hand on my arm. "Sketch, bringing the badass energy as usual."

I nod. Yoo just shakes his head, so angry he can't even speak.

"Next up," Pete says. "Staten Island, fools. We'll take the 1 train down to the ferry."

"Staten Island?" Yoo asks, looking at me.

I shrug. "Is that okay?"

"No. My mom will flip out. It was hard enough convincing her to let me come to Manhattan."

"Then don't tell her," I say.

Yoo stares at me as if I've slapped him. "What the hell is going on with you, dude?"

"What do you mean?" I ask, even though of course I know what he means.

"Uh-oh," Knapp says. "I'm sensing some tension, my friends."

"This isn't you," Yoo says.

I shrug, trying not to show how angry I am. "I mean, I'm standing right here, and I'm the one saying these words and doing all these things, so I guess it is me, you know?"

"Claws are coming out now," Bobo says.

"Rowr!" Pete adds.

Yoo looks at them, then back at me. "Whatever," he says, shaking his head again. He starts walking away from us.

"Where are you going?"

"Anywhere but here," he says, without looking back.

"Yoo, come on!" I say.

I'm about to run after him when Bobo grabs my arm. "It's okay," she says, her brown eyes looking directly into mine. "Just let him take a moment."

"Oh," I say. "Yeah. Okay."

I'm thinking that means we're all going to wait for him, but then seconds later Pete is bounding down the subway steps shouting "Onto borough numero dos!" and Knapp is too.

Bobo is still holding on to my arm.

"I should probably . . . ," I say, gesturing toward the direction in which Yoo walked. "Like, he seems really upset, so—"

"Your buddy is a sensitive guy, I understand that," Bobo says, rubbing her fingers up my arm in a way that feels really good and makes me feel really guilty. "But that shouldn't ruin your whole day, right? Please come with us. I want you to come with us."

"You two coming or what?" Pete shouts from the bottom of the steps.

I feel for Yoo, I really do. But if I go with him, I might be ruining these new friendships, the *only* new friends I've made so far. He'll understand. We'll work through it.

"Let's catch this ferry," I say.

Bobo howls triumphantly as we race down the stairs together.

9

THE SINKHOLE

Eric

Yoo isn't responding to my texts.

It's Monday, two days since we last saw each other, and I've checked in on him like five times. Nothing.

When I hadn't heard from him all day Saturday, I started to get worried that maybe he didn't make it home to Brooklyn, so I texted Smash Sunday morning. She said he's fine but that what I did really sucked. I said I know, but it was a tricky situation and please tell Yoo to text me back. She didn't respond.

At least I know Yoo is alive.

That said, I'm starting to find the ghosting really annoying. Like, almost babyish. If he were being grown-up, he would *talk* to me about this.

I don't know. I feel guilty, I guess. But at this point more annoyed.

On the plus side, we tagged all five boroughs and it was ridiculously awesome. Brooklyn was our last one, tagging an overpass in Dumbo, and by the time we finished it was nine at night. I headed to Dad's feeling amazing. A truly epic day and a truly epic accomplishment.

After checking my phone in the hallway, I walk into art class. I'm one of the first ones, though as usual, the tall, intense kid—who I've learned is named Ricky Martinez but enigmatically goes by Spooner—is already at it with his X-ACTO knife. He always makes the most interesting stuff, like work you might actually see in an art gallery. I walk past, getting close enough to see without intruding on his space, and he's going to town, cutting a series of spikes and spirals that look like some kind of dragon.

"Can't get over how sick that was," Pete says as he walks in, pulling my focus. We've been recapping Saturday pretty much nonstop since homeroom.

"The sickest," I say. And then I'm not sure why, but something compels me to call out to Spooner. "We're talking about how we put our handles all over the city during the weekend. In case you're wondering." It's probably that he's very cool, and I love his art, and I'm kind of desperate for him to like me. Or even just acknowledge me. "Like, different boroughs and stuff."

"Are you talking to me?" he says, looking up a few seconds later.

"Uh, yeah," I say. "I was just saying we've been, like, doing street art. All over."

"Tagging," Pete adds.

"Oh," Spooner says, eyes back on his canvas. "Congrats."

"You should come with us sometime," I say, and Pete scowls at me like *You can't just invite random people!*

Doesn't matter anyway because Spooner says, "Nah. I don't do that."

"Okay," I say, nodding as he silently continues working. Another fruitful exchange!

Pete and I walk to our table, reminiscing about the subway platform we tagged in the Bronx.

I check my phone as soon as Pete and I leave class, and my heart does a little leap when I see there's a new text.

It's not from Yoo, though.

It's from Beanie, texting the Monster Club group thread. We don't use it much these days—one of the last texts is from Yoo on Saturday: *me and SketchDoodles won't be around to hang this week, tending to some business in manhattan*, which of course reminds me how bad I feel.

Beanie's sent a short message—*this is so nuts*—along

with an article about a giant sinkhole that opened up in the ground last night near the City Hall subway stop. One parked car fell into it, but thankfully no one was in it. They think it happened because of old New York City infrastructure, possibly a corroded water main that sprang a leak, soaking the ground from below so much that it crumbled.

World is ending bro, Hollywood texts.

I wonder if Yoo will say something, or if his silent treatment extends even to the group thread.

Someone flicks my ear. "Stop being addicted to your phone," Bobo says as I look up. As always, she and Knapp have joined us in the hall on the way to lunch. "What's so captivating that you don't even notice us?"

"Oh, hey," I say. "Nothing. Just reading about this massive sinkhole that opened up last night by the City Hall subway stop. A car fell in."

"Whoa," Knapp says. "That is right near here, yes?"

"Yeah, why?" Bobo says. "You hoping one will open up beneath the school?"

"Let me see that." Pete grabs my phone, his mouth dropping as he looks at the photo of the sinkhole. He holds it up so we can see.

"Yo," he says.

His eyes ping-pong between the three of us, with a look on his face that screams *Are you thinking what I'm thinking?*

"It's, uh, for an art project," I tell Marcus the door-man as he asks why I'm leaving the building dressed in black pants and a black long-sleeved shirt at 1:30 in the morning.

I hadn't really factored in the whole doorman thing.

After much discussion, Bobo, Pete, Knapp, and I concluded that the high-profile and dangerous nature of this particular mission ("It's a sinkhole, not a play-ground, Pete!" Bobo shouted at one point) meant that it would be best attempted in the dead of night. Fewer people around, less chance of getting caught.

"An art project, huh?" Marcus says, making it clear he doesn't believe that in the slightest. "Just be safe, all right, kid? If your mom asks me about this, I'll sell you out in a heartbeat."

I shudder as I imagine that scenario. Actually, I thought for sure Mom was going to wake up as I was leaving the apartment, but somehow she didn't. So I'm doing this.

I can't believe I'm doing this.

"That's fair," I say. "You're a good man. Thanks, Marcus."

"Yeah, yeah, get outta here before I change my mind."

They call this "the city that never sleeps," but at 1:37 a.m., there are definitely fewer people around than during my morning commute. Some blocks are completely empty, which feels both thrilling and terrifying, like anything could happen to me and no one would have any idea.

I creep myself out so much that I run most of the way to our designated meeting spot, the corner of Broadway and Warren. I'm seven minutes early for our two a.m. meet-up time, so it's just me, standing around looking sketchy. Living up to my nickname, I guess.

I'm just starting to worry that maybe this is a prank and no one else is coming when a blue SUV pulls up at 1:59. Bobo and Pete get out of the back, both dressed in black like me, and the car pulls away. "Was that your family driver or something?" I ask, knowing that's possible with this crew.

"In a Subaru?" Bobo scowls. "Absolutely not. That was a Lyft, you sweet, naive child."

"You thought that was her driver?" Pete says, giggling.

"Oh, my bad," I say. "I wouldn't know, since *real* city people mess with cars as little as possible."

"Wait, did you *walk* here?" Bobo asks.

I nod. It hadn't even occurred to me there was another option.

"Wow, you really are hard-core," Pete says.

"That's why I love this guy." Bobo puts an arm around me and rests her head on my shoulder, giving me chills. The good kind.

"Yeah," Pete says, and again I see that disappointed look on his face before he nods twice, almost to himself, and puts out a hand for me to fist-bump. "Sketch is the real deal. And a true friend."

I can't tell if he's joking or what, but he seems sincere. It almost feels like a peace offering to acknowledge that it's cool Bobo is flirting with me instead of him. I extend my fist and bump his.

"Word," Pete says with a smile as he looks around. "Where's Knapp at? He's usually early."

"Well, he better get here," Bobo says, "because he has all our stuff."

We wait on the corner for almost fifteen minutes, Knapp not responding to any of our texts, when finally a red Honda Civic pulls up. Knapp and his backpack come bursting out the back.

"I'm sorry, I'm so sorry!" he says as the car pulls away. "The Ambassador was up late tonight. Couldn't sneak out until he went to bed." It turns out Knapp's dad is actually the secretary to the ambassador of Sweden. They all call him The Ambassador, though, because it's more fun that way.

"It's fine, dawg," Pete says, "but you could've texted us. We thought you bailed."

"I didn't want to, in case The Ambassador was monitoring my phone."

"Can he even do that?" Pete asks.

"Anything is possible with The Ambassador," Knapp says. I'm not even fully sure what that means, but I guess Knapp's dad is really intense.

"Man, my dad's like the opposite," Pete says. "He doesn't monitor anything I do. Unless it will help his clients."

"Wow," I say. I suddenly feel really lucky to have the dad I do.

Bobo ends the conversation by walking away, and we all follow.

As we approach the sinkhole area, surrounded by large cones, those caution sawhorse blocker things, and yellow police tape, I get a little nervous. Everyone else must be too, because we simultaneously start walking at a slower pace.

And then Bobo starts holding my hand.

It feels amazing but instantly takes me back to the moment when, running from the Noodle Monsters, Jenni did the same. I've been trying not to think about her, though. She texted last night that she heard from Smash how I wasn't actually sick last weekend, and that she's really upset about it. I didn't know what to say, so I didn't respond at all. I realize this makes me a hypocrite, since I'm angry at Yoo for ghosting me, but I feel like this situation is different somehow? But also maybe not.

Anyway, the point is, I am holding hands with Bobo, and it's very exciting, even as I understand it puts me in the running for Hugest Jerk of the Year. After a quick scan of the area to make sure no one's watching, Bobo pushes aside one of the sawhorses and slinks through the gap in the barrier she's created, pulling me along, with Pete and Knapp right behind.

The four of us line up a few feet from the edge of the sinkhole, staring down in awe. Nearby streetlights cut through the darkness to give us a sense of what we're looking at. The sinkhole is about twenty feet wide and thirty feet long, as if someone's aimed an X-ray at a New York City street, revealing the chaotic infrastructure below: pipes, dirt, wooden scaffolding.

"Dude," Pete says.

"It is quite sick," Knapp agrees.

Bobo releases my hand so she can reach out to Knapp for a spray can. "Hook it up." Knapp kneels down with his backpack, pulling out his phone flashlight to see what he's doing. He passes each of us a can. "I think we're the first to mark this thing," Bobo says as she creeps along the edge of the sinkhole.

"Hell yeah we are," Pete says, finding a spot he likes, then crouching over to tag it, looping his arm dramatically in the air.

I walk past Bobo as she's tagging, thinking I'll spray my Sketch tag right next to hers, but then I notice that just ahead of me, the edge of the sinkhole angles downward, forming a kind of ramp.

"You gotta tag down there," Bobo says practically into my ear, startling the crap outta me. "That's what you're thinking, right?"

"Maybe," I say, even though I wasn't at all, and the idea of following that ramp is pretty terrifying. "Seems a little dangerous."

"That's why we should do it," Bobo says, sliding her hand down my arm and interlacing her fingers with mine again. "Lead the way, badass."

"All right," I say, feeling more exhilarated than scared and also like I don't have much of a choice. As we slowly step forward into the darkness, I flick on my phone flashlight. Don't want Bobo or me to slip off the edge into the abyss. The ramp, made of intact pavement from the street that caved in, curves around a bend and down into a structure that's almost like a cavern.

It's very dark.

I'm about to stop and tag a large water pipe next to us when I hear sounds.

I know Bobo hears them too because she suddenly goes very still.

It's like a steady buzz or hum, intermingled with a sharp crunching, coming from ahead, deeper underground.

"Probably doing some repair work," I say. "Like, a city construction crew."

"Those noises are weird, though," Bobo says. "Let's go a little farther in. I wanna see what it is."

"Yo, what're you doing?" Pete's voice calls from a little ways behind us. "Let's split before we get caught."

"Slow your roll!" Bobo shout-whispers. "This won't take long." She lightly shoves me ahead, toward the symphony of crunching and buzzing.

I force my legs to keep moving forward.

We turn a corner, ducking our heads below wooden scaffolding, and suddenly I'm staring at these machines about fifteen feet ahead of us, these large cone-shaped drill bits spinning and corkscrewing down into the earth. There are three of them, each about three feet tall, which I can see because a couple of workers have big floodlights aimed directly at them.

"You were right," Bobo says, peering over my shoulder. "Construction. Boring." She turns around and starts walking back, but before I can do the same, I see something that makes it impossible for me to move.

One of the machines opens an eye.

And stares straight at me.

I shake my head back and forth, thinking I must be

imagining it, but no: above the rapidly spinning cone, there's a green eye staring at me.

A monster eye.

"Hey!" a man's voice shouts.

"Who's that over there?"

I squint and hold out my hands as a floodlight lands directly on my face.

Then I run.

"Get back here!" another man's voice shouts as they both stride toward me.

"Go go go!" I shout at Bobo, sprinting up the ramp. "They're coming!"

Bobo runs, even as she's cracking up. "OMG, they're chasing us? What dorks!"

"Maybe so," I say, "but I still think it's in our best interest not to get caught!" We catch up to Pete and Knapp. "Run, run!"

They do, and as the four of us crest the top of the ramp, skirt the edge of the sinkhole, and sloppily vault over the sawhorses, the men's voices drift farther and farther behind us. We speed across Broadway, then take a right, then a left, then another left, until we've for sure shaken them.

Just like after we tagged the playground, we stand on a corner catching our breath. Bobo, Pete, and Knapp are laughing, celebrating, but this time I don't join them.

Because I can't shake the feeling that something is very wrong.

"Sketch, did you even tag anything?" Bobo asks.

I shake my head no, and the three of them fall apart like it's the best punch line they've ever heard. I'm barely able to process that, though, because I'm still thinking about what I saw: not a digging machine . . . a digging *monster*.

And then my brain pieces together the other thing bothering me:

I recognized those men's voices.

They were the Vultures—Beard and Mustache. The two goons who worked for Pluto Properties, the evil real estate company that tried and failed to buy Dad's amusement park.

It couldn't have been them, though, right?

I must be imagining it. I'm sure I am.

Right?

Right?

10

PHASE ONE

Neptune

It's working.

It's actually working.

King Neptune stands inside the sinkhole, hidden in the shadows, watching in wonder as the monsters that he carefully drew into life do exactly what he intended them to, burrowing ever deeper into the bowels of Manhattan, creating a network of tunnels, all in service of The Plan.

He and his employees first broke ground last night in the basement of his building, directing the creatures to spin through the concrete floor. As soon as the monsters began, he felt a sense of euphoric calm, that this was the moment he'd been waiting for his entire life. Finally, his very own monsters.

It proved that persistence pays off. That if you wish and hope and work for something long enough, no matter how impossible it seems, you will be rewarded in the end.

King Neptune gets a little teary remembering those teenage years of wishing and hoping after his father threw him out of the house, the aimless days and nights he spent on the beach. The ink was the only thing that gave him even a sliver of hope, thinking about that living tattoo of the Neptune monster, how if he had power and strength like that, he could've stood up to his father. He wouldn't be unhoused.

He'd thought about the ink so much, in fact, that once he dropped out of high school his junior year—finally escaping the senior bullies whose abuse had only grown more intense once they learned he had no home—the only place he could think to go was Coney Island. Though King's Sideshow Extraordinaire had not reopened after the fire, he found some of its sideshow performers— the Geilio Brothers, the man with the tiny head, the bearded lady—working at another one, Sammy's Spectacular Sideshow. Sixteen-year-old King Neptune got a job there, taking tickets and sweeping—it was as if he'd won the lottery.

Over the next months, he got to know the sideshow performers, and it felt like meeting movie stars. Puberty ensured he looked different enough from who he was four years earlier that none of them recognized him. The performers all said working at Sammy's couldn't hold a candle to the joy they'd had working at King's. And they all missed Isaac King, who'd died of a heart attack two years before. They all agreed it was a broken heart from losing the sideshow. This, of course, made King Neptune feel horrible.

Eventually, the Geilio Brothers got so comfortable with the boy that they told him about Isaac's magic ink, including the highly confidential story of how Isaac first found it. It was the same story a much older King Neptune would many years later pass on to Isaac King's great-great-grandson, of how Isaac came to America and saved a mermaid, who later gifted him with some of her enchanted blood.

"Does someone still have the ink?" Neptune had asked eagerly as he mopped the stage between shows.

"No," Salvatore Geilio said, sitting on the stage next to his brother, Lorenzo, as they moved through their post-show stretching routine. "It's gone forever. Destroyed. That is what Isaac wanted."

"Yeah, right!" Neptune said. He'd heard something in the man's voice that made it seem like a lie. "Destroyed? When you could all be raking in the dough collecting bets on more monster battles? Gimme a break!"

He instantly knew he'd said too much. The Geilio Brothers froze in the middle of a stretch and stared at each other, as if melding their minds.

Lorenzo turned toward Neptune, a scary look in his eyes. "We did not mention any battles."

"Oh," Neptune stammered. "D-Didn't you . . . ? I guess I just assumed—"

"You are the boy," Salvatore said, sneering.

"The little snoop who ruined everything," Lorenzo agreed.

"What boy?" Neptune slowly backed away, mop in hand.

"Now you are the one who is telling the lie," Lorenzo said. "I cannot believe I didn't recognize you sooner."

"Uh," Neptune said, sure he was about to have his limbs ripped off one by one by their unnaturally muscular arms.

"Get out of here!" Salvatore shouted, slowly getting to his feet.

"But Sammy counts on me to—"

"We'll tell Sammy to fire you!" Lorenzo bellowed. "Now scram!"

King Neptune's mop clattered to the floor as he dashed out the door.

Yet another home lost.

But now he's the one with the last laugh, isn't he?

Because now he knows that the ink isn't gone forever,

as that strongman buffoon claimed. It's right here, in this sinkhole in downtown Manhattan, extraordinary magic happening before King Neptune's eyes!

As his employees Tim and Julio hold up floodlights to give Neptune the clearest view of the action, he watches his three monster machines with awe. Each is silver with small black tractor wheels for legs and a cone-shaped head that narrows to a sharp point, almost like a beak. On the back of each of their heads, there's a cylinder of coiled-up silver from which extends a long, rigid tail that ends in a thick hook. The monsters bounce off their wheels and dive beak-first into the ground, the cone head spinning so that it can corkscrew deeper and deeper, making noises that are simultaneously mechanical and animalistic.

As they start to burrow, their long silver tails slam down behind them, anchoring a hook into the newly formed ledge. When their digging is done, their elongated tails pull them back up to the surface, winding onto the winch-like cylinder at the tail's base. They are powerful and highly efficient monsters. Exactly as they were intended to be.

These first two days were meant to be a trial run, but they've been a resounding success. Sure, the sinkhole was an inadvertent byproduct, but so be it. Lower Manhattan won't be around for too much longer anyway.

King Neptune is transfixed as his beautiful monsters

begin to corkscrew down for another round when there's a yelp from across the sinkhole. Tim aims the floodlight across the way, where much to all their surprise, there's a teenage boy standing about fifteen feet away, his hands over his face shielding his eyes. Behind him, there's at least one other kid, maybe a few.

Damn teenagers. Always getting in the way.

The boy and his friends start to run. Julio shouts before he and Tim take off after them.

King Neptune remains with his monsters—his hard-working monsters—not particularly concerned about the interruption. Just kids looking for someplace to misbehave. And anyway, no amount of pesky teenagers can derail the inevitable.

Not too long from now, the tunnels will soon be finished, and then the next phase will begin.

Atlantis will be here.

And Neptune will finally be home.

11

THE EYE IN MY HEAD

Eric

I turn over in my bed for the fifty-eighth time in the last ten minutes.

I'm supposed to wake up for school in less than two hours, and I still haven't fallen asleep.

I can't get that eye out of my head.

Over and over, on a loop, I see it opening up, that bright green eye, staring right at me.

Unless . . . I didn't actually see what I thought I saw.

It *was* late. And dark.

But those dudes' voices definitely sounded like Beard and Mustache. I close my eyes and remember the sound of them threatening Dad: *Come Monday, when you're unable to pay up to the bank, everything on your side will belong to* us*!*

I guess I'm not totally sure. Shouting men have a

tendency to sound alike.

That's what Bobo, Pete, and Knapp think anyway. I felt compelled to mention what I saw, and they thought it was absolutely hilarious.

"Dude," Pete said, giggling like a hyena. "I'm sorry, but even one encounter with monsters is hard to believe. But *two* encounters? In totally different places? Nah, bro. Those were definitely machines."

"Yeah," Bobo agreed, rustling my hair. "You probably have PTSD. Which is actually kind of cute."

"I could give you the number of my therapist if you want," Pete said. "She's the dopest."

I didn't take the phone number. But maybe I should have.

I did go through something insanely traumatic this year. Not to mention my parents getting divorced. And I haven't once talked to a therapist or social worker, or even a guidance counselor, about it.

I pick up my phone. For at least the tenth time, I think about texting Yoo. He's the closest thing I've ever had to a therapist. But it's 4:31 in the morning. And anyway, there's no reason to think Yoo will be down to respond now when he hasn't in days.

Ugh, I still haven't responded to Jenni. I suck.

As I shift in my bed, I accidentally nudge Pepper, who's sleeping at my feet. She rouses slightly, and I seize the moment. "Hey, girl," I whisper. "Do you think I'm losing my mind?"

She blinks at me a couple of times before slowly rising and walking over to lick my face.

"Thanks, Pep," I say, laughing. She curls up next to me and goes back to sleep. "You're probably right. I just need to chill out."

I take deep breath after deep breath—*just chill out just chill out just chill out*—until finally I fall asleep, moments after I convince myself that Bobo and Pete were right.

12

PETE'S BAR MITZVAH

Eric

I am riding in a helicopter.

It is very rad.

Today is Pete's bar mitzvah out in the Hamptons, with a service at a temple, followed by a party at Pete's parents' beach house, which is supposedly a mansion. Every single seventh grader has been invited—Tinsdale's policy for bar and bat mitzvahs so that no kids get left out—and everyone's being bused out from the city.

Not us, though.

Bobo, Knapp, and I are with Bobo's parents on their *private helicopter.*

I still can't believe it. I assumed Bobo and her family might have a private driver, but I mean, a private helicopter? How rich do you have to be to have that?

I'm dressed in a new gray suit Mom insisted on getting me. I thought it was super fancy until I saw Knapp's silk blue suit and Bobo's dark purple dress, which seriously looks like what a famous person might wear. Now I just feel kind of embarrassed, even though Bobo and Knapp seemed genuinely into it. "It's shabby chic," Bobo said, running a hand down my suit sleeve. "You pull it off so much better than I ever could." I wasn't sure if that was a compliment or an insult, but I smiled anyway.

I convinced Dad to let me miss one of my weekend days so I could be here, which he was really cool about, even though it's the second weekend in a row of me skipping out on him. He made me promise to come to Brooklyn tomorrow morning, which I happily agreed to.

"Can you imagine if we had to be on a *bus* right now?" Bobo says, smiling at me in a way that makes me aware of my heartbeat. She's been sitting very close to me since we took off. Or lifted off. I don't know the helicopter terminology.

"Oh, come on, B," Bobo's dad says from his seat across from us. "The bus is fine too."

"If it's so fine, Daddy, then how come you never take it?"

Her dad laughs. "She's got a point there, Charles," Bobo's mom says.

"I think we should ride this thing to school every

day," Knapp says, chewing on a piece of salty licorice as he stares out the window. He already offered some to Bobo's parents, but they politely declined.

Apparently, this is a really fancy helicopter because you don't even have to wear noise-canceling headphones to block out the sound of the propeller; Bobo said it's designed in a way that makes the helicopter itself noise-canceling. Pretty sweet.

It also means that when my phone buzzes, and I see that Jenni has texted a voice memo, I can actually listen to it.

"Eric," Jenni says, and she sounds like she's been crying. Also very angry. "I don't know why you think it's okay to just fall off the face of the earth, but I hate it. And the message has been received loud and clear. You've got your new life now, I get it."

"Who is that?" Bobo asks.

"One sec," I say.

"But you could at least have the courtesy of telling me you've moved on so I don't have to, like, figure it out for myself. You're being such a jerk, and I know that's not how you actually are. So it's . . . I don't know. But this is done, okay? We're over. Enjoy your stupid life."

I feel so horrible, it's like my whole body is one giant cringe.

But, not gonna lie, I'm also kind of relieved.

"That was your girlfriend, wasn't it?" Bobo says, a little grin on her face.

"No," I say. "Well, like. She used to be. But now we're . . . Now she's not."

Bobo makes a sad face. "Aw. I'm sorry."

"It's okay," I say, and I realize it really is. Like, just look at me: I'm on a private helicopter to the Hamptons! Sitting next to the coolest, most popular girl in seventh grade!

Bobo puts her head on my shoulder, and intertwines her hand with mine.

"Want to cheer up with some salty licorice?" Knapp asks.

Bobo sits next to me during the service, which is on the beach next to Pete's parents' enormous summer home. It's an elaborate setup involving a stage, music stands, microphones, and hundreds of chairs lined up in the sand on this cloudy late-September day.

Bobo and I hold hands through the whole thing. Now that Jenni and I are broken up, I at least don't have to feel guilty about it. Or, at least, not *that* guilty. Pete does a really good job reading and singing in Hebrew, and it reminds me how much work I still have to do before my bar mitzvah in the spring. I try not to think about it.

Once the service is over, dozens of cater waiters swarm

in, some of them restaging the area for the party, some of them holding trays and offering us popcorn and root beer floats. Bobo, Knapp, and I slurp down our floats as a sharp breeze blows past.

"So, Sketch," Bobo says, putting a hand on her forehead like a sailor and dramatically looking back and forth from the beach to the ocean and back again, "see any monsters around here?"

Knapp cracks up.

"Yeah, yeah, laugh all you want," I say. "But no, I have not, as of yet, sighted any monsters at this location."

"Well, keep us posted," Bobo says, linking her arm with mine.

Each day that passes since we tagged the sinkhole, I feel a little more ridiculous about what I thought I saw. It makes no sense whatsoever, and I'm now all but certain I really was having some kind of trauma flashback. Good times.

"Yo, it's my homies!" Pete shouts, putting arms around Knapp on one side, me and Bobo on the other, and pulling us into an awkward huddle. "Glad you're here to watch me become a man!"

"You did amazing up there," I say.

"Yeah, great job," Knapp says. "You had very good passion."

"For real," Bobo adds.

"Thanks." Pete sighs. "You should tell that to my dad."

"Oh no," Bobo says. "What did good ol' Andrew say this time?"

"Nothing major," Pete says. "Just that some of my melodies and rhythms were off in the singing and I should have practiced more. Like, considering that over half the people here are connected to the music industry. And considering he dropped so much money on this party and everything. It's whatever. Not a big deal."

"Ew!" Bobo says. "Your dad is such a weenus!"

Pete shrugs, running a hand through his shaggy hair. "He's just a perfectionist. Which you gotta respect, you know? It's how he got to be as successful as he is. Gotta go the extra mile."

"The Ambassador spouts this kind of nonsense too," Knapp says.

As the party pops up around us, I notice red-and-white carnival tents. Also games like ring toss and squirt gun target races and Whac-A-Mole. And then I see a team of workers setting up a ten-foot-high replica of the Wonder Wheel.

What.

"Pretty dope, right, Sketch?" Pete says, seeing me checking everything out. "I was, like, inspired by you."

The theme of Pete's bar mitzvah is Coney Island.

"Definitely," I say. I'm flattered. But it's also weird.

"Hot dog! Anybody want a classic Nathan's hot dog?" It's being shouted by a guy with a tray who's dressed as a carnival strongman from the early 1900s, wearing a skintight one-piece leotard not unlike the one Yoo found at Dad's place.

"I do!" Knapp says. "I will take two."

"Here you go, buddy," the strongman says, thrusting the tray toward us. He's clearly trying not to shiver in his one-piece.

We all grab one (or two) as a few juggling clowns walk by.

I have never seen a clown on Coney Island.

But anyway.

The party continues like that. Fun but weird. Bobo is practically glued to my side, which is rad and exhilarating but also kind of a lot. Jenni and I literally just broke up *two hours ago*. Also Bobo keeps telling everyone how I'm from the actual Coney Island, and then I have to talk about how this party compares to the real place. It makes me wonder: Does Bobo like me because of who I really am or because of this whole Coney Island badass Sketch persona that's kind of me but also, as Yoo and Jenni have both not-so-sweetly pointed out, kind of isn't?

Three hot dogs, two root beer floats, and one cotton candy later, it's time for Pete to do the traditional bar mitzvah candle lighting, where different people who are close to him are called up with a special poem to help light each of the thirteen candles. His grandparents go up, various aunts and uncles and cousins, close family friends, that artist dude Fuller Hopkins, and then Pete reads this poem:

"This guy is fun, we always live on the edge. . . . For candle number nine, I call up my BFF, Sketch!"

Before I even understand what's happening, Bobo squeals and shoves me toward the stage.

I'm lighting a candle with Pete? I know he considers me a true friend, but I didn't know that meant I was his BFF!

I walk through the sand and up onto the stage, where Pete is waiting with a big grin. "Yeah, Sketch!" he shouts. "Let's do this, baby!"

As disorienting as it is, it also feels really good. I help Pete light the candle, aware of the professional photographers taking our picture, and then I'm back in the crowd. I'm assuming Bobo and Knapp will be called up for one of the next candles, but they aren't.

It's actually sort of shocking.

How was I chosen and not them? I didn't need to light a candle; I practically just met Pete! I can tell Bobo and Knapp both feel crappy about it too.

"Sorry," I tell them, "that's sorta messed up that—"

I'm interrupted by a gigantic scream from everyone around us.

I'm ready to make a run for it when I realize it's a happy scream.

"Lil Nas X is starting!" Bobo shouts, pulling Knapp and me toward the stage, where a crowd of our classmates has formed, the shouts and yells continuing as drums and a looping electric guitar hook kick in.

"Wait, like the actual Lil Nas X?" I ask. "He's here? Performing? Now?"

"Yes, idiot!" Bobo says, pointing at the stage with glee. "Look!"

Sure enough, Lil Nas X is bounding around the stage with a mic in his hand. He's wearing a top hat, suspenders, and a black suit jacket with tails. I'm trying to figure out why that outfit looks so familiar when I realize: he's dressed like a sideshow barker. And he looks exactly like my great-great-grandfather Isaac does in that photo of him and my great-great-grandmother Eva in front of the Parachute Jump.

I feel a little dizzy.

"Hey," I shout into Bobo's ear as she jumps up and down to the beat, "I really have to pee."

"Right now? He's just starting his set!"

"I know, I know, but— You stay here, I'll be right back."

"Fine, the porta-potties are over there behind the carnival tents. They're the fancy kind, so they're not gross."

"Oh," I say. "Great." I give her a kiss on the cheek, which actually surprises me as much as it does her. I'm worried it was too much, but her face breaks into a smile.

"Come back quick, loser," she says.

I do actually have to pee, but that's not the reason I needed to step away. This is all just . . . so much. In every way. I weave through the massive crowd, and I'm looking for those porta-potties when I hear someone say, "Oh, there he is!"

It's those girls from homeroom who were talking about their ridiculous trips on the first day, whose names I now know are Juniper (Tuscany) and Mirabel (Croatia). They're pointing at me.

"Hey, Sketch!" Juniper shouts. "Can we take a pic with you near the backdrop?"

I have no idea what she's talking about, but I know I'm not interested. "Uh. Don't you want to watch Lil Nas X?"

"Oh, come on!" Mirabel says. "It'll take literally thirty seconds."

"Okay," I say with a sigh. They walk me past one of the carnival tents toward the replica of the Wonder Wheel. Just past it there's a big airbrushed backdrop for people to stand in front of and take Instagram-ready photos.

It's a gigantic painting of the Parachute Jump.

I pose with Juniper first, then Mirabel, and then I need to get far, far away because I feel like I'm going to vomit. I walk straight past the luxury porta-potties, toward the ocean, where I can actually hear myself think.

I don't know what this twisted, Hamptons, rich-person version of Coney Island is, but I know it's not *my* Coney.

Or Dad's.

Or Aunt Betty's.

And definitely not Great-Great-Grandpa Isaac's.

Which brings me to the question I haven't asked since that first day at Tinsdale:

What am I doing here?

The sun has almost fully set, so it's getting darker by the minute. If it weren't for the light shining our way from the huge party lanterns, it would probably be hard to see much. I stand as close to the water as I can without getting my nice shoes wet and listen to the waves crashing in. It's the closest I've come yet to an actual Coney Island experience.

Something moves quickly by my feet, and I gasp.

It's a fish, silver and blue, flopping around on the sand.

Poor thing. I want to kick it back into the water, but

that seems unnecessarily violent, so I swallow hard and pick it up. I try not to think about how slimy it is as I flick it into the ocean.

I've never seen that happen before. Weird.

About ten feet to my left, I notice two more fish flapping around.

What. Is. Going. On.

I walk toward them and see that there are actually three. No wait, four.

Oh my god, no, there are *seven* wriggling fish washed up on the shore.

"What are you guys doing out here?" I ask aloud as I pick each one up, suppress a shudder, and chuck it back into the surf.

As I release the final fish, I see someone out in the ocean.

Maybe fifty feet away, there's a woman just floating there, her silhouette barely illuminated by the bleed of light from the party lanterns.

I think she's looking at me.

"Are you okay?" I shout.

No reply. She just stares. The party lights catch her pupils and they shine green like an animal's at night.

"You all right?"

"Yeah, man, why?" a voice says a little farther down the beach, startling me even more than the fish did. It's

Spooner, crouched down, tracing elaborate images in the wet sand.

"Oh," I say. "No, I wasn't talking to you. I was—" There's a splash. I turn back to the woman, but the silhouette is gone. All I can see is a quick glimpse of . . . a fin?

It disappears below the water.

13

BETTER THAN A MUSEUM

Eric

It's confirmed, then.

I'm absolutely losing my mind.

"Hey," I shout to Spooner as I walk toward him. "Did you see that just now?"

"See what?" He's focused on what he's drawing with his finger, some kind of stick figure. A green backpack is still on his back.

"There was, like, someone swimming out there."

"I didn't," Spooner says. "But I get it. It's the kind of party you want to escape."

Can't argue with him there.

I don't know what I actually saw out in the water, or where that woman swam to, but it doesn't seem like Spooner's interested in discussing it further. Add it to the list of Eric's Delusions and move on, I guess!

"Not a Lil Nas X fan, huh?" I ask.

"He's solid," Spooner says. "This just isn't the right venue."

"I feel that," I say, nodding as I watch Spooner work. What at first looked like a stick figure evolves into an intricate pattern of swirls and dots. It's the best sand art I've ever seen.

"You ever do this when you were little?" Spooner asks.

"Like . . . draw in the sand?"

"Yeah."

"Sometimes."

"All the best artists find inspiration in their child-hood." He emphasizes his words with swoops and points of his finger in the sand.

"Cool," I say, just trying to keep up.

The tide comes up the farthest it has while I've been standing here—it fills in Spooner's art with little pud-dles, washing much of the work away as it recedes.

"Because that kid is gone," Spooner says, looking up at me. "But he's also not, you know? The art lies in that negative space of his absence."

I nod, knowing he's saying something profound, some-thing I kind of understand but also kind of don't. "Yeah. For sure."

"Yo, you want to check something out with me?"

"Like . . . somewhere else?"

"It's not far. Short walk. You'll appreciate it."

I look back up to the party, half a football field away, where Lil Nas X's beats are still going strong. I'm sure Bobo is wondering what's taking me so long.

But I'm also beyond flattered that Spooner has deemed me cool enough to see whatever this is. And I know I can't handle going back up there yet.

"Sure," I say.

Spooner and I walk down the beach, away from the party.

Into the darkness.

Luckily the moon is, if not full, then pretty close to it, and its glow helps light our way. We don't say much as we trudge through the sand. It makes everything feel a little ominous. I trust Spooner, but I don't actually know him. Like, at all.

"Here," he says, after ten minutes. He points to this small, creepy building near the top of the shore, many of its dozen windows shattered.

"Um," I say. "What is that?" He's not suggesting we go *into* it, is he?

"An abandoned bunker," Spooner says. "From World War II. My older sister told me about it. Come."

It's funny to hear about Spooner having a sibling, or

any family really, since he seems like such a lone wolf. I reluctantly follow him toward the building. Maybe it once had doors, but it doesn't now, just wide-open entrances.

A text comes in as we get closer to it.

It's Bobo: *where the hell you at sketchball????*

I can't ghost her the way I did so many times to Jenni, so I say: *Party's not fully my scene. Found spooner. He took me to this bunker farther up the beach but I'll be back soon*

What??? A bunker???

He says it's worth seeing, I write.

She doesn't respond. I'm sure she's annoyed, but she'll get over it.

Right before we go in, Spooner reaches into his backpack and hands me a heavy flashlight. It's super legit.

"Use this," Spooner says. "I have one too."

I click it on, and we walk inside, our bright beams immediately making it clear why Spooner has taken me here.

The walls of the dilapidated bunker are covered with graffiti, a breathtakingly beautiful display. We can only see what our flashlights point to, so it's like taking in a mural one piece at a time: a cartoon face here, a huge grinning skeleton there, and hundreds of tags, of all sizes, everywhere.

"Wow," I say.

"Right?" Spooner says. "Better than a museum." He's digging into his backpack again and this time comes out with multiple cans of spray paint and several stencils, obviously created by him with that X-ACTO blade he's always carrying.

"I thought you said you don't tag!" I say.

"No, I said I don't tag with *groups*. Hit me with some light." I follow Spooner with my beam as he approaches a corner of the cavernous space, finds a blank patch of wall between a tag that says GINA in bright purple bubble letters and another in neon-green that says FREEX. He puts one of his stencils up against the wall and begins an impressively intricate process of spray-painting, changing stencils, spraying again with a new color, shifting the stencil, and so on. I'm in awe.

Spooner finishes up, stepping back from the wall. He's made something incredible. It's a series of yellow and orange silhouettes of children running and jumping, and—

Wait a second.

"Dude!" I say, so excited I drop my

flashlight, which makes a surprisingly loud thud. I pick it up. "I saw your work on the fricking Manhattan Bridge! I can't believe that was you! You're so good!"

Spooner shrugs and smiles. "Good is subjective. I'm just in the flow. The artistic outcome is less relevant."

He says such smart-sounding stuff, it makes my head spin a little. "Right on," I say.

"You want to partake?" he asks, holding out his can of spray paint.

The truth is I feel immensely intimidated. I'm supposed to make my measly Sketch tag now that I've watched him create a masterpiece before my eyes? Nevertheless, I say "For sure" and take the can.

I'm scanning with my flashlight, staking out a spot on the wall, when we hear voices and loud laughter quickly approaching the bunker. I'm nervous we're about to confront a group of jerky teenagers when I realize who it is.

"Shame on you, Sketch," Bobo's voice rings out from the entrance. "Ditching us like that."

"You are in big trouble, Mr. Sketch," Knapp says with a huge smile in his voice.

Even in the near dark, I can see the disappointment on Spooner's face. He clicks off his flashlight and starts packing up his gear. He doesn't do groups. I probably shouldn't have texted Bobo where we were.

"Yo, what is this place?" Pete asks.

"Whoa," I say, startled to hear his voice. "You left your own bar mitzvah?"

"Hell yeah," he says, shining his phone flashlight on the walls. "And I'm glad I did. I've lived here eight months and I've never found this place! It's sick."

"You're such an enigma, Sketch," Bobo says, suddenly right next to me, smelling good as always, like coconut and a hint of strawberry. "Vanishing into the night like that."

"Sorry," I say. "Needed some air."

She puts a hand on my chest and lightly shoves me.

"I am kicking myself for not bringing my stuff," Knapp says, walking through the bunker.

"Sketch has a can!" Pete says, gesturing to the one I forgot I was holding. "We can use his!"

"That's mine," Spooner says. "And I need it back." I shine the flashlight and see his hand extending toward me. "Need the light too."

"Yeah, sure," I say, handing both over. "Sorry about this, man."

The bunker is darker, now lit only by Pete's and Knapp's phone flashlights.

Pete hovers over Spooner. "Dude, *please* can we borrow that one can?"

"Nah," Spooner says, putting it into his backpack.

"Please please please!" Pete begs. "I just became a

bar mitzvah, man! This can be part of my gift from you. Please!"

I'm glad it's dark so no one can see how hard I'm cringing.

Spooner sighs so loud, it practically echoes in the bunker. He hands Pete the can and heads for the exit.

"Oh thank you thank you!" Pete says. "You are a champion among men! Seriously, you're the dopest."

Spooner gives no indication that he's heard Pete's gratitude as he slinks out the door. I run out after him. "Hey, Spooner, thanks for bringing me here," I call out into the darkness. "Sorry that, you know, everybody else showed up."

If he responds, it's too quietly for me to hear.

"Anyway, I guess I'll see you Monday! In class. So. All right."

Here I am again, watching someone I genuinely like walk away from me. Bobo, Pete, and Knapp are great, but I wish they could coexist more easily with other people. Maybe I'll talk to them about that.

When I walk back into the bunker, they're all cracking up in the dark as they take turns tagging different walls. "Yo, Sketch, what do you think?" Pete says, shining his phone light on a tag that reads *P13*, with his usual lightning bolt cutting through. "The *13* is in honor of my bar mitzvah."

"Yeah, I got that," I say, laughing. "Give me the can, I haven't put anything up yet."

"Hold on," Bobo says, taking my hand and pulling me away. "I need to show you something first."

She walks me across the bunker, deeper into the shadows. It's so dark, it's a little scary. Finally, she stops us at one of the far corners.

"So," I say, "what did you want to—"

And then Bobo is kissing me.

It catches me off guard, especially since, even this close up, I can't really see her.

But I like it.

I put a hand on her face and kiss her back as my mind, so full a moment ago, goes completely and utterly blank.

14

NO SLEEP TILL BROOKLYN

Eric

It's early.

Way too early.

And this train car is smelly.

Way too smelly.

I'm riding back Sunday morning from the Hamptons on the LIRR (Long Island Rail Road), which is, unsurprisingly, way less glamorous than a luxury helicopter. There are just three other people on my train car—all adult males riding by themselves like me—and one of them is farting up a storm. I've given up trying to pinpoint which one, though.

I really wanted to stay out in the Hamptons longer with Bobo and Knapp at Bobo's family's absurdly humongous mansion, especially since Bobo is kind of my girlfriend now. But I know that would be supremely uncool to Dad, who's already put up with me bailing a couple of times. Plus, we're doing a Monster Club hang this afternoon, which I'm pretty sure Yoo will be attending, so he and I will finally be able to patch things up.

All of which explains why I'm here on the 7:47 a.m. train, riding the almost-three hours to Atlantic Terminal in Brooklyn, where I'll switch to the Q line and make my way to Dad's.

I rest my head against the window and close my eyes, hoping for some much-needed sleep. I'm too jumpy, though.

I can't stop thinking about Bobo.

Last night, Knapp and I were sharing one of the approximately four hundred guest rooms in Bobo's house when she woke me at two in the morning. We snuck into this weird lounge on the third floor and talked and kissed for hours. It was amazing. I learned so much about her—that until third grade she was really shy, that she wants to be a curator at an art gallery when she's older, that her actual name is Bernice but she hates it. I finally went back to sleep at six, just in time to wake up at seven and get driven to the train by their family driver, Maritza.

So I'm simultaneously jittery and wrecked.

As we pull out of Patchogue, I'm finally falling asleep,

but then the mystery farter lets another one rip and I'm jolted awake.

It's definitely the guy two seats in front of me.

Sigh.

"So you really like her, huh?" Dad asks.

We're sitting at the kitchen table, finishing up Dad's classic incredible eggs and bacon and drinking coffee. I told him about Bobo. I've never actually had coffee before, but I felt so tired when I showed up, I decided it might be worth a try. Dad was hesitant until I said Mom lets me drink it sometimes. Which is, of course, a lie.

"I think so, yeah," I say, followed by a sophisticated sip from my King's Wonderland mug. "She's really cool."

"So I assume things are officially done with Jenni, then?"

"Yeah, she dumped me," I say, feeling a little sheepish. "I mean, it was my fault because I . . . I kind of stopped being in touch."

"Ahh," Dad says, wincing. "You gotta be careful the way you treat people, Eric. If you stop liking someone, you gotta be brave enough to tell them that."

"I know, I know. I messed up. I'll apologize to her."

Dad takes a long sip from his coffee, staring at me in a way that makes me uncomfortable. "I'm glad you found these new friends, bud," he says. "And that you've connected with this girl Bobo. Just try not to lose who you are, you know? Make smart choices."

"Everyone keeps saying that!" I shout. I think the caffeine is kicking in. "I haven't lost myself! I'm still me!"

"Hey, hey, of course you are," Dad says, reaching across the table to put a hand on my arm. "I'm just giving you some fatherly advice. I've heard stories about Manhattan private school kids, how they go off the rails sometimes, so I . . . I just want to make sure you don't. Who else is saying that to you?"

"What?"

"You said everyone keeps saying you're losing who you are."

"Oh," I say, retreating into my coffee mug. "Nobody. It doesn't matter."

"Gotcha," Dad says, giving me that look again, like he's shooting lasers into my brain. "Is Yoo coming by today to go through some boxes?"

"Uh." I take yet another sip of coffee. "I don't think so. He's busy. Doing stuff. But I'll see him when I hang with Monster Club in an hour. So."

"Busy," Dad says. "Interesting. Meant to tell you, we're visiting Aunt Betty at four."

"Again? We just went!"

"True. But you owe me for giving me two straight one-day weekends, so I don't wanna hear any complaints."

When Dad gets intense like this, he is very intimidating. "Fine," I say. I've had close to zero sleep, so of course hanging out later at the nursing home sounds like something I'd love to do.

"Good."

We sit in silence for at least a minute, Dad flipping through some yellowed newspaper from, like, 1948 that he found in one of his new boxes. (And by "new" I mean "ridiculously old.")

"How's Mom doing?" Dad says without looking up.

"Mom?" I'm not sure how much I'm supposed to share or not share about her life. "Oh, yeah, she's good." And I'm also not sure why we can't seem to find a topic of conversation that doesn't make me squirm.

"I know about this Terry guy she's seeing. Mom told me."

"Ah, yeah. Good. It's weird, Dad. It's so weird."

"I'll bet. What's, uh . . . What's he like?"

"He's okay," I say. I want to give Dad some good dirt, but the truth is Terry seems like a nice guy. He's been cool to me every time I've seen him. And I still think those titanium special edition D&D dice he gave me are incredibly rad. "Seems like kind of a dork."

Dad laughs. "A dork, huh? That's helpful. I can work with dork."

I laugh too, mainly from relief. "You're way cooler,

Dad. Do not worry about that."

"I miss you, bud," Dad says, still smiling even though his eyes are a little teary.

I nod and realize my eyes are getting teary too. "I miss you too, Dad," I say. Then I look away and finish off the remains of my coffee.

By the time I'm biking up to the stretch of boardwalk where Monster Club is hanging out, it's starting to rain.

"Well, look who's decided to grace us with his presence!" Hollywood says, standing on a bench in a red leather jacket as I hop off my bike and flip down the kickstand. Everyone's there except Jenni: Hollywood and Keiko, Beanie and Lynsey, Smash and Yoo. No one seems particularly happy to see me.

"Yes, I've deemed you all worthy," I say, playing along.

Yoo hasn't looked my way yet, but I hear him scoff.

Hollywood smiles and jumps off the bench. He gives me a hug. "What's up, man?"

"Hey," I say. "I'm good. How're you?"

"Tight, yeah," Hollywood says. "Other than this dang rain. We were just talking about going somewhere else."

"Cool," I say, putting my hood up after my head gets pelted with a few fat drops. "How're you all doing?"

Beanie, Lynsey, and Keiko nod and offer some half-hearted "Good"s. Yoo and Smash, sitting side by side on the rail overlooking the sand, say nothing.

I was expecting things to be tense, but not *this* tense.

The rain starts coming down harder.

I decide to address the problem head-on. "So, Yoo, you no longer believe in texting? Or communicating in any form?"

Yoo sighs, still not looking at me.

"Yo," Hollywood says, "let's not—"

"He believes in texting," Smash says, almost like she's spitting out the words. "Just not with people who don't respect him!"

"Oh, come on," I say. "Of *course* I respect him!"

"You straight-up abandoned me last week, Doodles!" Yoo says, the words bursting out of him like a jack-in-the-box. He hops off the rail and steps toward me.

"I'm Sketch now, okay?" I say. "And *abandoned*? *You* walked away from *me*!"

"Yeah, because you and your new friends were being terrible!"

I know there's some truth to that as soon as he says it. But I also think he's overreacting.

"Well," I say, "it's not their fault you were too worried to come on the ferry with us!" We're now a few feet apart, shouting in each other's faces, the rain slowly soaking our hair and clothes, with everyone else surrounding and watching like it's a monster battle. Which is funny

134

because Yoo is wearing his AC/DC T-shirt, just like what he drew onto BellyBeast. "And honestly, taking a ride on a ferry isn't even that wild a thing to do, so, I mean—"

"It obviously wasn't just the ferry," Yoo says as a strong breeze blows past us. "That guy Pete made fun of my Kiss shirt. And then that girl made fun of my voice. And you didn't even defend me!"

"I did!" I say, but I'm worried I might be remembering wrong.

"Yeah, keep telling yourself that, Doodles." Yoo turns and walks away.

I follow after him. "It's *Sketch*, okay? I go by SKETCH now!"

"Doodles, Sketch, who cares what you go by?" Smash says, stepping in front of me to block my path. "How about we just call you Giant Tool?"

"All right, all right," Beanie says, holding a blue-and-white umbrella over herself as she walks toward us. "Can we all just bring a little chill to this conversation?" She puts a hand on my shoulder. "Eric, you okay?"

"Definitely," I say. "Absolutely. I'm actually doing better than ever. I went to a bar mitzvah in the Hamptons yesterday. And you want to know how I got there? Private helicopter! For real! It was insane!"

"Oh," Smash says, "so you're a giant tool *and* a poser too. Wonderful."

135

"I'm not posing, Smash! I'm just—" I run a hand over my face and through my hair to wipe the rain away. "Look, all of you were always telling me I needed to grow up, right? So that's what I'm doing! Experiencing new things!"

"I get that," Beanie says. "We're always evolving. That's just life."

"Right, exactly!" I say, grateful for Beanie. I see her look over to Lynsey, who's put on a green raincoat, and they exchange little smiles. It suddenly occurs to me that maybe Lynsey is Beanie's *girlfriend*.

"Yeah, fine," Yoo says, walking back toward me. "But I wish you weren't evolving into a huge jerk."

"Oh man," I say, rolling my eyes, maybe because it hurts so much to hear him say it. "This is getting so boring! Am I a giant tool? Or a huge jerk? Or a poser? Which is it?"

"All of the above!" Smash says.

"But don't you see what's happening here?" I ask. I notice that Keiko is pointing her phone at me, obviously filming, which is kind of annoying, but whatever. "I've apologized already, several times—"

"Not really," Yoo says.

"—and still it's not good enough for you! I don't know why, maybe you're jealous. I would be! Private helicopters are sick! And oh, by the way, I have a new girlfriend too. And she's *very* hot and *very* cool."

"Wow," Yoo says. "You actually straight-up suck now."

"True that," Smash says. "And great job breaking Jenni's heart, by the way. Also very cool."

"It's more complicated than that," I say. "But maybe you're the ones who aren't grown-up enough to understand. Maybe *you're* the ones who are scared of the slightest bit of change. Maybe that's why you can't stop whining!" I know I'm probably going too far, but my rage and exhaustion and all that coffee I drank have twisted themselves up into an unstoppable force. I make my hands into fists and move them by my face like I'm a baby. "WAAA WAAA WAAAA YOU'RE SO TERRIBLE, DOODLES! OH NO, THEY MADE A JOKE ABOUT MY SHIRT, DOODLES! YOU'RE SUCH A POSER, DOODLES! WAAAA WAAA WAAAA! Maybe you should grow up and get over yourselves!"

I hop onto my bike and pedal away as fast as I can.

Nobody tries to stop me.

15

PHOTOBOMB

Eric

"I can't go to Aunt Betty's" is the first thing I say when I walk into Dad's house, soaked to the bone.

"You're going, kid," Dad says without a moment of hesitation as he closes the dishwasher and starts a load. "We already talked about this."

"But I'm all wet!"

"Yeah, it's called rain. Change into something else and we'll leave. Tante Betty's expecting us."

"I know, but . . ." I can tell Dad's not going to bend on this, but I feel so crappy, I need to try. "It's not just the rain. I just— I got into an argument with . . . some of my friends, and it sucked, so I'm not in the mood to—"

"Which friends? Yoo?"

"Uh. Yeah. Mainly Yoo."

"That's why he wasn't here this morning, right?"

I look down. I nod.

Dad lets out a mammoth sigh. "Eric, geez. You can't just burn all these bridges. These people mean something to you!"

"I'm not burning anything! It's not my fault that—"

"I don't want to hear it." Dad glares at me. "Go change and we'll leave."

"Okay," I say. You don't mess with Dad when he glares.

In my room, I realize I only packed clothes for the bar mitzvah and today, so I don't have another outfit to change into. I'm about to raid Dad's closet when I get a text from Bobo:

i miss you so bad. today is no fun

It's the first thing all day that makes me smile. It's nice to be reminded that my life is more than just super tense arguments and smelly fart trains.

oh man, I say. *today is the most unfun. miss you so much*

I head downstairs without changing. Suddenly my wet clothes don't bother me that much.

"Have you never heard of an umbrella?" Aunt Betty asks seconds after we walk into her room. "You're drenched."

I shrug. "I have a hood."

"Couldn't stop for flowers, Tante Betty," Dad says,

giving her a hug. "Rain was coming down too hard. Sorry about that."

"Oh stop," Aunt Betty says. "The flowers are always lovely, but the real treat is seeing you two. Especially my Eric—get over here." She pulls me in for her classic sloppy kiss on the cheek, which I don't mind as much this time. I'm soaked anyway, right?

Aunt Betty sits down on her small couch and gestures for me to plop down next to her. "I've been thinking since you were last here," she says as I sit, "about how much you don't know about my life. So this time I'm prepared." She reaches below the couch and hefts a big, fat reddish-brown book up into her lap. "This is what was known in my day as a *photo album*. Basically my generation's Instant Gram."

"It's actually Instagram, Aunt Betty."

"Oh, whatever. My point is—"

"Hello, hello," her caregiver Renee says, gliding into the room with a smile and a vase in her hands.

"No flowers today, honey," Aunt Betty says.

"What?" Renee says, opening her mouth in pretend shock. "No flowers? Then who is going to eat the cheeseburger and fries I have ready to feed them?"

Dad loudly guffaws. I don't understand until I realize she's referencing his terrible plant food joke from last time. I can't believe she remembered that.

"I'm sure we could find a hungry bouquet somewhere in this place," Dad says.

"I hope so," Renee says, laughing.

"Oh, while you're here," Aunt Betty says to Renee, "can you talk to my nephew over here about that switch in my medication schedule? He's good with that stuff. Just run it by him."

"Sure," Renee says.

"But not in here!" Aunt Betty shoos Renee and my dad toward the door. "Take it outside, I don't need to get stressed out hearing you talk about it in front of me. And take your time!"

"All right, all right," Dad says, walking behind Renee toward the door. "Geez, Tante."

"I'm a particular person, what can I say?" Once they're gone, the door closed behind them, Aunt Betty gives me a wink. "This way you and I get some private time."

She opens up the massive photo album and starts touring me through the pictures. Although I've seen a couple of them, most are new to me, which is actually surprising—I'm still caught off guard by how much I don't know about my own family, how much I never even thought to ask.

"This is your great-uncle Paul and me on our honeymoon," Aunt Betty says, gesturing to a picture of them, young and smiling in front of some large mountains. "The Catskills. Never been so sick in my life."

"But you look happy," I say, laughing.

"Oh, we were!" Aunt Betty says. "But something I ate didn't sit well with me. A few hours after this picture was taken, I was spending most of my time in the bathroom."

"Ew," I say.

"What? It's the truth! Oh, look, here's your dad and your uncle Harry." The two of them are sitting side by side on the King's Wonderland Express, a train kiddie ride—Dad looks about eight, completely serious, with Uncle Harry about five, waving at the camera. "They'd just lost their mother—your grandma—a year or so before. Your father was very sad for a long time. Harry was too, but he was younger, so he bounced back quicker."

I stare at this little kid version of my dad, imagining how devastated he must have felt. I've always known Dad's mom died when he was a kid, but I've never fully thought about how hard that must have been for him.

Aunt Betty takes me through page after page, and it's actually the most amazing escape from how awful I was feeling after my fight with Yoo and Smash, losing myself in the stories of my family, learning about relatives I've never met and understanding new things about the ones I have.

As we reach the end of the book, I see a small stack of photos tucked into the back pocket of the inside cover. I grab out a square black-and-white pic at the front of the stack, which features an Aunt Betty who looks even younger than she did on her honeymoon. It turns out it's attached to another photo below it, like it's from a photo booth. In both, Aunt Betty is smiling and laughing with a young man who definitely isn't Uncle Paul. In the first, their faces are right next to each other; in the second, the man is giving Aunt Betty a kiss on the cheek while she giggles with delight.

"Looks like you found Oscar," Aunt Betty says, with a little twinkle in her eye.

"Oh wow," I say. As uncomfortable as I am seeing my aunt all flirty with someone who's not my uncle, it's fun to at least see what this first love of hers looked like.

But as I stare at the twentysomething man in the photo, I get the strangest feeling that he's familiar to me. Something about his smile.

Wait. It can't be . . . can it?

I look closer, and even without the white beard and the wrinkles and the long gray straggly hair, I'm suddenly sure of it:

My great-aunt Betty used to date King Neptune.

16

OSCAR = NEPTUNE

Eric

I can't believe it.

The resemblance is unmistakable.

"That's . . . ," I say. "That's—"

"Yup," Aunt Betty says. "Oscar. My first love."

I have no idea if she's aware that Oscar is now a dirty man in a toga who walks the boardwalk claiming to be King Neptune, god of the sea. Don't get me wrong, I think King Neptune is a good-hearted person, and he was really helpful in giving me advice about the ink and ultimately destroying it so we could make sure it never falls into the wrong hands, but I don't want to be the one to share with my aunt how far his mental state has declined.

"What, um, what was he like?"

"Handsome," Aunt Betty says. "That's what I remember the most, how handsome he was."

"Seriously?"

Aunt Betty gives me an exaggerated scowl. "Is that so hard to believe, that I'd be able to attract someone so handsome?"

"No, no, it's not that, I just— Well, how did you even meet him? And what made you break up?"

"Oh boy, I haven't really thought about any of the details in a long, long time. Feels like several lifetimes ago."

"So just tell me what you remember," I say.

Aunt Betty taps her mouth with a finger and stares at the ceiling, as if some of the details have been scrawled up there.

"Okay," she says finally, looking right at me. "Here's how it went."

17

THE STORY OF BETTY AND OSCAR

Betty

Betty King was nineteen years old when she first laid eyes on Oscar Weissberger.

It wasn't love at first sight.

It was more like immediate intrigue.

It was July 1963, and Betty was working at the newly opened King's Wonderland. Fourteen years after King's Sideshow Extraordinaire had burned to the ground, Betty's father and uncle had finally raised enough money to use the land to open up a theme park they thought would properly honor the memory of *their* father— Betty's grandfather—Isaac.

As exciting as it all was, Betty very quickly grew bored of the job, which in her case meant selling ride and game tickets, hour after hour, mostly to families with loud children or to packs of loud teenagers who she wanted nothing to do with, in spite of how close in age they were to her.

That's why Oscar's presence in line stood out so much.

"I'll take twenty tickets," he said, a little jumpy, sliding the bill across the counter, his blue-green eyes so vivid, Betty almost felt like she was staring into the ocean.

"Sure." She slid him the tickets.

"Thanks." He gave her a smile and a wink and then ran toward the rides with the enthusiasm of a young child. Betty had assumed he'd be meeting someone, but instead he went onto the Tilt-A-Whirl, all by himself.

She couldn't help but wonder: *Why is this man in his twenties alone at King's Wonderland?*

The question only grew more pressing when Oscar came back the next day.

And the day after that.

"Isn't it obvious?" her best friend, Sharon, asked after Betty told her about this frequent visitor to King's. "He wants to go out with you!"

"Oh please," Betty said as her face turned fire truck red. She wasn't used to that kind of attention and didn't want to get her hopes up. She'd started to notice how handsome Oscar was. It was in his eyes, yes, but there was also something magnetic, something unpredictable about him, not to mention a slightly wounded quality, like he needed someone to take care of him.

Someone like Betty.

It was during Oscar's fourth consecutive visit when Sharon was proven correct.

"Would you like to get a burger sometime?" Oscar asked across the counter.

Though she wanted to scream yes, Betty tried to sound every bit as casual as when she'd handed him tickets: "Sure."

And from that first date onward, they became Betty and Oscar, Oscar and Betty, almost inseparable. He was always making her laugh, always making her feel special, even as he rarely shared much about himself. Betty knew he worked at the New York Aquarium, which had recently relocated from Manhattan to Coney Island, and she knew he was an aspiring artist, but otherwise, he was a mystery she was constantly trying to solve. It was quite thrilling.

"I want to know who you are," she would say to Oscar in those early months, as they held hands and walked down the beach.

"I'm Oscar," he would respond with a sly smile. "One half of the legendary duo, Oscar and Betty."

"But who are your parents? Where do you live? What are your dreams?"

"Well, let's see," Oscar would say. "For the hundredth time: I don't get along with my parents, I live near here, and my dream is to walk down the beach with a beautiful gal named Betty King. Look at that! My dream has come true!"

Betty would giggle and blush and let it go.

She was nervous to introduce Oscar to her parents, knowing they'd prefer her to pair up with a doctor or lawyer rather than an aquarium worker. But, thanks to Oscar's charisma and charm, her parents loved him instantly. The first time he came over for Sunday night dinner, the four of them sat chatting at the table for almost three hours.

Oscar became a regular fixture at these dinners, which warmed Betty's heart to no end. Yet the Mystery remained. During these visits, Oscar would sometimes disappear—Betty would assume he was in the bathroom, but instead would find him in random rooms of the family's row house, just gazing around. "I'm sorry," he would say, looking down. "I've always loved exploring other people's homes. Probably because the home I grew up in was . . . Well, it wasn't much of a home. Let's leave it at that."

In those moments, Betty couldn't help but want to hold this damaged soul close, give him whatever it was that he'd never had when he was growing up.

"I'd like to take you somewhere tonight. Somewhere special. Would that be okay?" Oscar asked her one day, five or so months into their relationship.

"Sure," she said, gazing into those deep ocean-green eyes.

She thought for sure she was finally going to see Oscar's home. *Keep all your judgments to yourself, no matter how small or dirty it might be*, Betty reminded herself. But it turned out Oscar was sneaking her after-hours into the New York Aquarium, where it turned out he worked as a janitor.

A few slick-haired hooligans in their twenties loitered near the entrance, wolf-whistling at Betty, taunting Oscar that she was way out of his league, but that all faded away once Betty and Oscar made it inside and Oscar locked the door behind them.

"I hope you ignored those guys," he said.

"Ignored which guys?" Betty said with a smile.

He smiled back, relief emanating from him like cologne, and took her hand in his.

It was easily the most romantic night of Betty's life up to that point.

Holding her hand the entire time, Oscar gave her a private tour of all the sea creatures (the ones that weren't asleep, anyway). He referred to them as if they were his friends, which was perhaps the most endearing thing Betty had ever experienced.

"You know," Oscar said, "you're always asking about my home. Where I live. But truthfully, I've felt more at home here than anywhere. At least, until I met you."

He led her to a candlelit table he'd set up next to one of the tanks, bowing before helping her into her seat. They ate sandwiches and laughed at the octopus that hovered for a minute, as if it wanted to join them. When Oscar stared into Betty's eyes, the glow from a passing jellyfish shining on his face, Betty knew for sure:

She was deeply in love.

As the months went by, it became clear Betty and Oscar were on a path to marriage. Not only did her parents approve, but Oscar became so close with her father that plans were discussed for him to leave his job at the aquarium and join the family business for the upcoming summer. He would help manage King's Wonderland.

"Isn't this fantastic?" Oscar asked as they walked down the boardwalk near King's during the off-season, one of those warmer winter days that promised a glorious springtime would be here soon. "Maybe one day you and me will be running this whole place! We could bring back Isaac's tattoo business. Heck, maybe even bring back the sideshow too!"

Betty was thrown to hear Oscar talk so familiarly

about her grandfather when he'd never once mentioned him before. "Maybe," she said. "I didn't realize that was something you'd be interested in. . . ."

"Well, sure!" Oscar said, with a little too much enthusiasm, clearly on the defensive. "You know I'm an artist. The tattoos could be a venue for my art, like they were for Isaac."

"How do you know so much about what my zayde did?"

"Well, because . . . Isaac is a Coney Island legend. And your dad told me about him."

Betty made it clear she wasn't buying this.

The Mystery was no longer thrilling or intriguing. It needed to be solved.

"Look," Oscar said, suddenly solemn. "I never told you this, but . . . I saw King's Sideshow Extraordinaire when I was a kid. And I loved it. It . . . It changed my life."

"Oh," Betty said, trying to keep her head from spinning.

"Your grandfather Isaac was a real inspiration to me. Not that I ever met him. Well, not officially anyway."

"How come you've never mentioned this, huh?"

Oscar looked off toward the ocean. "I . . . I didn't want to seem peculiar. I thought I might seem like a . . . crazed fan or something."

"Are you?"

"No!" Oscar shouted, with an intensity that was a little frightening. "Of course not!" He seemed like he might start to cry.

"Okay, okay." Betty led them to a bench and ran a hand down Oscar's back, trying to calm him down. She'd never seen him like this before. "I know that's not who you are. You're my dear, sweet Oscar. I know you, right?"

Oscar nodded, unable to speak, and collapsed into Betty's arms.

She rocked him, almost like a baby.

"I'm sorry," Oscar said. "I love you, Betty."

"I love you, Oscar." She forgave him, the moment passed, and she thought that was the end of it.

She was wrong.

It was a few months later, less than a week away from the opening of the summer season at King's. Oscar had started his management job with the family, though he was still holding on to some hours at the aquarium to save as much money as he could for the life he and Betty were planning together.

He was over for Sunday night dinner, and, for the first time in a while, he'd disappeared.

Betty searched through all the rooms, including the

bathrooms, but there was no sign of him. As she was passing the door to the basement, though, she heard something.

A gentle banging.

She pulled open the door as quietly as possible and moved down the steps, careful not to make them creak. Halfway down, she saw Oscar.

He was at Betty's father's padlocked cabinet, his back to Betty as he used a hammer to try to crack the padlock off.

Betty couldn't believe what she was seeing.

The cabinet was filled with her father's World War II memorabilia, but Oscar might not have known that.

He clearly thought something valuable was inside.

Betty suddenly understood that the countless other times Oscar had disappeared in her home were likely motivated by more than a simple desire to "explore."

She felt betrayed. Angry. Devastated.

And she was so stunned and overcome that she couldn't voice any of it.

As Oscar continued hacking away at the lock, Betty crept back up the steps and silently shut the door behind her.

Betty didn't say anything about it for the next few days.

King's Wonderland would be opening to the public

on Friday, and there was much to prepare. Steeplechase Park, one of the other Coney Island amusement parks, was kicking off its season on Thursday, and Oscar had suggested they take a ride that night on its most famous attraction, the Parachute Jump. It was rumored that this might be its last summer in operation.

"Sure," Betty said, thinking, perhaps irrationally, the ride would be the perfect moment to confront Oscar about his attempted theft. They would be on an island in the sky, and he wouldn't be able to run away from any of her questions.

Thursday night came, and Betty tried to remain calm as they boarded the ride, seated side by side on a canvas bench.

They began to ascend into the sky.

Betty swallowed and was about to speak, but Oscar beat her to it.

"Betty," he said. "My sweet Betty. I am so excited about this life we are building together." He reached into his jacket pocket and pulled out a small box. "You are my everything, and so I want to ask you a question." He started to open the box, and Betty felt a panic rising in her as quickly as they were rising above Coney Island. "Betty King, will you ma—"

"Did you find what you were looking for?" Betty asked, no longer able to keep her cool.

Oscar was confused. "Well, yes. It's you, Betty. I want to spend my life—"

"I'm not talking about that," Betty said, staring out at the steadily expanding view of Brooklyn. "I saw you trying to break into my father's cabinet."

Betty watched the blood drain from Oscar's face.

"Wait," he said, "break into your—? I did no such thing, Betty!"

"I watched it happen, Oscar," Betty said, a volcanic rage roiling within her.

"Betty, it's not what you think."

"So tell me what it is!" They were now at least two hundred feet up in the air. "Because I'm not going to marry a lying thief!"

"Okay, okay," Oscar said, looking pale but composed. "I was looking for ink. Magical ink that belonged to your grandfather. It has immense—"

"Oy vey! That's the best you could come up with? Magic ink? Do you think I'm an idiot?"

"Of course I don't. This ink is real. I saw it with my own eyes. The night King's burned down."

Betty recoiled (at least as much as one can when seated on a tiny bench twenty stories in the sky). "What are you talking about? You're having a mental breakdown, Oscar!"

Their bench stopped. They'd reached the apex of the

ride. The view of Brooklyn and Manhattan and all of New York City was breathtaking, though neither of them could take it in.

"All I wanted was to know who you are," Betty said, her emotions erupting, tears streaming down her face. "It shouldn't be this hard."

She felt her stomach bounce as the ride began to descend, the white parachute opening up above them.

"You know who I am," Oscar said, trying to turn the charm back on. "One half of the legendary duo, Betty and—"

"You know what I mean! We've been together almost a year, and I've never even seen your home!"

"You are my home, Betty!"

Betty shook her head and wiped her face. "I'm not fall-ing for your flattery anymore. All the snooping," she said. "All the mystery. I don't know who you are. And I don't know how I can possibly trust you now."

"Of course you can," Oscar said, but even he knew his words seemed hollow.

"You tried to break into my father's things. You won't

tell me even the most simple facts about yourself."

"Please," Oscar said, clutching his small box as the ground rose up toward them. "It's not— It was a mistake!"

"I can't do this anymore," Betty said. "And I've already told my father what happened. So I would resign if you don't want to be fired."

"No. Betty. No!"

Their seat jerked to a stop, the bench swinging back and forth.

"I'm sorry," Betty said as she lifted her lap bar and stepped down.

The ride was over.

That was the last time Betty saw Oscar.

She was heartbroken, but she knew it was the right thing to do. This was only further confirmed when she found out Oscar had gone to the New York Aquarium later that night and smashed a bunch of tanks, killing many of the sea creatures he had once called his friends. He was a troubled man.

Almost two years later to the day, Betty met and fell in love with Paul Grossman. She moved on, got married, lived her life. Even though she'd once hated Oscar for the way things ended, for the way he'd hurt her, taken advantage of her, that faded over time. Because she knew there had also been something real there. Even the best con man couldn't fake the magic of that night together at the aquarium.

Going through her things one afternoon, she stumbled upon pictures of her and Oscar from the King's Wonderland photo booth, taken a couple of months after they started dating. She was about to throw them in the trash when she had second thoughts. She was a different person now, but that experience was still a part of her, one she didn't want to forget.

She decided to keep the photos.

18

VIRAL IN THE BAD WAY

Eric

So I'm pretty shocked.

Aunt Betty thought she was going to *marry* King Neptune? He would have been my uncle!

That is too weird to process.

Really, that whole story was.

"I can't believe he was trying to break into your dad's stuff!" I say, though in some ways I guess I can. King Neptune was definitely intense about destroying the ink, even decades later.

"I know. He was desperate." Aunt Betty slowly stands from the couch and stretches her arms. "I later found out from Tony at the auto repair place that Oscar had been homeless the whole time I knew him. Mainly was sleeping at the aquarium. Or under the boardwalk.

Can you believe that?"

Well, yes. Yes, I can.

"So, in some ways," Aunt Betty continues, "as much as I hate him for scamming me, I also don't fully blame him. And, look, it all worked out in the end, boychik."

"But, Aunt Betty . . ." I'm trying to figure out the best way to articulate my next thought. "You know that your grandfather Isaac really did have that ink, right? I found it in an old box. That's what caused all that chaos at the beginning of the summer."

"Oh, I know. Kind of ironic, right? I was in shock when your dad told me. Maybe Oscar wasn't so nuts after all, huh?"

Well.

I should tell her the truth about who he is now, that he walks around in a toga and crown genuinely believing he's a god. She can handle it.

"And you really haven't seen him since you broke up that night?" I ask.

"Nah," Aunt Betty says. "Apparently he went on to do very well, though. Inherited his father's business."

Very well? I'm pretty sure he still has no home, all these years later.

"Um," I say. "Aunt Betty, there's something you—"

The door opens, and Dad walks into the room loudly laughing. "I'll believe it when I see it!" he calls out to

Renee as she walks away down the hall. Guess he was out there talking to her this whole time. "You didn't mention how hilarious she is, Tante Betty."

"Who? Renee? She's amazing. She's a genius. I love her."

"And an incredible cook too!" Dad takes a bite out of something, then holds it up. "Fried plantain! Or, uh, bannann, I think she called it."

"Oh," Aunt Betty says, eyebrows raised. "She offered you some of her cooking? That's the VIP treatment."

Dad looks down at the floor and maybe even . . . blushes a little? "Ah well, I enjoyed talking with her. And we, uh, squared away everything with your new medication schedule. What've you two been talking about in here?"

"Oscar," Aunt Betty says, giving me another wink.

"Oh god, not this guy again," Dad says, covering his ears.

After I hug Aunt Betty and Dad goodbye, I detour to the beach instead of hopping right on the subway back to Mom.

I need some space to think.

It's a chilly day, and it's even chillier down by the water. I walk parallel to the ocean, dodging the tide so my sneakers don't get wet. There's a couple in their sixties sitting on the sand in beach chairs, but otherwise it's empty here.

I want to make sense of everything, but I can't yet.

Aunt Betty was once in love with King Neptune.

And he might own a business and make a comfortable living, even though he seems like he's poor and unhoused. Maybe Aunt Betty is confused. Or maybe he had the business for a while but then lost everything. That would make more sense.

The other thing I don't fully get is why Neptune was so obsessed with getting that ink if his plan was to destroy it. Was he *that* concerned that it would fall into the wrong hands? How could someone trying to do good be that cruel? To the extent that he would want to date Betty just for, like, the good of the world?

It's all so weird.

I slide my hands into my jeans pockets and realize the photos of Betty and Oscar are in one of them. Oops. I must've put them there during her story. I'll bring them back on my next visit.

Betty looks so happy, but honestly so does Oscar. It's obvious even in black and white. If he was just using her to try to snoop through her family's stuff and find the ink, he was a very good actor.

As I continue walking, sudden movement in my peripheral vision pulls my focus from the photos.

I don't believe it.

There on the shore are seven fish—some green, some blue, some black—flopping around out of the water just like the ones at the Hamptons yesterday.

Do I seriously have to do this *again*?

I feel too bad not to save them, so I start frantically picking the fish up one by one, but then I wonder . . .

I turn to look and, sure enough, I see her.

That woman again. She's floating about fifty feet out, bobbing in the waves as the sun is starting to set, the sky turning pink.

"Who are you?" I call out.

No response.

"Are you watching me?"

There's a splash as she goes under. A flick of green fin. Another small splash on the surface. And she's gone.

Again.

This time I don't think I'm losing my mind.

I know it.

'Cause it's either that, or I just saw a mermaid.

Please hit me back when you can, I text Yoo. *I get why you have every reason not to, but please*

I'm back in Manhattan at Mom's, sitting on my bed before I join her and Terry for dinner. I texted Yoo seconds after I saw the mermaid, seeing as he's the only person in the world who will understand the full impli-cations of what it means (beyond it just being generally insane to see a real-life mermaid), that it was a mermaid who gave my great-great-grandfather Isaac the magic ink so many years ago (the ink that is actually, um, *her blood*).

Come to think of it, Yoo isn't the only person in the world who would understand; King Neptune would too, seeing as he's the one who told me and Yoo that story in the first place. But even if I did have some clue as to where he is, I'm too confused about his deal. That's another thing I desperately need to talk to Yoo about.

But no matter how many times I text him—there was one other attempt, on the subway ride back to Mom's—he hasn't responded. I get it. I was a little ridiculous to him and Smash, and really all of Monster Club, this afternoon.

Which is why I haven't been able to bring myself to text the group thread, no matter how badly I want to. I pull up the text I composed:

So, first of all, I'm sorry about this afternoon. I was kind of a jerk. But more importantly . . . I think I saw a mermaid???? And also turns out King Neptune used to get with my aunt 😹 I am SHOOK

I can't send this. I left on such a horrible note. They'll probably all ghost me, just like Yoo.

It doesn't help that Bobo hasn't texted back yet either. I messaged her from the train, letting her know my afternoon got much weirder and I can't wait to tell her about it. I know she's not ghosting me, but it would be nice to talk to *someone*. She's probably on the helicopter home. Maybe her phone died.

I stare at my phone, willing some message to come through.

Nothing.

I get up from my bed, pace around.

In the other room, I hear the sound of the table being set and a brown paper bag crinkling, which means Terry's gotten back home with our take-out Thai.

"Eric, food's here!" Mom calls through the door.

"Be out in a minute!" I say. I'm not ready to go out there yet. Too restless.

I find myself opening my closet door, pulling out the plastic bin labeled "Monster Club." I paw through all my old notebooks, filled from cover to cover with drawings of Brickman in a zillion different poses. There are piles of old tournament brackets and score sheets. It wasn't all that long ago, yet it feels like such a different time.

I miss it.

I didn't think I did, I've been trying to convince myself everything is better now, but there's so much I miss about how things used to be. It felt easier then.

My phone buzzes and I spring across the room to see who it is.

It's Knapp.

I would have preferred Yoo or Bobo, but I'll take it!

Have you seen this yet, he's written, with something attached.

I bet it's some goofy pic from the bar mitzvah or a random image of salty licorice to troll me with.

"Eric, come on," Mom shouts, "your food's gonna get cold!"

"Yup, coming!"

It's actually a TikTok video. I look closer at the link, and I'm surprised to see my own face—I'm angrily shouting in the cover photo with the red title words on a diagonal from my waist to my shoulder: "Hero/Zero 😂"

Oh no.

It's been posted by EmptyMirror. Keiko. The footage she took of me earlier.

I don't want to watch.

I watch.

It starts with an interview I did with NY1 after the Crumple Noodle Incident, the reporter asking me how it feels to be a hero.

"Good, I guess," I say. "I just did what I had to do, though. I don't know if I'd call myself a hero."

Then the video cuts to me today, saying to Yoo and

Smash, "Am I a giant tool? Or a huge jerk? Or a poser? Which is it?"

A subtitle appears that reads "(all of the above)."

Then it cuts back to Past Me doing the interview. "Really, I'm just glad all my friends are okay."

Again back to the mortifying scene from this afternoon. "Maybe you're jealous!" I shout at my friends. "I would be! Private helicopters are sick! And oh, by the way, I have a new girlfriend too. And she's *very* hot and *very* cool."

Oh god. I can see how out of line I was. But also I cannot believe Keiko posted this. I quickly check to see how many views it has.

10,924.

And it was only put up two hours ago.

It's going viral.

Like, in the bad way.

Which is why Knapp has seen it.

Which means that Bobo has probably seen it too.

Which is probably why she's not responding to my texts.

No.

No no no no no no no.

"Eric," Mom says, knocking at my door. "Your pad thai's gonna get cold, sweetie."

I grunt a response, watching in horror as the me

on my phone goes into his epic "WAAAA WAAA" baby tirade, complete with baby fists.

"Are you okay?" Mom asks.

"Yeah, totally," I'm able to spit out. "Be right there, sorry."

"Okay." Mom sounds unconvinced, but she walks away anyway.

The video is over, and I see there are already twenty-six comments, and I am so embarrassed, and so angry, and so shocked.

I go back to Knapp's text to respond, but suddenly I feel the need to run to the bathroom instead.

I get there seconds too late and throw up all over the tiles.

19

EVERYTHING IS TERRY-BLE

Eric

I'm not eating my pad thai.

I'm too focused on the phone in my lap, watching this catastrophe unfold. Mom and Terry are chomping on curry as they have some stupendously boring conversation about the Woolworth Building, where she works.

"They get all the elevators working again yet?" Terry asks.

"Ugh, no," Mom says, "three of them are still down for repairs. I have to allot ten extra minutes every morning for the wait in the lobby. Eric, put the phone away, please."

"One sec," I say. Bobo still hasn't texted me back.

What happened to "missing me so bad"?

"More like the Woolworthless Building, am I right?" Terry says.

"That was really bad," Mom says.

The video has passed 20,000 views.

People in the comments think it's hilarious.

More than 20,000 people have watched my freak-out.

I swallow hard in the hopes of avoiding another trip to the bathroom.

"Would you say it was Terry-ble?" Terry asks.

"Oh boy," Mom says. "We might have to end this." Mom snaps her fingers at me. "Eric. Phone. Down. Now."

I nod and pull up the Monster Club thread.

Why did Keiko post that vid, I write.

Hollywood responds within seconds.

Cause she thought it would get a lot of views

She was right, he adds. *Lol*

I know I acted like a jerk to all of you, I furiously type, *and I'm sorry. but could you ask her to take it down*

Oh NOW you apologize, Hollywood writes. *I see how it is*

I want to scream.

"Will you get your face out of that phone?" Mom says.

"Oh. Yeah. Sorry. It's . . . Uh, yeah."

"Well, look at that!" Mom has shifted into full sarcasm attack mode. "Your neck is actually able to lift your head up so you can acknowledge us."

I offer an attempt at a smile and then look back down at the text that's just come in.

She should take it down, Ahmed, Beanie says. She always uses Hollywood's real name when she's being serious. *No matter how big a jerk Sketch is being, he doesn't deserve this*

"Give me the phone, Eric," Mom says, reaching a hand across the table.

"What? Why?"

"Why? Because you got to skip half a weekend with Dad to go to the Hamptons, now you're finally home and you can barely say a word to us! I'm sick of it!"

"I'm sorry." There's no way I'm giving her my phone. "It's because something important is going on, like actually something really bad, and—"

"Eric," Mom says, in that tone that sends a chill soaring down my spine. "I honestly don't care what's happening on there. You need to give it to me right now or I will take you off our family plan and you'll have no phone at all. Don't try me. I'm not bluffing."

I know she's not bluffing. But I also know the phone is my only way out of this heinous mess. I need to convince Keiko to take the video down, and then maybe I can post a vid of my own to explain my side of the story.

"Can I at least explain to you what's—"

"I'll grab my laptop now," Mom says, rising from the

172

table. "I'll be able to take you off the plan within a couple of min—"

"No, don't!" I shout. "Fine, here's my phone, okay?" I push it across the table as Mom sits back down, and it feels like I've given up a vital organ. Like my liver or something. "Just don't read the messages."

"Of course I won't," Mom says, leaning over to place the phone beneath her chair. "Thank you, Eric. I'm sorry I had to do this."

I feel so angry and powerless. For the first time in a while, I consider how great it would be if I were Brickman—I could use my wrecking ball to demolish everything in my path.

"You did the right thing, bud," Terry says, giving me a solemn nod.

Stupid Terry.

When I wake up in the middle of the night, for a moment I think the video of me going viral was just a horrible nightmare.

But no.

It actually happened.

And the situation has probably gotten even worse, though I have no way to know for sure BECAUSE I DON'T HAVE MY PHONE.

I also have no idea what time it is without said phone,

so I creep out to the kitchen to check the microwave.

1:42.

I'm kind of bummed to be awake, seeing as it took me an hour of restless, infuriated rolling around to fall asleep in the first place.

But now that I am, I'm ready to seize this moment.

Time to get my phone back.

I tiptoe down the hallway and into Mom's bedroom, where she's in her usual position, lying on her back, lightly snoring. I can't believe I'm doing this. I'm relieved to see Terry didn't stay over—one less person to catch me in the act.

Okay: If I were my mom, where would I hide my son's phone?

I start by grabbing her purse off the dresser and rooting around in there. This feels scary. I'm honestly more terrified of Mom waking up and catching me snooping through her purse than I was of Crumple Noodle. I can't see well in the dark, so I take it down the hall into the bathroom. After five minutes of focused inspection, I've found nothing.

I creep back into Mom's bedroom, and I'm depositing her purse on the dresser when she suddenly snorts and mumbles my dad's name. I freeze. She tells Dad to stop making so much noise, then returns to snoring.

Hmm. Okay. Not sure what to do with that.

I oh-so-carefully open each of Mom's drawers, run my fingers around the borders and underneath her clothes.

My phone is nowhere.

I step quietly toward Mom's nightstand, open up its single drawer and feel around. Nada. I check the time on her phone, which is charging there. 1:56.

It occurs to me that, duh, I could get onto my Tik-Tok account on *her* phone, at least to quickly check what's going on with That Horrendous Video. I pull the charging cord out and start walking toward the door.

I stop in the middle of the room. Mom might figure out that I'd been on here, and I'll have phone privileges taken away for even longer. Maybe permanently.

I'm walking the phone back to her nightstand when I notice one drawer of the filing cabinet next to the dresser is ajar and realize that's exactly the kind of weird hiding spot Mom would choose. She'd pick some random folder to slip my phone into, like some case she argued in 2018.

With a flick of my thumb, I turn on her phone's flashlight, keeping a close eye on her to make sure she doesn't wake up again. I slowly slide open the top drawer of the filing cabinet, then proceed to methodically go through each folder, shining the light to the bottom of each one to see if it's stashing the dark rectangular object I desperately need.

Nothing, nothing, a whole lot of nothing.

I pull open Drawer #2, relieved it's unlocked, and begin my process, now thinking there's no way Mom put my phone in here.

Nothing, nothing, no phone, boring papers, no phone, nothing.

But wait.

A name jumps out at me from one of the thousands of papers I'm rifling through.

I flip back to where I saw it.

Oscar.

Oscar Weissberger.

The folder is labeled "Pluto Properties," filled with the legal documents Mom examined in June when she established the case for why their evil company couldn't buy up Dad's business.

And there it is, in numerous spots on the page, clear as day:

Oscar Weissberger, CEO of Pluto Properties.

What?

This must be a coincidence. Another Oscar Weissberger.

There's no way Pluto Properties could be the business King Neptune inherited. That would make no sense.

Because if it is . . .

Well, that would mean I gave the last supply of the all-powerful magic ink to the owner of Pluto

Properties—aka the company that tried to take over my family's land.

No.

Why would the same guy trying to buy up Coney Island, destroying hundreds of lives for his own selfish benefit, also be on a lifelong mission to destroy—

Oh my god.

The sinkhole near City Hall.

Those digging monsters.

Beard and Mustache.

Oh no.

Something big and very bad is happening here, though I can't fully put together what it is.

I do, however, know this:

I have much bigger problems than what people think of me on the internet.

20

PHASE TWO

Neptune

King Neptune does one final lap around the nurse sharks, concluding his midnight swim, before climbing out of the tank and down the ladder, toweling himself off, ready to focus on his art.

He walks down the brightly lit corridor between two other tanks teeming with sea life, water still dripping off his body, until he arrives at his collection.

His shells.

They're lined up in rows in a towering glass cabinet.

Thousands of them.

It's a collection that dates back to when he was small, walking on the beach with his mother while Dad was at work.

"How do I know which ones to pick up?" he remembers asking.

"You pick up the ones that sing to you," his mother said.

"I'll actually hear the shells singing?"

"No," she said, giving his hand a squeeze. "But you'll *feel* them."

Neptune loved that time with his mother more than anything. Collecting shells, examining the creatures that washed up in the tide, feeling loved. He'd thought then that her love for him would always keep him safe.

But no. In the end, his father was stronger than that love.

What really wrecked King Neptune was that, even after his father died a decade later, his mom *still* didn't reach out. Too ashamed of how they'd treated him, perhaps.

He, of course, could have reached out to *her*, but he wasn't going to do that. And risk being rejected yet again? No, thank you.

It was only once his mother died, when King Neptune was forty-one years old, that he realized she might have been happy to hear from him. In her will, she'd passed to him the family's commercial real estate business along with various other properties she and her husband had owned, including this penthouse atop the Woolworth Building that he's standing in right now.

He was moved, yet also crushed by regret.

And though he was proud, he did not reject her offering. The business was a tool he could use for his own ends. And this historic building he owns a piece of has become the nexus of his final plan.

Neptune's fingers run along the shells on the third row from the bottom, coming to rest on a large clamshell close to the wall. He delicately pulls it off the shelf with both hands, cradling it like a newborn. The most precious shell in his collection.

With a sudden and almost violent twist of his wrists, he turns the shell's top and bottom in opposite directions, producing a satisfying click.

This shell is more than just a shell.

He turns the two halves again. Another click.

It's a stainless steel puzzle box fused together with his favorite shell that he'd collected with his mother. (Oh, how that shell had sung!) He'd commissioned an engineer to make the box for him soon after the arrival of his surprise inheritance.

King Neptune turns the halves once more, in the reverse direction, before sliding a fingernail into the crack in the clamshell—the mouth pops opens wide, revealing its contents:

A magic marker and a pen.

To those who don't know any better, securing these items would likely seem ridiculous.

But that's only because they don't know what's inside them.

The powerful, wonderful, awe-inspiring substance.

He still can't believe it's finally his.

He'd searched and searched for it, even once started a romance in the hopes of getting his hands on it. But that romance turned out to be—

It doesn't matter. The point is, his patience has been rewarded.

There's a finite amount of the ink, so he needs to be very deliberate with how he uses it. He's carefully transferred the remaining supply from the boy's marker into this pen.

A marker is far too crude a tool for such a precious resource.

The pen, however, is intended for drafting, with a long needle point that etches thin, thin lines and uses only as much ink as is necessary. It's what Neptune used to make his glorious digging monsters, and it should allow him to stretch the ink so there's just enough to complete his masterpiece.

At least he hopes so.

He locks the clamshell back up, with the magic marker inside, and places it back on the shelf. The pen travels with him across the penthouse apartment to the large corner he's been using as his studio.

King Neptune adjusts the lighting just so, puts "La Mer" by Claude Debussy on the record player, and kneels down in front of the giant paper canvas—twelve feet by ten feet, to be exact—he's been working on.

There's a cloth tarp covering the parts of his monster he's already drawn, for he knows as soon as he reveals the entire piece, it will come to life.

And when it does, everything will change.

He uncaps his pen and gets to work.

21

NOT SO HEROIC AFTER ALL

Eric

"You handled that really well, my love," Mom says as she passes my phone back across the breakfast table. "I'm impressed with how mature you were about this."

I nod and try to smile, but my face is too tired. I wonder if she'd still be impressed if she learned I snooped around her room for half an hour in the dark like an incompetent cat burglar and never even figured out where she was hiding it.

I barely slept after I snuck back to my room.

Too busy trying to figure out how the King Neptune I know could possibly be the same person calling the shots over at Pluto Properties.

It makes my head spin.

As I take slow bites of Mom's French toast—not cooked well enough, like usual, so it tastes all slimy—I'm relieved to have my phone back but also dreading what I'll find inside. Almost twelve hours have passed since Mom took it from me.

The first thing I see are dozens of new texts on the Monster Club thread, too overwhelming to read closely. The most important thing I take in is that Yoo hasn't chimed in, nor has he texted me individually.

Great.

When I open TikTok, I'm nauseated to see Keiko has not taken the video down.

Whether Hollywood never asked her to or she just refused, I don't know.

I do know that it's at 875,263 views.

Which is a lot of views.

There are also hundreds of comments, but I tap out of the app before I'm tempted to look at any of them.

I scan my texts again.

Bobo still hasn't responded.

This is not a good sign.

Knapp, on the other hand, for some reason has taken it upon himself to send me every scrap of video-related evidence he can find: articles with clickbait headlines like "Coney Island Hero Kid Not So Heroic After All" and "Watch Footage of Coney Hero Boy Freak Out." I'm not sure why he's texting this stuff to me. Does he think I like seeing this?

Because I don't.

I definitely don't.

"Eric, you okay?" Mom asks. "You look a little ill."

"I'm fine," I say. "This phone is sort of nauseating."

"Right? That's how I feel," Mom says, putting her empty cereal bowl into the sink before grabbing her camel coat out of the front closet. "Maybe I need to take it away from you more often! That would probably feel good."

"Probably," I say.

She kisses the top of my head and leaves for work.

I slide my phone back across the table.

I hold my breath as I approach Tinsdale, hoping, praying, *begging* that not many people have seen the video.

"Private helicopters are sick, bro!" some kid I don't know shouts from just outside the entrance, cracking up the other kids around him.

I put my head down and keep walking.

Everyone has seen the video.

Inside the school, I'm hit from all sides of the hallway with my own quotes: "Maybe you're jealous!" and "WAAAA WAAA WAAA!" and "You're such a poser, Doodles!"

"Yup," I mutter under my breath. "Okay. Keep it coming." Really, though, I wish it would stop immediately.

"My new girlfriend is *very* hot and *very* cool!" someone shouts in this exaggerated nerd voice and of course right at that moment, Bobo walks by, Pete and Knapp alongside her.

She notices me, I know she does, but she keeps her eyes straight ahead as she keeps moving, that classic small smirk on her face.

It's like I don't exist. Though, honestly, not existing sounds pretty good right now.

Pete's the same way, even though I'm going to see him in homeroom in approximately five minutes. Only Knapp acknowledges me, stopping in the hall as Bobo and Pete continue onward.

"Yo, Sketch!" he says with a big smile. "This is rough what is happening to you, man, yes? Did you get my texts?"

"I did," I say. "Sorry I never wrote back. It's been . . . a lot."

"Yeah, I'll bet! You really had a freak-out in that video! Very funny to watch. But probably not as funny for you."

"No. Not really."

"Anyway, I gotta jet, but you should take some of this." He hands me—what else?—some salty Scandinavian licorice. "The delicious taste will distract from your troubles."

I'm so touched he's even talking to me that I don't

have the heart to reject it. "Sure, yeah," I say, taking the licorice and stashing it in my jacket pocket with the rest of the pieces I keep forgetting to trash. "Thanks, Knapp."

He runs to catch up to Bobo and Pete, and I stand in the hall for a moment, feeling like a ghost until some girl shouts "WAAAA WAAA" at me while making baby hands.

I walk toward my locker.

Pete doesn't talk to me in homeroom, so I make no attempt to engage with him.

No one else in class talks to me either, unless it's to make fun of me to my face. That's how it is all morning. Well, my teachers talk to me, but that doesn't count. Within a day, I've become a total pariah.

When it's time for lunch, I decide to go to our usual table and see what happens.

I sit down with my tray. "Oh," Knapp says. "Hello."

"Hey," I say, choosing to ignore the intense what-are-you-doing-here vibe.

Bobo and Pete are deep in animated conversation. They don't stop to acknowledge me. I start eating my eggplant rollatini in silence, thinking the two of them will reach a natural pause, but they never do. Finally I speak.

"So you're just gonna pretend I'm not here?" I ask.

"Oh, I *know*!" Bobo says, laughing as she puts a hand on Pete's arm, continuing to completely ignore me.

"Seriously?" I say. "This is stupid." I stand up, trying to salvage the tiny remnants of my dignity.

"Sorry, man," Knapp says, but he's smiling, like it's pretty amusing.

I march off with my half-eaten rollatini, slowly circling the cafeteria like a plane waiting for an open runway. I notice Spooner at a corner table by himself, and a jolt of hope bounces through me. I didn't even know he was in this lunch period.

"Cool if I join you?"

"Yeah, man," Spooner says, looking up briefly as he leafs through some thick art magazine while forking couscous into his mouth.

We sit there quietly for a minute.

"Sorry about the other night," I say. "When I told them where we were. In the bunker. Didn't mean to blow up your spot."

Spooner shrugs, wipes his mouth with a napkin. "It happens. What do you think of this?" He holds up his magazine, points to a page with a painting that features a two-by-two grid of squares, each one a different color and texture.

It looks fine to me, not particularly special. I can't tell from his tone what answer he's looking for, so I try to answer honestly. "It's okay."

"I think that's too generous," he says. "I think it's a piece of crap."

"Oh, yeah, for sure."

"Doesn't it feel like it's *trying* to be something? Instead of just being what it is?"

"Definitely." I have no idea what he means, but I'm so happy to be having a conversation with someone.

"It's by Fuller Hopkins," Spooner says. "That chump who was at the bar mitzvah. Such a poser."

Having been called a poser recently myself, I feel weirdly defensive of Fuller, so I don't say anything other than "Yeah."

"Why are you sitting here anyway?" Spooner asks. "Aren't you usually over there with those . . ." He flaps his hand in the air to finish the sentence. I get his meaning even if I don't know what words he's aiming for. Those *privileged judgmental jerks*, perhaps?

"Yeah," I say. "But . . . they're kind of not talking to me right now. Because of that TikTok?"

Spooner looks at me blankly. I believe I've found the one kid in school who has not seen it. "I try not to pay attention to stuff like that," he says. "And even if I had, I don't let the machines determine my opinions. I think for myself."

"Oh. Nice. Yeah."

"What's in the video that's so bad?"

"Well, it's . . ." I move my eggplant rollatini around on my tray with my fork. "I got in an argument with some of my Brooklyn friends. And I kinda freaked out in this, like, really embarrassing way."

"And they *filmed* that?"

"One of my friend's friends did, yeah."

"That's messed up! That's, like, an invasion of privacy. You could sue them."

It's the first time I've thought about it that way. Like, yes, I was a mortifying mess, but there's no reason that should have been put out into the world. "I guess it is."

"Do you know any lawyers?"

"Yeah, actually. My mom. But I don't think I could actually sue someone for this."

"Maybe not. But anyway, my assessment of the situation is: no bueno." Spooner takes a swig from his bottle of iced tea, as if to emphasize his point, then turns back to his magazine.

"Hey," I say, suddenly wanting to pick Spooner's brain about everything in my life that's stressing me out so he can make me feel better. "Can I ask you one other thing?"

"You just did," Spooner says without looking up.

"Right. Yeah. Ha. I mean—"

"Shoot," Spooner says.

"Okay. If I gave someone something that they said they needed so they could destroy it because it was too dangerous for anyone to have, and then I later found out that they *hadn't* destroyed it and that was actually a lie so they could keep it and use it for themselves. Maybe for, like, evil causes. . . . How guilty should I feel that I was such an idiot?"

Spooner stares up at the ceiling, deep in thought. "Wow," he says. "That's a highly specific situation."

"Yeah."

He looks back at me. "You shouldn't feel guilty at all. It sounds like you were dealing with a master manipulator. Not your fault."

"Oh. Okay." Spooner is my new god.

"I guess the bigger question is: What are you going to do about it?"

"Huh?"

"Well, you're saying this person manipulated you into getting this dangerous thing to do evil with or whatnot, so . . . shouldn't you try to stop them?"

"Maybe, but—"

"You need to check in with yourself."

"Uh. What?"

"Maybe you don't know what to do, right? But maybe you will. Or maybe you already know, but you don't *know* that you know." Spooner uses a piece of pita bread to scoop up the last bit of couscous on his tray. "We all have layers. Things we have. Things we used to have. Explore the negative space."

"Okay," I say, though, as usual, I don't fully understand what he's saying.

I close my eyes.

I try to think about what it is I know. Or don't know. My layers or whatever. What I used to have. And, much to my surprise, immediately something clicks.

I know what I need to do.

22

WAITING FOR YOO

Eric

I'm standing on the sidewalk in front of my best friend's house, directly across the street from the house where I've spent most of my life, so it's weird that I'm so nervous I'm shaking.

I hopped on the subway to Brooklyn as soon as school ended—I knew I had to do it fast, before I gave myself time to change my mind—and went straight to Yoo's house.

No one was home when I knocked on the door, so now I'm here on the sidewalk.

Waiting.

And shaking.

Looking at meaningless stuff on my phone so I don't seem sketchy to my neighbors.

Yoo was the first person I saw when I checked in with my past. The things I used to have. And what I also saw was how awful I've been to him the past couple of weeks. The viral video made it glaringly obvious, but I think deep down I already knew. It's almost like part of me has been pushing him away on purpose.

I hope he accepts my apology.

Yoo comes around the corner on his bike and starts heading down the block.

I'm about to wave and shout when Smash comes around the corner just behind him on her skateboard.

I definitely owe her an apology too, but I need to talk to Yoo on my own first. Is it because I'm too scared to talk to both of them at once? Absolutely. But it also feels right that he and I have a moment alone—we haven't had one since before he met up with us in Manhattan and I completely screwed things up.

I make a mad dash for the side of Yoo's house, where I put my back against the wall and hide in the shadows, sketchier than ever. I don't think they noticed me.

"We have lemonade," Yoo says as they walk into the house through the front door. "Two different kinds."

"You are such a dork," Smash says.

The door closes.

I'm glad I hid. I really don't want to intrude on their time together.

They're probably gonna make out or something.

I stand in the shadows for a while, thinking. I know it would probably make sense to walk the fifty steps across the street to hang out at Dad's house, keep an eye out for Yoo from there, but I'm worried if I don't stay here, I'll miss my moment and be forever resigned to a life of Yoo ignoring my texts and calls and maybe even doorbell rings.

I think a lot about King Neptune, how he was so determined to get that ink that he broke into Aunt Betty's dad's stuff. I think about the moment in the spring when Yoo and I saw him on the boardwalk and told him we'd found the ink, the way he absolutely flipped out. That makes a lot more sense now.

I can't stop wondering: What is he using the ink for?

The front door opens.

"Bye, Yooby," Smash says, jumping onto her skateboard and weaving down the front path to the driveway. It's starting to get dark out.

"Later, Smashy," Yoo says, holding a glass of lemonade. "Let me know you got home safe, babe!"

"I will, dork!"

Yoo watches as Smash skates away, and I hop out from the side of the house to make sure I catch him.

"Hey, man," I say.

"Wahhh!" Yoo drops his lemonade.

"It's me, it's me! Sorry, sorry."

"Ugh." Yoo picks up the glass, which landed on their doormat and thankfully didn't break, and stares at the spilled lemonade. "You scared the crap outta me, Doodles. I thought you were a robber or something. What are you doing here?"

"I'm really sorry. I've been waiting over there since a little before you came home, and I—"

"Since *before* I came home? You've been lurking outside my house like a creeper for two hours?"

"Oh wow, it's been two hours? Yeah, I guess so."

"That's super weird, dude."

"No, it's not," I say as the timer light above Yoo's front door turns on and gives me a better look at his weirded-out face. "Because I really needed to apologize. For so much."

Yoo sighs and tries to take a sip of his lemonade before he remembers that it's empty. "Man, this is, like, an abusive cycle. You realize how many times you've been a jerk and then apologized to me in the past year?"

"I know, but—"

"A *lot* of times."

"I really do know, and I'm so sorry. I want to end the cycle. That's why I waited out here so long."

"Just . . . If you think you're gonna win me over again with ink monsters like last time, you're wrong. It's not gonna work."

"I don't," I say, hands in the air. "No ink monsters."

Yoo stares at me a moment, then puts out a hand like, *Well? Go ahead.*

"So," I say. "I'm really sorry about what I did. I hate that I didn't stay with you on that day we went tagging. That I didn't defend you more. I hate that I flipped out on you and Smash and everyone and acted like such a giant poser tool."

"And you hate that Keiko put it on the internet for everyone to see."

"Yeah. That too. But it did help me understand how out of line I was, you know?"

"You were out of line. Very out of line."

"I know," I say. It's gotten colder now that the sun's gone. I zip my jacket. "I think . . . I don't know. I think going to this new school, making these new friends, living this new life in Manhattan with my mom and her new boyfriend, Terry—it's all really confusing. Like, you said I'm not acting like myself, and you're totally right. I'm trying to be this other person, or I feel like I *have* to be this new person, like I have no choice if I want to fit in. But it isn't working, and so . . . It's just a mess."

Yoo nods. "I get that."

"And then there's this whole other situation going on with King Neptune, which definitely isn't helping."

"Wait. What?"

"Yeah," I say, so relieved to actually be talking to a friend who gets it. Who doesn't laugh at me when I talk about this stuff. "It's nuts."

"Just come in already," Yoo says, waving me inside. I know this means we're good again, and it's the best feeling in the world. "Want some lemonade? We have two kinds."

A minute later, we're planted on the green, cushy couch in Yoo's living room with pink lemonades, me telling him everything about what's gone down with Neptune: the digging monsters in the sinkhole, the voices of Beard and Mustache chasing us, the uncomfortable relationship Neptune, aka Oscar Weissberger, had with my great-aunt, and his role as CEO of Pluto Properties.

"Whaaaa?" Yoo says. "There's no way that dude is a CEO. Where does he conduct his business, from the breakers?"

The front door opens and Yoo's mom walks in from work. "Hi, Alan. Oh, Eric!"

"Hi, Ms. Pai," I say.

"We're friends again," Yoo explains.

"So happy to hear that!" Yoo's mom says as she takes off her jacket. I'm embarrassed that she knows we briefly weren't friends. "Great to see you, Eric. Please join us for dinner if you'd like."

"Okay, thanks," I say. "I'll have to check with my mom."

She asks how my mom is doing, and I tell her good, and I think about mentioning Terry but I don't because I still think the whole situation is kind of gross.

"So, let me get this straight," Yoo says, once his mom has left the room. "You think King Neptune *didn't* destroy the ink and is using it for some nefarious purposes?"

"Pretty much."

"That would explain why the dude was so desperate for us to give it to him. Remember after he told us that story on the beach, how he said we should go home and get the ink?"

"Oh, right!" I say. My phone buzzes, probably Mom checking in, but this feels too important to interrupt. "Yeah, he probably never for a second intended to actually destroy it."

"You think he's connected to those new sinkholes? They're right in the same part of town as that first one."

"New sinkholes?"

"Dude!" Yoo gets up from the couch to reposition himself next to me with his phone. "It was on TikTok. There was one in City Hall Park and one under this old hotel." We watch a video that cuts together footage of both sinkholes, with police setting up barriers as people stand around gaping at it. Both holes are pretty big, about the same size as the one we explored.

"This has gotta be him," I say. "And it's my fault. I don't know what he's doing, but he's using the ink to do it. The ink I gave him."

My phone buzzes in my pocket again.

"So I think that means it's on me to try and stop him," I say, remembering Spooner's words.

Yoo opens his mouth, and I'm sure he's going to tell me it's a bad idea or it's not my responsibility, but instead he says:

"I'm in."

I love him so much.

"Awesome," I say. "Not that I have any idea how we begin to do that. I mean, he's an adult, a CEO, and he has magic ink. We're middle schoolers with bikes and skateboards."

"Do you think that shell still exists?" Yoo asks.

"Shell? What shell?"

"Remember when Neptune told us that whole story about your great-great-grandfather? Or was it three greats? No, two, right?" I nod. "Okay, great. I mean, great-great. So Neptune said the mermaid gave her blood to your great-great in that shell, and it kept refilling itself. Do you think it still exists somewhere?"

The shell. I'd totally forgotten about that part of the

story. "Wow. I have no idea."

"Because if it does, and it's still able to make ink—"

"Then we have a way to fight back. Resurrect our own monsters to battle his. You're brilliant, Yoo."

"I do what I can," he says, clicking his tongue as he gives me a wink.

"I'm really sorry I've sucked so much lately."

"I forgive you. Just don't let it happen again."

"I'll do my best," I say. I'm wondering if being a jerk might just be one of my layers (as Spooner calls them), but I definitely want to work on it. I'm so happy Yoo and I are friends again, it feels like I won the lottery.

"So the shell," Yoo says.

"Right, yeah. I guess we start by scouring my dad's house. I don't remember seeing any shells in that box I found the ink in, but we should definitely check. And then I guess I could ask Aunt Betty if she remembers her grandfather having any shell."

"Wouldn't she have told you that by now?"

"Well, maybe. Probably not." I'm thinking of how much I didn't know that I didn't know about Aunt Betty until the past few weeks. Like, really, I've always just thought of her as this old lady who's related to me who wears tons of perfume and gives very moist kisses. But if I'd actually let her have a conversation with me sooner, I would've learned she's way cooler than I thought. And way more than just my great-aunt. She used to be young like me, doing stupid stuff and making mistakes and falling in love with the wrong people. "But I'm sure Neptune already asked her about the shell back when they used to date—"

"That's super nasty, by the way," Yoo says.

"I know. But he wasn't old then. So it kind of wasn't." I take the two photos of Betty and Oscar out of my backpack to show him. I've been carrying them around, like a lucky charm or something. Kind of cheesy, I know.

"Huh," Yoo says, staring intently. "Your aunt's actually kind of hot. They both are, really."

"Dude," I say just as my phone buzzes in my pocket yet again. It's Dad.

"Hey, Pops, what's shakin'?" I ask.

"Why aren't you answering your phone?" Dad sounds super intense. "I shouldn't have to call this many times."

"I'm sorry, I'm at Yoo's. I was apologizing to him."

"Oh," Dad says, his voice softening ever so slightly. "Look, Eric. Aunt Betty had another stroke this afternoon."

"Oh no, is she okay?"

There's a pause that feels absolutely epic but is probably closer to five seconds.

"No," Dad says. "She passed away, Eric. Aunt Betty is gone."

23

GONE

Eric

Aunt Betty is gone.

I'll never see her again.

I'll never speak with her again.

I'll never get one of those sloppy, wet-cheek kiss-licks again.

She's dead.

Dead.

The word is hard to think, let alone say out loud.

So final. Like a punch to the gut.

Dead.

Even now, two days since Dad dropped that bomb over the phone, I still don't believe it. I literally just sat through Aunt Betty's funeral service, heard eulogies from Dad and Uncle Harry and various other people, and it still doesn't feel real.

Aunt Betty can't be gone.

I'm in the back seat of Mom's car, Mom driving with Dad in the passenger seat, heading from the temple to Greenwood Cemetery, where Aunt Betty will be buried. I'm wearing the same new gray suit I wore to Pete's bar mitzvah; it's not black, but it's all I have. I haven't driven in a car with both Mom and Dad in many months, since before they separated. Just the weird cherry on top of this devastating and surreal crap sundae.

No one's talking. Dad's staring out the window. He had to pause during his eulogy to wipe his eyes. I had to look away. He doesn't lose it like that very often.

"You know we can talk about any of it," Mom says to Dad in a quiet voice. "Anytime."

Dad nods, still looking out the window.

"I know how much she meant to you," Mom says. "She was such a wonderful woman."

Dad looks to Mom and nods, even slightly smiles, and I suddenly realize: even though Mom is maybe falling in love with Terry, and Dad is using his best terrible jokes to try to impress Renee, these two still love each other. Not, like, romantic married love. But still love. Maybe it really always will be a part of them. Layers.

Mom looks up into the rearview. "That goes for you too, Eric. We can talk whenever."

"Thanks, Mom."

When we get to the cemetery and step out of the car, the air has some serious bite to it, as if Aunt Betty's death has been so seismic, it's nudged the temperature down. The rabbi is already standing near the plot of land that will soon become Aunt Betty's grave. It's right next to Uncle Paul's.

Uncle Harry and his husband, Anuj, walk up to the grave at the same time as us.

"How you doing, buddy," Uncle Harry says, the skin around his eyes raw and red, putting an arm around me. "Was that your first funeral?"

"Yeah," I say. There was, of course, the moment last spring I watched Brickman die as he tried to save my life. But as hard as that was, it was different. Brickman wasn't a person. And there was definitely no funeral.

"I'm sorry, E," Uncle Harry says. "Death sucks."

Once everyone's arrived—a crowd of about fifty people—the rabbi begins to speak. I'm nestled between my parents and Uncle Harry and Uncle Anuj. The rabbi holds up a shovel and hands it to Dad. As is Jewish tradition, everyone takes a turn digging up dirt and putting it onto the coffin, literally taking part in the burial.

I try to hang back, but then Uncle Harry is putting the shovel into my hand, and, whether I'm ready or not, it's my turn. I stab the shovel into the earth, placing my foot on the back of the spade to get more leverage the way I just watched Dad do. I balance the heap of dirt on the blade and heave it onto the coffin down below, where it lands with a series of staccato thuds.

Aunt Betty is down there in that box.

Vibrant, funny, loudmouthed Aunt Betty.

In a box.

It doesn't make sense.

I pass the shovel to Uncle Anuj and take a few steps away to try to process it all when someone taps on my shoulder. I turn around to see a group of familiar faces, and I don't know if I've ever been so happy to see them.

Monster Club.

Yoo's in front, with Smash, Beanie, and Hollywood right behind, and I give each of them a huge hug.

"Thanks for leaving school to be here," I say. "Means a lot."

"Of course," Beanie says, leaning down for her hug because no matter how much I grow, she's always way taller than me.

"Yeah," Hollywood says. "So sorry, man. And, you know, also sorry about that whole situation with Keiko."

"It's okay," I say, and I mean it. It's hard to stare at a box containing a recently alive person you loved and still feel upset about a stupid video. "And I'm sorry I was terrible. Smash, you were completely justified in calling me every single one of those things."

"Well," Smash says, "I prolly could have handled it a little better. But thanks for saying sorry."

"Yo, let's huddle up," Hollywood says, putting an arm around all of us and holding up his phone.

"Ahmed," Beanie says. "It's very poor form to selfie at a funeral."

"Hey, I met Betty once," Hollywood says. "She was a cool lady, she'd be into this." He takes the picture. I smile, but in a very subtle way to keep it respectful.

I notice that Renee, Aunt Betty's caretaker from the nursing home, is here. She and Dad are near the grave having what looks like a serious conversation, Renee doing most of the talking as Dad nods, his eyes looking glassy. Renee has just put her hand on his arm when I notice, down the hill by the paved road, two men in black suits and sunglasses standing next to a black car.

Two familiar men.

Beard and Mustache. The Pluto Properties goons.

They recognized me at the sinkhole.

They know I saw their monsters.

And they've found me here.

But then, hovering on the periphery of the crowd, I see another man. He's also in a suit and sunglasses, with slicked-back white hair and a silk scarf around his neck.

I see through his disguise.

It's the Pluto Properties CEO.

King Neptune.

He turns his head and looks straight at me. Like a challenge.

Like a threat.

Whatever it is he's planning to do with the ink, he doesn't want me to interfere.

He holds his stare for another few seconds before turning and walking toward his car.

"Hey," I say, trying not to make a scene as I dash after him down a grassy hill, leaving my friends and the rest of the crowd. "King Neptune!" I whisper-shout. "I know you kept the ink, and I know you're up to something!"

He stops.

It seems like he's going to turn around, but then he lets out a huff of air and keeps walking.

Within moments, he's in the back seat of the car, the Vultures in front.

"Wait!" I shout.

He shuts the door, and they pull away.

24

MONSTER CLUB ASSEMBLE

Eric

"I can't believe he showed up to intimidate you at *your aunt's funeral*," Yoo says.

"I know," I say. "The very aunt who he tried to scam, like, sixty years ago. It's, like, a power move. They want me to know they can find me anywhere."

"That dude is cold," Hollywood says. "And out of his mind."

I'm chilling with the two of them, Smash, and Beanie in my bedroom in Dad's house. Just like old times. Downstairs, Dad is having people over for the first night of shiva, the Jewish tradition of hosting folks for seven days after a family member dies to gather and grieve together. We were down there mingling with everyone for a while, but after my eighteenth conversation with some old-person friend of Aunt Betty's I'd never met before, I decided I'd earned a break.

"Of course he's out of his mind," I say, pacing back and forth near the foot of my bed, where Yoo and Smash are sitting. "He thinks he's King Neptune. Like, for real. And now we can't just dismiss it as some whimsical, quirky behavior—he's somehow also the powerful CEO of a terrible company and he has the ink, which makes him legitimately dangerous."

"All right," Beanie says, standing near my desk fiddling around with a paper clip, "so Yoo mentioned this magical ink-producing shell that once existed, but it's not here." She gestures down to the floor, where, shortly after coming upstairs, we dumped out the contents of the horrible box from my closet. "Sounds like it could be useful to find that shell if we want to stop him."

"It's not a matter of *wanting* to stop him," I say. "I *have* to stop him. I'm the one who gave him the ink like a total idiot. It's my fault. And he thinks I'm just a child. Well, he's wrong."

"Fine," Beanie says, flipping the paper clip, now vaguely in the shape of a shell, onto my desk. "Point being: How do we go about finding this thing?"

"If it even still exists," Yoo says.

"Right," Beanie says.

"It has to exist, though," Hollywood says, spinning

around in my desk chair. "If you got a magic shell, you don't just give it away! You take good care of it. Because it's magic."

"True that," Smash says. "For something that powerful, you'd wanna keep it somewhere close but also well hidden."

"Or you keep it really *far* and well hidden," Yoo says. "Like buried in Siberia."

"Or you do neither of those things because you die before you have a chance to hide it and you haven't told anybody in your family that it was magic," Beanie says, adjusting her glasses. "If his family thought it was just a regular shell, it wouldn't have necessarily seemed that special. Could have ended up in the trash. Or in some other random box of crap, like this one where you found the jar of ink. Did your aunt Betty ever mention Isaac being into shells?"

"Not that I remember." I grab a grape off the plate we assembled from the five hundred food platters downstairs and pop it into my mouth. "She was definitely never told anything about the magic ink, and I'm sure she didn't know about the magic shell either. Yoo and I were gonna go visit her to ask about all this, but then . . . Then my dad called and . . . we couldn't."

"Really sorry, Sketch," Smash says.

"Thanks." I blink down at my feet. "It's okay if you

call me Doodles. Or Eric. Or Sketch. I'll go by whatever."

"But Giant Tool is still out, right?" Hollywood asks.

"Probably, yeah." I grin at him through my tears.

Smash kneels down and sifts through the stuff we dumped out of the box. "And we're sure there are no shells in here?"

"I was very thorough," Beanie says, seeming insulted.

"Okay, true that," Smash says, standing back up with her hands in the air. "Figured it couldn't hurt to double-check."

"Other than the tattoo pen and the jar of ink," I say, "it's all photos and useless junk. Just like the rest of the house."

"Wait a second," Yoo says, still sitting on the bed, eyes wide. "Wait a second, wait a second! Where's all your dad's stuff?"

"You mean the stuff that's usually lying around everywhere?"

"Yeah!"

"We shoved all of it into the basement this morning," I say.

"Perfect!" Yoo sprints out of the room and downstairs.

We all stare at each other for a moment. "I guess this is the part where we follow him?" Beanie says.

We all shrug and nod and run after him, bouncing down the stairs and rolling through the swarms of people in the living room—it seems like even more folks have arrived while we were in my room—toward the basement stairs.

"Eric," Dad says, wrapping an arm around my shoulder to halt my momentum in the kitchen as my friends keep moving. "There you are."

"Yeah. Hey, Dad." I'm hoping I can squirm out of this quickly. "We went upstairs for a second."

"I want you to meet Marsha." Dad gestures to an older woman with short, poufy black hair standing next to him. "She used to play bridge with Aunt Betty."

"Hi, love," Marsha says, giving me an overly squinty smile. "So sorry about your aunt."

"Thanks." Marsha seems nice and all, but talking with her is not my priority right now.

"Your aunt mentioned you a lot, you know," Marsha says. "She really loved you."

"Oh," I say, feeling genuinely moved by this but also impatient to end this conversation. "Cool."

"All right, get outta here," Dad says, rustling my hair and shoving me along on my way.

In the basement, Beanie, Smash, and Hollywood are standing around watching as Yoo bounces through the messy space like a pinball, digging into box after box with a maniacal energy. "This will pay off, I swear!" Yoo says. "Just gotta find it."

"Okay," I say.

He keeps swirling around us like the Tasmanian Devil, madly ransacking boxes, until finally he says, "Jackpot!"

Yoo is holding up the moldy strongman outfit he found in Dad's stuff weeks ago, a huge smile on his face.

"Uh," Beanie says.

"Though I am delighted by the idea of you wearing that," Smash says, "how is it going to help us find the shell?"

"Hold on!" Yoo says. He chucks the strongman outfit to the floor and digs back into the box at his feet that it came from until he finds what he's looking for: a framed black-and-white photo. He rubs some dust off the glass, then nods vigorously as he hoists the frame into the air. "I knew it was in the same box as *this*!"

We rush forward for a closer look. The wooden frame is starting to rot and come apart, but the photo is captivating. Standing in a line looking at the camera—none of them smiling—are two strongmen wearing similar outfits to the moldy one Yoo just held up (or maybe that *is* one of their outfits), a tall woman in a dress with a beard, and another woman in a dress with two heads.

"Dang, Doodles, your family might be even weirder than mine," Hollywood says.

"I think these are performers," I say. "From King's

Sideshow Extraordinaire."

"Yeah, and look what they're standing next to," Yoo says, pointing at the lower half of the photo.

It's a tombstone.

For the founder of the sideshow. My great-great-grandfather Isaac King. 1893–1951.

The tombstone's border is decorated with shells, up and down both sides and across the arch at the top. Not just images or drawings but actual shells from the ocean embedded into the stone.

"Oh my god," I say.

"Maybe he had all these put in his tombstone so he could hide the magic shell among them," Yoo says. "Know what I mean?"

"Close but well hidden," Smash says.

"Or maybe the guy just really loved shells," Beanie says.

"No one loves shells that much!" Yoo says. "I'm sorry, but unless you're, like, a professional shell collector, that seems ridiculous."

"Not necessarily." Beanie cleans her glasses with the bottom of her shirt. "For some people, shells are a symbol of the beach, so it's possible he—"

"This picture," Smash interrupts. "Is that the same cemetery where we were today?"

"Yeah, I think so," I say. "It's a family plot."

We all stare hard at the picture, like we're trying to find Waldo.

"Hollywood," I say, without taking my eyes off the photo. "Let's see that rude-ass selfie you took at my aunt's grave today."

"Oh hell yeah," Hollywood says, taking his phone out of his pocket and finding the pic. We all shift our attention to his screen, where he zooms in past our faces to a spot in the distance behind us. There's a small gap between two people dressed in black through which you can just barely see a couple of tombstones.

Hollywood zooms in further.

It's blurry but unquestionable:

The border of one of the tombstones is embedded with shells.

25

PACKET IN YOUR POCKET

Eric

"Should we just come back tomorrow?" Yoo asks.

We're stopped on our various forms of transportation—bikes for me and Hollywood, skateboards for Smash and Yoo, homemade e-scooter for Beanie—staring at the main gate of Greenwood Cemetery. It's locked. It's 6:16 p.m., and the cemetery closed at 5:00.

"Probably," Hollywood says, scratching the back of his head.

"No," I say. "We'll find a way in."

My friends all look at me, maybe impressed, maybe shocked.

"Weird, right?" Yoo says. "Now that he's Sketch, he's fine doing illegal stuff."

"It's not that," I say. "I mean, it's kind of that, but . . .

I just have this feeling like we don't have time to put this off. If we can get our own supply of magic ink from Isaac's tombstone, then we need it, like, ASAP. And anyway, I think what King Neptune has planned is significantly more illegal than breaking into a cemetery."

"So what do you suggest?" Beanie asks.

Fifteen minutes later, we've made it from the main gate on Fifth Avenue over to the north side of the cemetery on Twentieth Street. I don't have much of a plan, other than knowing that, if we're going to jump the fence, we need to do it in a spot that's less obvious than the main entrance. And entering from the north puts us closer to Isaac's grave. I think. I could be wrong about that. I don't have the best sense of direction.

"All right, let's stop here." I try to say it with conviction, as if I'm some sort of expert on climbing fences and not just picking a completely random spot. We lock up our vehicles to the gate itself, and then everyone looks to me for what to do next.

"Okay," I say, staring at their faces, which are in varying levels of darkness based on the way light is hitting them from the nearby streetlight. "So, the plan is this: we'll hop the fence, then find Isaac's tombstone as fast as we can."

"Ha!" Hollywood says. "Yo, that's not really a plan."

"I'm curious to understand how you think we'll achieve that," Beanie adds.

She has a point. This isn't a chain-link fence like the one I climbed to tag the Manhattan Bridge—this one's made of tall black metal posts with pointed triangular tops. There's not really anywhere to get a foothold.

"What if, like, one of us leans over and the others step off their back?" I ask.

"Like in a cartoon?" Beanie says.

"Well, yeah," I say, trying to defend my stupid idea, "but they do it in some movies that aren't cartoons too—"

"I think it'll work," Yoo says. He walks over to the fence and bends his torso forward. "Step off me."

None of us makes a move.

"Seriously!" Yoo says. "Someone step off me. Let's try it."

"Nah, if we're doing this," Hollywood says, striding to the fence, "everyone should be steppin' off me. 'Cause I'm the tallest."

"You are *not*," Beanie says. "I literally have a nickname based on my height."

"But beans aren't tall," Yoo says, getting out of his leaned-over position. "They're round and small."

"I'm not named after the beans!" Beanie says. "My grams called me this because I shot up in height like a

219

bean *plant*. Bean plants are known for growing fast, ya doof."

"Ohhhhhhhh," Yoo says. "I seriously never understood your nickname till just now."

"I think we're getting off topic," I say.

"You're not the tallest, though," Hollywood says, ignoring me as he walks toward Beanie. "Not anymore."

"Fine, let's do a test," Beanie says. She and Hollywood stand back to back, while Yoo, Smash, and I examine the height differential. Sure enough, Hollywood was right—he's grown a bunch and now he's taller by, like, an eighth of an inch.

"BOOM!" Hollywood says, strutting around the sidewalk in the dark, doing a little dance with his shoulders. "Don't hate the player, hate the game."

"Yeah, okay, congratulations," Beanie says. "Your prize is we get to use you as a stepstool, so don't get too excited."

That definitely kills some of Hollywood's buzz, but he tries not to show it, continuing a less exuberant version of his dance as he moves toward the fence. He reaches out an arm to grip one of the fence posts and leans over to form his body into an L. "Let's go," he says.

"I'll be first," Beanie says with a smirk. "Gonna enjoy this."

She climbs onto Hollywood's back, at first like she's

220

going to get a piggyback ride. Then she shimmies into a position where she can put one purple sneaker on his back after another, so she's crouched down facing the fence, holding on to two metal posts. She slowly lifts herself into a standing position, Hollywood's body trembling beneath her.

"You okay down there?" she asks.

"Me? Yeah, this is nothing. This is easy. But, yo, could someone film this?" He somehow stretches a hand into his back pocket and extends his phone toward us. "This content will be fire."

"Uh, okay," I say, starting to record as Beanie tries to straddle a leg up and over the top of the fence, finally getting it on her fourth try. She lifts the rest of herself up too, then falls down to the grass on the other side, her glasses falling off as she lands shakily on her feet.

"Gotta say," Beanie says, picking up her glasses and cleaning them off. "I'm surprised that actually worked."

"I'm not," Hollywood says, upright again, twisting his body back and forth to stretch. "Because I'm a beast! Let's go, let's go!"

Smash goes first, then Yoo, then me, each of us far less graceful than Beanie. And since we're all considerably shorter than her, it's way harder to get a leg over the top of the fence. But somehow we manage it, with me standing next to Hollywood to reach up my arms and

221

give Smash and Yoo an extra boost. (I have to stop filming for that.) I'm very glad I thought to exchange my suit jacket for my hoodie before we rushed from my Dad's place to Greenwood.

Once I make it over the fence, we realize Hollywood obviously can't step on his own back.

"Sorry you can't come with us," I say through the fence.

"Yeah, thanks for getting us all in," Smash says.

"Anything for Monster Club, right?" Hollywood says. "I'm good here. I got some dope content to work on while I wait. Good luck. Make me proud."

We all fist-bump him through the fence before finally making our way into Greenwood Cemetery. It's really gigantic, which is even more apparent now that it's dark and we're having an impossible time finding our way back to the spot we were in this afternoon. For at least twenty minutes, we follow various paved paths in various directions until finally Beanie shines her phone flashlight around to locate some key landmarks and orient herself. She cross-checks what she's found with her maps app and within three minutes, she's steered us toward the small plot of land devoted to the King family.

Four graves down from Aunt Betty's freshly filled burial site, there it is:

My great-great-grandfather's tombstone.

"How're we gonna do this?" Smash asks. "Just start pulling at all the shells?"

"Hold on," I say. I crouch down to stare at the tombstone, like I need to make proper eye contact. "Hey, Grandpa Isaac." Yoo, Smash, and Beanie are looking at me, but I don't care. "Good to, um, see you, I guess? Sorry I didn't realize you were here earlier. I was pretty focused on Aunt Betty. But anyway. We're hoping one of these shells on your tombstone is the one that mermaid gave you, the one that makes more ink? It's pretty important because . . . Well, this guy has the ink who shouldn't. So we need to stop him. And. Yeah. So that's what we're doing here. I just don't want you to think we're, like, trying to desecrate your grave or whatever. Because we're not."

I take a deep breath and give my friends a nod, then shine my phone's flashlight along the border, trying to assess which shell is The Shell.

"I liked your speech," Yoo whispers. "Very moving."

"Thanks, man."

Without really discussing a strategy, the four of us start employing Smash's suggestion of tugging and pulling at each of the shells, seeing if one of them will loosen or come off or start spraying ink at us.

"It was a snail shell, right?" Yoo asks as he carefully pokes his index finger into a spikier shell jutting out of the tombstone's bottom right.

"Huh?" I say.

"I think Neptune said the magic shell was a snail shell."

"Oh." I'm impressed that Yoo remembered that and embarrassed that I didn't since it's *my* family. "Yeah, that does ring a bell."

"What kind of snail?" Beanie asks.

"There's more than one kind of snail?" Yoo says.

"Yes, Yoo." Even in the dark, I can tell Beanie is rolling her eyes. "Way more."

"Moon snail," I say, the words rising to the surface of my brain from who knows where. "It was a moon snail shell."

"Oh, easy." Beanie runs her phone's light over the tombstone until she finds what she's looking for, stopping at a round, brownish-white shell. "It's that one."

"Whoa, you sure?" I ask.

"Of course I'm sure. It's science."

"You're very good at this," Smash says.

"It's what I do," Beanie says.

I run my finger over the smooth shell, feeling awe that this might be the very object handed to Isaac by the mermaid. More of my family's history. Beanie, Smash, and Yoo crouch next to me and peer over my shoulder as I pull at the shell. I tap it. I try to twist it. Absolutely nothing happens.

"Hey, Beanie," Yoo says, "can you use some science to figure out what the heck we do next?"

"Any of you bring water?" Beanie asks.

"I did," Smash says, pulling an aluminum water bottle out of her bright green backpack. "Have as much as you want."

Instead of sipping from the bottle, though, Beanie directs a splash right at the moon snail shell. We stare at the shell, thinking something will happen. Nothing does.

"You trying to clean it?" Yoo asks.

"No, just experimenting," Beanie says, standing up and pacing around the grave. "Because I'm thinking: What's different now? As opposed to when ink was flowing out of it? And, well, the obvious answer is, back then it was *wet*. So I thought maybe water could act as a catalyst to activate its magical properties. But I was wrong."

"Good idea, though," I say.

"But if water were a catalyst," Yoo says, "this thing would be turning magic every time it rained. People probably would have discovered that sometime in the past seventy-five years."

I stand up from the grave. "I hate to be a downer, dudes, but I don't think this thing works anymore. Assuming this even is the actual shell, seems like Isaac just stored it here so he would seal it off from the world for all time. Kinda like what Neptune said he was gonna do with the ink but never actually did."

"It does seem pretty stuck in there," Yoo says, standing up to join me.

"Right," I agree. "So I say we let this go and focus on figuring out—"

"Salt water," Beanie says, still crouched by the tombstone with Smash.

"What?" Yoo says.

"You're not going to find tap water in the ocean, right? Maybe activation requires salt water."

Yoo and I stare at each other, Yoo shining his phone flashlight up toward his face so I can see him shaking his head and making skeptical eyebrows.

"So," I say, trying not to laugh, "you're saying we need to go to the ocean?"

"Not necessarily." Beanie is speaking in that slow way that means her brain is actually moving a thousand miles a minute. "If we can find some salt, we can probably make our own."

"Oh, that'll be easy," I say, "because we all carry salt with us all the time."

"Just everyone check anyway," Smash says, backing up Beanie. "Like, maybe you have a salt packet in your pocket or something."

"Packet in your pocket," Yoo repeats with a chuckle.

"How many packets of pocket did Peter Piper pick?" I say, cracking up.

"If you're going to put a packet in your pocket on the picket," Yoo says, cracking up with me, "make sure you peck it before you pack it in your pocket."

"Okay, okay," Beanie says. "This is the opposite of helpful."

"True that," Smash says. "Tongue twisters haven't been funny since second grade."

But we can't even see their faces because we're standing in a cemetery at night, and suddenly all of this seems like the funniest thing in the world to me, like what are we even *doing* here? Why are we splashing a tombstone with water? I cannot stop laughing.

It's been a long day.

"I'm sorry," Yoo says, trying to stifle his giggles. "Really, I know this is serious."

"Me too!" Even though I completely mean it, I'm still laughing so it doesn't sound like it at all. Yoo and I haven't laughed like this together in months. "It's im*pec*-*ca*bly serious!"

Yoo snorts and breaks into another giggle fit.

"Okay, whatever," Beanie says, standing up. "Let's go, Smash."

"Yeah, you guys are being idiots," Smash says.

They start walking away, and that's when I happen to

slide my hands into my hoodie pockets.

"Oh my god, wait!" I shout. "I do have salt in my pocket!"

"This joke stopped being funny about five hours before you first made it," Smash calls back to us.

"Wait up, Smashy!" Yoo says, running after them, his giggle fit finally concluded.

"I'm not joking this time!" I pull out the four pieces of Knapp's nasty salty licorice that I keep forgetting to throw away. "I have salt! I truly have salt!"

The conviction in my voice is enough to stop them from walking anymore.

"You for real found a packet of salt in your pocket?" Smash calls out.

"Not a packet, no, but it's this horribly disgusting salty candy this Swedish kid at my school insists on giving me all the time. I never threw it away. Which it seems might be an amazing move on my part."

I hear my friends' footsteps crunching through the grass toward me.

"All right," Beanie says, plucking the licorice out of my hand. "This is worth a shot. But no more of that tongue twister nonsense, okay?"

"Promise. Cross my heart and the packet in my pocket."

"Doodles."

"Sorry."

"Light me up," Beanie says. Yoo, Smash, and I direct our phone beams at her as she sets up a (very) makeshift lab right there next to Isaac's gravestone. She's about to put all four pieces of Knapp's licorice into Smash's water bottle when she stops. "You know what? This probably has a better chance of working if we soften the licorice up first."

"What? Really?" Yoo says.

Beanie throws us each a piece and keeps one for herself. "Just chew it up and then spit it in the bottle."

"Ew!" Smash says. "That's my favorite water bottle!"

"You'll live." Beanie holds up her piece. "Ready? Go!"

We all start chewing.

"Good lord!" Yoo says. "This is supposed to be candy? This is like gnawing on a piece of the Grim Reaper's cloak!"

"Yeah, told you it's bad," I say, wincing.

Smash is gagging too hard to speak.

"I'm kinda into it," Beanie says.

One by one, we spit our licorice into Smash's bottle. Beanie puts the cap on and vigorously shakes it up, almost like she's trying to kill something inside it. After a solid minute of this, she unscrews the top. "Here goes nothing." Beanie splashes the shell with her freshly made salt water.

We stare at the moon snail shell. Nothing.

But then there's something.

A single drop of a thick black substance that emerges from the shell's opening, then plunks to the ground.

"Did you see that?" Yoo asks.

"Yes," Beanie says.

"Splash it again," I say.

Beanie does, and within moments, multiple drops are free-falling out of the snail shell down to the dirt. She splashes it once more, and the drops turn into a thin black stream oozing down the side of Isaac's tombstone, as if a faucet's just been turned on.

"Oh my god," I say, "it actually works!"

"Science!" Beanie yells.

"You sure that's not just, like, licorice juice?" Smash asks.

"No way!" Yoo shouts. "Don't you smell that? That unmistakable fishy, garbage-dump odor? The magic is back, baby!"

As I fumble with the zipper on my bag, my eyes are tearing up, both because of the horrendous smell—I forgot how bad it is—and because I cannot believe this actually worked. It feels like Great-Great-Grandpa Isaac is looking out for me. I pull out the four empty mason jars we brought and hold one under the sludgy stream of ink, watching with astonishment as it slowly fills to the top.

26

REBIRTH

Eric

Well, here I am again, lying in bed in the middle of the night.

Wide awake.

I'm at Dad's house, the four now-full mason jars stashed safely in my closet and the snail shell on Isaac's gravestone safely "turned off" by drying it with leaves (no one had a napkin). We need to come up with a plan. Which I guess is dependent on us first figuring out what King Neptune's plan is.

Good luck to us.

It's weird to be here on a weeknight. I mean, I used to *always* be here every night, but now I've grown accustomed to the routine: weekdays with Mom, weekends with Dad. This is my third straight weeknight here. It's a bit unsettling.

I listen to the house to see if maybe Dad is up too, padding around the kitchen downstairs. He has trouble sleeping sometimes.

I don't hear anything.

I can't lie here awake another minute.

I step out of bed and start quietly hopping around the room, trying to tire myself out or just burn off this restless energy. Without meaning to, I end up in front of my closet, as if it's pulled me in with a magnetic tractor beam.

I open the door and reach back behind my old soccer cleats.

I take out one of the mason jars.

I rummage through the detritus of my desk drawer until I find what I'm looking for: a magic marker.

This one's red instead of black, but it shouldn't make a difference.

I snap off the back.

I unscrew the mason jar and make sure not to inhale.

I pour the sludgy ink into the marker.

This all feels very familiar.

Only thing I need now is a blank piece of scrap paper, which inspires an epic three-minute search before I remember to look in my backpack.

I center the piece of my paper on my desk.

I hold up the magic marker.

Am I really about to do this?

Yes. Yes I am.

I begin to draw.

And, obviously, there's no question in my mind as to what.

The marker moves over the white paper, the color of the ink automatically shifting as needed to match what I'm creating.

Most of the time, though, it's a rich brownish red.

I lovingly detail a torso of tightly packed bricks.

A left hand firing cement from its fingers.

A right hand attached to a wrecking ball on a chain.

Eyes filled with a playful, almost human warmth.

Only seconds after I've applied the finishing touches, the paper begins crinkling inward.

I take a dozen steps backward as a huge grin forms on my face.

The paper continues crumpling up until it's a ball and then:

POP!

It explodes into white confetti. There on the desk is my old friend.

Brickman.

"Hey, buddy," I say, reaching out for him.

He gives a joyful grunt, that familiar sound like gravel rubbing together, and gives my hand a hug.

"It's good to see you too," I say, laughing. "Because, Bricky . . . I think we might need your help."

Brickman looks up at me, concerned.

"Eric," Dad's half-awake voice says through the door. "What was that? You all right?"

"Oh," I say. "Definitely. I, uh, accidentally knocked over . . . some books. When I was walking to the bathroom. Yeah. So it made that sound. I'm really sorry."

"You sure you're okay?"

I look down at Brickman, who gives me a thumbs-up.

"Yeah," I say. "I'm okay. I'm very okay."

27

THE NIGHT EVERYTHING CHANGED

Oscar

King Neptune sits in the back of his black car, irritated and restless as it carries him back toward Manhattan.

He takes off his scarf, loses the suit jacket, hating this costume he's always forced to wear when he wants people to believe he's merely human.

"Lower the heat," he barks at Tim and Julio up front.

"Sure thing, boss."

He isn't quite sure why he went to the cemetery. He hadn't thought about Betty in a very long time. But seeing that obituary . . . It was like he needed to go.

Maybe it's because the last time he saw her was also the night everything changed.

"Wait," he says to Tim. "We need to stop somewhere."

Though it's in Brooklyn, the new destination isn't

convenient in the slightest, thirty minutes in the wrong direction.

But he started this journey into the past, and now he needs to finish it.

When they arrive, the black car turns into the parking lot and stops at the curb. King Neptune steps out to get a better view.

As many times as he's passed the New York Aquarium since that night—after all, it's right there in Coney Island—he's never, in all those years, allowed himself to stop and take it in like this.

For seven years, this place was his home, back when he still thought he was a man named Oscar Weissberger. He'd gotten a job there as a janitor when it first opened in 1957.

Oh, how he loved that job, being with all the sea creatures every day.

It reminded him of those walks on the beach with his mother when he was little.

Many nights he would secretly sleep over at the aquarium, literally making the place his home. It meant he had to walk past the bullies from his high school days, who often took up residence outside the entrance—smoking, drinking, looking for easy marks to pickpocket, and taunting Oscar that, almost ten years later, he *still* didn't have a home. It was worth it, though: once he went through those doors and locked them carefully behind him, the hooligans receded into his past, and he was in a different world.

A world that calmed him, the light bouncing off the water in the tanks as he watched the fish, imagining he was King Neptune, in command of it all.

He even took Betty there one night.

But then, even as his life seemed to finally be coming together, he'd gotten sloppy.

He let Betty find him as he was trying to get into her father's locked cabinet. He hadn't even known of the cabinet's existence until that week—in fact, he'd more or less given up on finding the ink. But then her father mentioned something about the King's Wonderland archives being stored in his cabinet in the basement.

And, well . . . He hadn't been able to resist.

So she ended their relationship.

Done. Finished. Another one of his homes burned to the ground.

He'd staggered away from the Parachute Jump that night, almost in a trance, until he found himself here, at the New York Aquarium, the only home he had left. It was closed at nighttime, so he used his keys to get in.

And, likely because of the devastated, disoriented state he was in, he did something he'd never done before:

He left the entrance door open behind him.

Once inside, he found in his wallet the two photos of him and Betty that they'd taken in a booth early on in their courtship. She'd been so happy. She'd torn the strip in two, handed him half, and said, "Now we'll each be able to remember this forever, huh?"

Forever? he thought. *Ha! She's probably already torn hers up, already trying to forget me.* He did the same to his, ripping apart the photos and dropping them like a trail of bread crumbs as he wandered through the building. He stared at the tanks, feeling worthless, losing himself in the animals the way so many people nowadays lose themselves in their screens.

His mistake with the door became apparent when he heard voices.

And smashes.

Oscar ran toward the sounds in a panic and was horrified to see his bullies from a decade earlier, egging each other on as they took turns gleefully swinging the metal handle of his mop at the tanks like they were piñatas. He arrived just in time to see them crack one panel of glass open. Various fish and manta rays and nurse sharks came pouring out, flopping helplessly around on the floor as the water thinned out beneath them.

Oscar was livid. "THESE ARE MY CREATURES!"

The hooligans laughed. "You really are a freak, Weissberger."

"Yeah," another one said, "guess you'll have to take

your lady friend out to an actual restaurant now."

"Or to your house," the third one said, cracking up. "Oh wait, I forgot. You don't got one!"

Oscar charged blindly toward them, reaching to snatch away his mop. One of the bullies shoved him to the ground without breaking a sweat, as if Oscar were a fly that could easily be swatted away. They laughed harder than ever.

Oscar stumbled back to his feet, but no sooner had he begun to charge than one of the other hooligans tripped him, sending him careening to the floor.

Cackles echoed around him, and it felt like high school all over again:

Oscar wasn't strong enough to stand up for himself.

Not like the mythical King Neptune could have.

There on the floor, inches from his nose, was a blue-fish, still flopping its tail around but not as wildly as a minute ago. Oscar looked into one of its dying eyes and all he could think was *I'm sorry, I'm so sorry.*

He began to hyperventilate, a helpless panic invading every inch of his body.

And then something changed.

Oscar began to have a vision—or more like a *realization.*

He saw himself swimming through a sparkling ocean, his body laden with powerful muscles. He had a long beard, and he was holding a trident.

He was the god of the sea.

As the vision faded and reality came back into focus, Oscar was staring at his hand. He saw that right next to

it, shattered glass from the tank had landed in such a way that it formed *the shape of a trident*: one long rectangular piece for the shaft and three smaller pointed triangles on top for the prongs.

This was no coincidence.

This was *a sign*.

The vision he'd had was real!

Oscar had never actually been Oscar—he was King Neptune.

With this new knowledge coursing through his veins, he rose to his feet and walked with confidence toward the sound of the hooligans, who had moved farther through the building on their path of destruction.

How dare they intrude upon his kingdom.

"This ends here, mortals," he said as he came upon his tormentors. He handled the tallest one first, delivering a quick, sharp knee to the groin that sent the man sprawling to the floor.

They weren't laughing anymore.

"You're gonna regret that, Weissberger, you pathetic square," the goon with the mop said.

240

"Gods don't regret," King Neptune said, jabbing his fist into the man's throat with a speed and precision that surprised even himself. The mop fell from the man's hand as he lurched backward, gasping and holding his neck. "It is mortals like you who are destined to always traffic in regret," King Neptune said, basking in his triumph. "For you are the—"

He didn't finish his sentence, for the third hooligan had picked up the mop and whacked the handle into his skull, knocking him unconscious.

When he came to hours later, surrounded by dead sea creatures, shattered glass, and the mop, the sun was rising, and the intruders were gone. The aquarium looked like a war zone, and no amount of cleaning King Neptune could manage before other employees showed up was going to change that.

He was fired, of course. It was devastating, being let go from both of his jobs in the course of twenty-four hours, but also a relatively small price to pay for the gift of learning who he truly was.

And now he also knew that his only true home was the sea.

Before he left the aquarium that day, he'd picked up the mop and the three shards of glass. Eventually, he'd had the handle plated with gold, the mop head removed, and the shards fused to the top.

His trident.

It was all meant to be.

If Betty hadn't broken things off, he wouldn't have discovered all that.

"Thank you, Betty," Neptune says quietly as he stares at the aquarium's entrance doors for a long moment. Then he lets out a sharp sigh and turns away, angry at himself. "Gods don't regret."

Betty had served her purpose in his life, and, in the end, the ink had come to him anyway. Through her gullible nephew! So victory was his.

He steps back into the car, aware that he can't afford to waste any more time, especially not with that nephew knowing he has the ink, threatening to interfere with his plans and screw things up.

The time has come.

For, though he's known for so many years that he is a king, he's never had his kingdom.

And now everything's in place.

He used the final drop of the ink this morning—he'd apportioned his supply out just right—to complete his monster masterpiece.

It's covered by a tarp in his studio.

Waiting to come to life.

Tomorrow's as good a day as any.

"Drive," King Neptune says.

They pull away from the aquarium.

28

BIGGER FISH TO FRY

Eric

After spending so much time with Monster Club, it's hard to go back to Tinsdale, where my friend count is hovering at a precarious . . . 0.5? Maybe a total of 1 if you add my sort-of friendship with Spooner to my sort-of friendship with Knapp.

Regardless, I feel pretty pathetic as I walk up those stone steps into school.

Mom and Dad said I didn't have to go, that I could take another day to grieve, but honestly, I'm ready for a day that feels more normal.

I went back to Mom's place early this morning and dropped Brickman, along with the magic marker and mason jars of ink, in my closet. Definitely not taking my chances bringing Bricky and the ink to school. Already saw how *that* works out.

As I walk down the hallway to homeroom, no one is making fun of me anymore for my viral temper tantrum, so that's a plus, but no one's really acknowledging me in any way at all. I'm like this invisible presence, ghost-gliding to class. When I sit down at my desk, Pete confirms this status by picking right up where he left off on Monday, completely ignoring me. Well, that's not entirely true. He looks at me for a moment, almost like he's going to say something, but then thinks better of it and turns away.

Whatever.

I've got bigger fish to fry.

Namely, the king of all the fish. I have no clue when Neptune is going to strike next, but I know we have to be ready.

Thinking about this consumes my mind throughout the morning, to the extent that, when art class rolls around, it feels only natural that Neptune be the subject of my work. I sketch frenetically, funneling my anxiety into the image, a hybrid of the man I know and art I've seen featuring the actual mythical god.

"Yo, that's sick," Spooner says, stepping away from a nearby table to get a closer look.

"For real?" Spooner's never given me a compliment before.

"Yeah. You're, like, tapping into something. Like, it

244

has an energy, you know? Did you draw stuff like this when you were younger?"

"Well," I say. "Kinda."

"I feel that." Spooner sits down in the chair next to me, pointing to details in my picture. "This drawing goes deep, man. It's you. All of you. There on the page."

"Wow." I don't know what else to say. I didn't realize how much of myself I was putting out there. "Thanks. Maybe it's 'cause . . . Well, my great-aunt just died. A few days ago."

"Aw, shoot," Spooner says, seeming genuinely distressed. "I'm sorry, man. I know how that goes."

"Oh. You do?"

Spooner looks down at his hands. "Yeah. My mom. She died a few *years* ago."

I don't know how I would've known this about him, yet I'm still surprised to learn it. And honored that he's chosen to tell me.

"That sucks," I say. "I'm so sor—"

"I'ma get back to work," Spooner says, patting me on the shoulder before returning to his table. I'm completely confused until I realize Pete's been watching and listening from a couple of tables over. Which obviously scared off Spooner. Just like this morning, Pete immediately glances away when I look at him. What a chump.

I want to continue my conversation with Spooner, but he's already deep into his cutting.

When the final tone sounds, I'm glad the school day is over. It wasn't so bad, but it wasn't so good either. It just was. I grab what I need from my locker, and I'm walking toward the front exit when I see Bobo, Knapp, and Pete clustered ahead of me in the hall, speaking in hushed, intense tones.

I'm about to move right past them, but instead I stop. I'm tired of this.

"So what," I say, "we're not friends anymore? Just like that? Because of a stupid video?"

Pete looks at me for a second as they continue their conversation, like I'm a mosquito he can't even be bothered to swat away.

"Are all of you seriously this shallow?" I continue. "Bobo, I thought you liked me. You said you missed me."

"Look," she says, taking off the sunglasses she's wearing indoors. "We met, and I thought you were Sketch. A real badass. But it turned out, you're actually Doody."

"You mean Doodles," I say.

"Same difference. The point is, we had a good time. Had some fun. Then it ended. What's so hard to understand about that?"

I'll be honest, it crushes me a little. But I'm also disgusted.

"You guys feel like that too?" I ask Pete and Knapp.

Pete looks uncomfortable, glancing at Bobo, then back at me. Knapp just shrugs and smiles. "I don't think her words exactly capture what I am feeling," he says, smoothing back his blond hair with one hand and gesturing with the other. "I am more of a neutral party, you know what I mean? I still think you are a cool guy, Sketch, but . . ." He shrugs again, as if that explains anything.

"I . . ." I'm at a loss for words. "I can't— I can't believe I thought you were my actual friends."

"Ooh, sick burn," Bobo says, putting her sunglasses back on and walking toward the exit, Pete and Knapp of course following her lead.

My heart feels kind of broken. Not just for these friendships, but also for the way I chose these people over Yoo and Smash and Hollywood and Beanie. The way I was just as cruel to my friends as Bobo, Knapp, and Pete just were to me. I'm so lucky they've all forgiven me. But I cringe when I think about how I treated Jenni, the way I completely stopped communicating with her. Ugh, it's mortifying.

I pull out my phone and dash off a quick text:

Hey Jenni. No need to respond to this but I wanted to say I'm so sorry about how I treated you. You are so great and I was so awful. Switching to this new school has been weird and I'm just sorry

I send it and start walking toward the exit, glad that the Tinsdale Three have gotten far enough ahead of me that I won't have to interact with them again.

When I make it outside, though, they're still there, standing at the top of the steps along with a bunch of other kids from school.

Within seconds, I see what they're all staring at:

A massive ten-foot-wide sinkhole has opened up in the street, almost directly in front of the school. Police cars and news vans are already starting to gather around it.

"There's seriously another one of these?" Bobo says, disgusted. "What is going on in this trash city?"

"Check out that CRV!" Pete shouts and points. A blue Toyota CRV that had been unluckily parked right near where the sinkhole opened up is now precariously perched on the edge. It slowly tips over and careens down out of view into the sinkhole. "Oh, sick!"

This is bad. This is so bad.

There's a roar of panicked screams and shouts, and a crowd of people rush out of the nearby Fulton Street subway station. They're all soaking wet. "It's flooding!" a woman shouts as she sprints away. "Yo, get some plumbers down there or something!" a man shouts. "That ain't normal!"

It's definitely not normal.

But it's no mystery to me what's happening and who's behind it.

It's go time.

29

CHAOS REDUX

Eric

Of course this is happening. It's Murphy's Law: if you leave your pet monster and your magic ink at home, that's exactly when the insane supervillain will choose to strike.

"Another Neptune sinkhole!" I shout as soon as Yoo picks up. I've already sprinted away from Tinsdale, heading west toward Mom's place, leaving Bobo, Knapp, and Pete in my dust.

"Oh man," Yoo says, "this guy works fast."

"Yeah. It's right in front of my school. And the Fulton subway stop nearby is flooding. Whatever his plan is, it seems like it's in effect. So avoid the trains and get yourself and Monster Club to my mom's as soon as you can. I'll text you the address!"

"Word!"

I keep running, leaving Fulton Street to run down John Street instead. As soon as I turn onto it, I'm greeted by a line of emergency vehicles, sirens blaring and lights flashing as they rush by. Of course this reminds me of the chaos when Crumple and all the other Noodles took over Coney Island. And just like then, this is all my fault: that time it was me letting Darren Nuggio get his hands on the ink; this time it was me literally handing it over to King Neptune.

Either way, it's on me to make things right.

As I pass the Cortlandt Street subway stop, it's the same madness: commuters emerging soaked and terrified. It's not even raining, yet there's flooding through multiple subway stops.

I repeat: very bad.

I turn up Trinity Place and no sooner have I made a left back onto Fulton toward Mom's than I see a crowd of bystanders gathered on both sides of the street, many with phones held high, traffic completely stopped. Cars are honking, people are cursing each other out and shouting "Move!" I'm expecting to see that the holdup in the street is more flooding, maybe exploding from a manhole or something, but it's even worse.

There are three digging monsters spread out in roughly ten-foot intervals, the same cone-shaped creatures on wheels I saw that night at the first sink-hole, like machines with eyes. They're spinning down into the pavement, I'm assuming to hit more water sources, turn this area into even more of a disaster zone than it already is.

I cautiously step through the rows of people watching, knowing that, when it comes to ink monsters, I'm the closest thing there is to an expert. "Excuse me," I say, with authority. "Coming through here." Granted, I'd be better equipped for the moment if I had a posse of my own monsters and/or a water blaster filled with the ink beasts' kryptonite—nail polish remover—but this is at least worth a shot.

"Hey, you destructive little cretin!" I shout at the near-est one, just starting on a new hole. The silver monster pauses in its spin-digging, its big ol' green eye opening up and swiveling quickly in my direction. If I can dis-tract all these things enough to stop them from doing any more damage, that would be a win.

The monster goes back to its work a second later. So much for that.

"Hey!" I shout, louder this time, stepping even closer to it. "Stop digging. NOW!"

The monster pauses again, and I think I'm onto some-thing.

But no.

A mouth opens up just beneath the monster's eye, roaring at me. "Okay, okay," I say, stepping back as the creature suddenly lifts its silver tail and extends it straight toward me. The tail, which has a big ol' hook on the end of it, seems to have the weight and heft of solid steel. I dodge out of the way, barely, as the crowd behind me gasps.

This is an ill-conceived plan. I need reinforcements.

"Whoa there," Frank the doorman says as I hoof it through the lobby of Mom's building. "Don't forget to catch your breath, chief."

"Thanks, Frank, you too." I hop into an elevator.

Once I'm through the door of Mom's condo, I go straight to my bedroom without even taking off my hoodie or sneakers. I grab a large sketch pad, then dive into the closet to grab the four mason jars, the new magic marker, and . . .

Brickman is gone.

"Bricky?" I search every corner of the closet before tearing like a lunatic through my bedroom, leaving no nook, cranny, or crevice unexamined. "Brickman," I say, hearing the panic bubbling in my own voice, "if you're here, buddy, you should come on out. I need you."

I take my investigation out to the rest of the apartment, and Brickman's whereabouts quickly become far less mysterious. The kitchen is a total mess, with various snacks and boxes littering the floor, and Brickman and Pepper are in the middle of it all. Brickman is holding a veggie straw like it's a hockey stick, whacking a chunk of cheddar cheese across the tiles, dragging his wrecking ball behind him, trying to weave past Pepper, who's having the time of her life, panting and barking and pouncing and not letting him by. Brickman has set up a sideways cereal box on each side of the kitchen, presumably a goal on each side of the "field." If I weren't so stressed, I would find it hilarious.

"Brickman," I say, accidentally startling him. He trips and slides across the floor, and the veggie straw cracks in two. "Oh shoot, sorry about that. You okay?"

Brickman hops to his feet and gives me a thumbs-up.

Pepper goes over and licks his head.

"Bricky, you weren't supposed to leave the closet, remember?" I crouch down to his level. "If my mom came home, or the neighbors heard you, that would be a big problem."

Brickman nods and grunts apologetically.

"But I get it. This game you came up with does seem pretty rad."

Brickman grunts again, this time happily.

"And anyway, none of that matters now because we have an emergency. You ready for battle, buddy?"

My monster raises his brows, surprised and delighted, before hopping up and down and swinging his wrecking ball over his head like it's a lasso. (I have to move a step back so he doesn't accidentally hit me.)

"All right," I say, laughing. "Amazing."

I zip my backpack shut and strap it on before picking up Brickman and heading out into the hallway so we're downstairs in time to meet Monster Club. We step onto the elevator, and the doors are just starting to slide shut when Pepper bounds in, leash in her mouth.

Shoot. I must have not fully shut the front door.

"Aw, you weren't supposed to come with us, girl."

Pepper barks two times, which is her usual signal for wanting to go outside.

"You sure you want to come? May get wild out there."

Two more barks. And the elevator's already descending. No turning back now, I guess.

"Okey-dokey, then," I say, wrapping Pepper's leash around my wrist. "Let's get the band back together."

30

THEY'RE BACK

Eric

The Monster Club text thread has been reactivated and man, does it feel good.

On our way, Yoo texted twenty minutes ago.

In the remaining forty seconds it takes Brickman, Pepper, and me to descend in the hyper-fast elevator from the seventy-seventh floor, I have time to suddenly get nervous.

Because honestly: What the hell do we think we're doing?

Sure, we have the ink, we have Brickman, but we still don't have any kind of plan. Entire subway stations are flooding, and I'm expecting my foot-tall monster to handle that?

"Stay still for a minute," I tell Brickman as the

elevator doors open out to the lobby. I walk briskly past the front desk, Pepper right beside me.

"Hey, cool figure!" Frank says.

"Thanks!" I say, without stopping.

Once we step outside, I look up and down the street for any sign of Monster Club.

I see someone else instead.

"Hey," Pete says, his shaggy hair bouncing as he gives me a little nod.

"What are— What are you doing here?" I'm so confused. And suspicious. How does he even know where I live?

"Yeah," Pete says. "I, um . . . I hope this isn't weird, but I looked up your mom's address on the internet. I kind of knew already because you said you lived in Battery Park. So."

"Okay," I say, feeling that Brickman, who had started to relax as we went through the doors, has again gone rigid in my hands. I know it's exhausting for him to hold that position, so I appreciate it. "But I guess my question is more: *Why* are you here?"

"Oh," Pete says, rubbing his hands together nervously. "Right. Well. I guess it's because I want to help. I heard you on the phone when you were walking away. Talking about, like, a mission to deal with the sinkholes."

"Is this some kind of trick or something? There aren't

gonna be any famous people involved in this mission."

Pete winces and nods. "I know that. But fair enough, dude. That's fair. I deserve that." He scratches Pepper behind the ear, and she pants happily with her tongue out.

I stare at Pete, waiting for more. Brickman starts trembling in my hands.

"I just," Pete says. "I'm really sorry I've been, like, not talking to you. And ignoring you. Bobo said we should. So I did. Which is stupid and pathetic, I know. Because you're my friend. Like, for real. I miss hanging out with you."

It's kind of a trippy experience for me to hear him say those words because it's such a similar apology to the one I gave to Yoo and Smash and the rest of Monster Club. Having been on both sides of this situation, I know that, regardless of which one you're on, it feels kind of horrible. He seems sincere, so I decide to trust him.

"All right," I say. "Thanks, Pete. We're good. You can help."

"Yeah!" Pete raises his arms in triumph as Brickman finally goes slack in my hands, collapsing and taking deep, grunty breaths.

"Whoa!" Pete says, literally jumping back and holding his hands in front of him like he's ready to fend off an attack.

"Pete," I say. "Meet my friend Brickman."

Pete takes two cautious steps forward. "The monster stuff is *real*?"

I stare at him like, *of course.*

"I kinda thought those videos of you on the Parachute Jump with that monster were, like, deepfakes or something."

"No. It's all real. Very real."

As if they've been summoned by my words, Yoo, Smash, Beanie, her friend Lynsey, Hollywood, and the infamous Keiko roll up at that moment, riding the usual collection of skateboards, bikes, and a scooter (Beanie).

"Monster Club assembled," I say, almost involuntarily. "I'm so happy you're all here." (I could do without that traitor Keiko, but we definitely need every ounce of help we can get.)

"It's kind of a mess out there," Yoo says.

"Lots of streets closed off," Beanie adds.

"Yeah, that's why we gotta act fast," I say.

"Brickman's back!" Hollywood vaults off his bike. "What's up, my dope little dude?" Brickman makes happy grunts as Hollywood rubs his trapezoidal head.

All of us hug and fist-bump and say hey and Pepper gallivants around smelling everyone. I introduce the group to Pete, who's incredibly excited to meet some more "real Coney Island people." Yoo is giving him some serious stink eye, but before I can try to smooth out the situation myself, Pete walks over to him.

"Hey. Yoo, right?" he asks. "I get it if you think I'm, like, an obnoxious snob. Because I was that day we hung out. Sorry. But I would love a redo." He puts out his hand. "If, you know, that's cool."

Yoo stares and nods, leaving Pete hanging for a few long seconds before breaking out in a smile and shaking his hand. "Yeah. Okay. That's cool." Classic Yoo. Most wonderful and forgiving human in the universe. He and Pete pat each other on the back, and I'm relieved.

Then I bring everybody up to speed on what's going on, the digging monsters I encountered on Fulton Street.

"So let's get to it, then," Smash says.

"It?" Pete says.

"Yeah," Lynsey says, looking to Beanie, whose hand she's holding. "What is 'it'?"

"You'll see," Beanie says with a small grin. "Don't worry, it'll be impossible to miss."

I lead us all to the side of the condo building, in the hopes of being a little less conspicuous, before ripping off pieces of paper from my sketch pad and passing them around.

"I'm so freaking excited!" Yoo says as he takes his paper.

"Hey," Keiko says quietly in my direction. I pause in

the middle of tearing off another piece of paper. "Just so you know, I deleted that video of you. It's down."

"Oh," I say. "Uh. Okay. I mean, deleting it when I first asked, like an hour after you posted it, would have been better—or, actually, not posting it at all—but thanks. I appreciate that."

Keiko nods. "I still think it's pretty hilarious. But since you can't take a joke . . ." She shrugs and walks away, somehow leaving me feeling worse than if she'd said nothing.

I finish handing out pieces of paper, and I pass Yoo the marker. "All right, do the honors."

"Wow, all right," Yoo says, placing his paper down on the sidewalk as all of us watch. "It's been a while. I have to remember how to even draw him."

"You got this," Smash says.

"Like riding a bike, my dude," Hollywood says.

Yoo takes a deep breath and shakes out his entire body like an athlete warming up for the big game. Then he closes his eyes and puts both hands together in front of his chest like he's praying. "Namaste," he says.

Seconds later, he's attacking the paper with a vengeance, the ink magically providing every color needed for BellyBeast: blue fur, yellow fangs, camouflage shorts, black AC/DC T-shirt with red letters. In no time at all, we're staring at a detailed rendering of that familiar creature, a gorilla-like beast with four arms and an immense attitude.

"Done!" Yoo shouts, and the paper begins to crumple up.

"What the . . . ," Pete says.

Keiko starts to hold her phone up, but Hollywood pushes her arm down. "Just watch. With your eyes."

When the paper has contracted into the size of a tennis ball, it explodes with its classic *POP!* Everyone flinches as shreds of paper float through the air. Pepper barks. Pete covers his head and runs fifteen steps away.

"Belly!" Yoo shouts, crouching down to his monster, who pounds his chest with all four arms and roars before giving Yoo a double fist bump.

"So you just draw something with that ink," Lynsey says, looking shell-shocked, "and it comes to life?"

"Not anything," Beanie says. "Has to be some kind of monster."

Brickman charges toward BellyBeast at full speed and clotheslines him to the ground. BellyBeast quickly recovers and lifts Brickman into the air, spinning him around a few times before hurling him into the wall of Mom's building.

"This is the sickest thing of all time," Pete says, cautiously walking back toward us, eyes glued to the monsters, who laugh as they tumble around on the sidewalk.

"Not to mention a content gold mine," Keiko says, and you can almost see the number of views ticking up, up, up in her eyes.

"Forget about that for now," Hollywood says. I'm glad he's saying it and not me. "We're not posting any content featuring our monsters until we kick Neptune's aquatic arse. Gimme that."

He grabs the marker from Yoo and within minutes there's another *POP!* RoboKillz rolls around on its tank treads next to BellyBeast, who greets it with a happy growl. RoboKillz raises and lowers its laser cannon arm as it whirs the buzz saw on the other one.

"Robo, my love!" Hollywood shouts.

"Looks like something out of the *Terminator* movies," Pete says, totally awestruck.

"You know it!" Hollywood puts an arm around Pete. "I like this guy!"

Smash goes next, resurrecting Skelegurl, the badass winged skeleton with a pink Mohawk holding two majestic blades, who soars around all our heads before landing on Smash's shoulder.

"Missed you, Gurl," Smash says as Skelegurl raises one of her swords triumphantly to the sky.

"Hey, Eric," Frank says, rounding the corner in his fancy doorman suit. "You guys can't be setting off firecrackers out here, okay? You—" He stops short as he takes in our monsters.

"Do you like our action figures?" I shout in a panic.

"Yeah, action figures!" Yoo agrees, Smash nodding along vigorously.

"Wow," Frank says, seeing BellyBeast riding around on Brickman's back as RoboKillz fires a laser at both of them. "Those are . . . action figures?"

"Yup, definitely," I say. "With smart technology in them. Amazing, right?"

"I'll say. Wow."

"They also make realistic sound effects," Beanie says, "which is probably what you thought were firecrackers."

"You gotta tell me the name of those things," Frank says. "My grandkids would go bananas for 'em."

"Oh, definitely," I say. "These are beta versions, so they're . . . not available everywhere yet. But soon."

"Hopefully in time for Christmas!" Frank says. "Thanks, Eric, sorry to bother you all. Maybe keep the sound effects down if you can."

"Sure thing, Frank!"

We all stare at each other as Frank disappears around the corner and heads back inside. Then we crack up.

"Okay, okay," Beanie says, "let's make this quick so we can get out of here." She holds out her hands, Smash throws her the marker, and she draws DecaSpyder with her usual focus and mathematical precision. The eight-legged aluminum monster pops to life and immediately fires a web that ties BellyBeast, Brickman, and Robo-Killz together. "Still got it," Beanie says.

"All right," I say as Skelegurl flies down from Smash's shoulder and cuts through the web with her swords. "So that's the whole squad. Welcome back, crew." The monsters amiably nod, shriek, growl, and grunt at me. "Who knows how soon Neptune's flooding is gonna make it out this far west, so we should get mov—"

"Can I make one?" Pete asks.

"Huh?" I say.

"A monster. Can I make a monster?"

"Uh . . ." All of us original Monster Club members look at each other warily. Which is to say, they're all looking at me like *NO NO NO NO DEFINITELY NOT NO WAY.* We all remember quite well what happened the last time someone who wasn't us made a monster, and it wasn't good.

"Please?" Pete says. "You know I'm good at drawing.

I'll make a helpful one, I promise."

"Do you have a monster in mind?"

"Not exactly, but I have ideas."

"Fine, fine," I say, "just do it fast."

As Smash reluctantly passes Pete the marker, Yoo looks at me like *What the heck, dude?* I look back like *It's fine, maybe it really will be helpful!*

"And Lynsey and Keiko," I say, turning to them, "if you wanna take a stab too, you—"

"No, thank you," Lynsey says, shaking her head. "The most monstrous part about my drawing would be my lack of talent."

"And Hollywood asked me to film him creating his," Keiko says. "So."

Pete sketches quickly, narrating as he does. "This is StarPower," he says, drawing a yellowish-orange fanged monster whose body is in the shape of a star. "He can shoot debilitating star energy from each one of his, like, star points. And he bounces really high. Also he uses his fangs to bite stuff."

"Okay," Beanie says, radiating dubiousness. "Interesting."

"That's not all," Pete says, clearly making this up on the spot. "He also has immense charm, so he can talk his way into clubs and VIP areas and stuff."

"That's weird," Keiko says.

"StarPower can speak?" Smash asks. "Like, English?"

"Well, maybe," Pete says as he lifts the marker from the paper with a flourish to signal he's done. No crumpling happens, though. "Why isn't it doing it?"

"I'm not sure." I look closer at the drawing and notice a lack of definition in his monster's face. "Those look like scribbles instead of eyes."

"Geez, okay," Pete says. "This ink is picky, dude." He fixes the eyes, making them rounder and more clearly defined. The paper instantly starts to fold inward.

"StarPower!" Pete shouts as his monster explodes into being. It manically bounces around us, wildly babbling in some gibberish language that definitely isn't English.

Okay. Maybe helpful. Probably not.

My bad.

I avoid making eye contact with Yoo and the rest of Monster Club as I let out a rallying cry—"Let's do this!"—and we set out from Mom's building, ready for the chaos.

31

MONSTERS TAKE MANHATTAN

Eric

"So they're like machine monsters?" Yoo asks, once we break through the crowd enough to get a decent view.

"Yeah," I say. "They're corkscrewing their giant-ice-cream-cone-looking heads down into the pavement. The idea must be that they'll dig down to the water supply, to cause all the flooding."

I've led everyone back to Fulton Street, where the digging monsters' work is still in full effect, now a block farther west than they were when I left them. They're moving down the street, systematically boring deep tunnels into the pavement.

We watch as one of the digging monsters is pulled back up to the surface by its tail, the tail winding onto a cylinder on the back of its head. Once it's out of its hole, it lifts its tail hook from the ground and rolls about five feet to a new patch of pavement. As it moves, three police officers slowly approach, each of them holding their batons high, ready to strike.

In quick succession, the digging monster knocks the batons out of their hands with its steel tail, and the police officers retreat, hissing and moaning and holding their fingers as they rejoin a group of about a dozen other officers, all of whom clearly have no idea how to handle the situation.

With the officers handled, the digging monster bounces off its wheels and dives headfirst into the asphalt to start creating another hole.

"Whoa, that was nasty," Pete says as StarPower springs annoyingly up and down by his side. "But you didn't make these other monsters?"

"Nah," Hollywood says. "Some old dude who thinks he's a god did."

"Whoa," Pete says. "So our monsters are gonna battle the old dude's monsters?"

"Yup," I say. "Pretty much."

"Love it! No offense to old people, but we're obviously gonna be better at making badass fighting monsters."

"I hope so."

We gather in a tight circle on the sidewalk, our monsters in the center of us. "Okay, Monster Club," I say.

"You see your targets, right? The goal is to stop those three monsters from tearing up the street anymore. Ideally, you'll eliminate them, but immobilizing them works too. Use any and all of your weapons, and we'll back you up however we can. Understood?"

The monsters nod, visibly buzzing with excitement to get into the proverbial ring.

"Fight smart," Beanie says. "These beasts are bigger than you, so outthinking them is your best shot."

We all look at each other, like *Are we ready?* before we all nod, like *Yes we are.*

"Okay," I say. "ATTACK!"

The monsters barrel onto Fulton Street, Brickman calling out audibles for them to disperse into pairs, one for each digging monster. Brickman and RoboKillz charge toward the one that's farthest away, BellyBeast and Skelegurl head toward the one in the middle, and DecaSpyder and StarPower skitter/bounce to the last one.

Just as when I shouted at them, the digging monsters are clearly caught off guard by the interruption. Brickman wastes no time, spinning his wrecking ball in the air twice before smacking it into the monster while it's mid-spin. The digging monster screeches as it's knocked over onto its side.

"Yes!" I shout. "Go, Brickman!"

RoboKillz rolls in to finish the job, lowering its buzz saw right in the center of the digging monster's cone-like body.

The crowd is gasping, cheering, everyone with their phones out. So much for Hollywood's no-filming policy. But I don't blame them. Our monsters are amazing.

BellyBeast has a digging monster lifted above his head with its wheels facing up, Skelegurl hovering nearby ready to use her blades.

DecaSpyder has webbed up the last digging monster, blocking its ability to spin down into the ground, as Star-Power fires some yellow energy stuff at it and shrieks, "Rapeela Gratzo!!!!" (Whatever that means.)

All of us in Monster Club are freaking out, jumping up and down, so proud.

But then RoboKillz's buzz saw makes contact with the digging monster's body. Dozens of bright orange sparks shoot into the air, and there's a high-pitched screeching sound so awful I have to cover my ears.

Whatever this monster is made of, RoboKillz can't cut through it. Robo lifts up its whirring blade and is about to lower it again for another try when the digging monster jerks back up onto its wheels and rolls out of the way. It then proceeds to raise its silver tail like a hammer, with RoboKillz as the nail. Three quick hits, and RoboKillz explodes into a puff of black dust.

"Aw, come on!" Hollywood says.

Things aren't going much better for the other monsters.

The digging monster BellyBeast is holding above his head starts spinning so fast in his hands that it burns them. BellyBeast howls and lets go of the monster, which unfortunately happens at the exact same moment that Skelegurl slices downward with both of her blades to attack. She accidentally cuts BellyBeast into pieces instead of her intended target and he too puffs into a cloud of black ink dust. Skelegurl lets out a screechy scream of pain and remorse.

Smash puts a hand over her mouth.

"No no no no no no no!" Yoo says, holding his head.

"It was an accident!" Smash cries.

The webbed-up digging monster realizes its tail is free and uses it to quickly hammer-smash DecaSpyder into dust—"Dangit!" Beanie shouts—while Brickman, in spite of a valiant effort to fire cement at his adversary, receives the same treatment, swiftly hammered into black dust particles.

It's devastating to watch.

Not only because our monsters are being killed, but because I'm realizing how out of our league we are, how stupid I was to think that just because we got our own supply of ink, we'd somehow be able to save the day.

Forget taking on King Neptune—we can't even handle a few of his monster sidekicks.

"Yo, check out StarPower!" Pete says.

The star monster is babbling incomprehensible words at the webbed-up digging monster, whose big green eye peers at StarPower with something resembling curiosity. "He's charming it, see? He's charming it!"

The digging monster hammer-smashes StarPower into dust with one hit.

"Aw man," Pete says. "I thought he was charming it."

The digging monster lets out a roar that blows DecaSpyder's webbing off its body, then returns to corkscrewing into the pavement, just as the other two monsters have. It's like our attempt at stopping them never even happened.

Skelegurl is the last monster left standing. Or, in her case, flying.

"Forget about it, Skelly!" Smash shouts from the sidelines. "They're too strong! We'll come up with a new plan!"

Skelegurl is still furious about BellyBeast's death, though. She ignores Smash, flying at top speed toward the digging monster who murdered her friend, her swords at the ready as she screeches out a high-pitched war cry.

For a moment, things look hopeful, as the digging

monster doesn't seem to realize another attack is on the way.

Once Skelegurl gets close, though, a second tail peels off the monster's main tail that's anchored to the ground. It wraps around Skelegurl and, like a frog tongue, pulls her down into the hole and into the digging monster's small mouth.

While continuing to shatter the ground to pieces, the monster chews Skelegurl to pieces too.

"Aw geez," Smash says as Yoo puts an arm around her.

To add insult to injury, the monster farts out a black cloud of dust ten seconds later.

"Rest in peace, Skelly," Yoo says.

"Rest in peace, *all* our monsters," Hollywood says. "That was a total bust, yo."

"It did not go well," I agree. That's an understatement, of course. I'm feeling hopeless and lost and defeated, without a clue what to do next.

"Because we need nail polish remover!" Beanie says. "It's the only way."

Of course it is. I've been so stupid. I wanted to believe our monsters alone would be able to handle it, but that's not how it went with the Noodle Monsters, and it's not how it's going now. Beanie is totally right.

"Yeah," Smash says, "but getting to my mom's salon

in Coney isn't exactly an option."

"So let's do some googling," Lynsey chimes in. "We'll find some drugstores and buy all the nail polish remover they have."

"And we can get water blasters too!" Yoo says. "Fill 'em up with nail polish remover like last time and go to town on those monster jerks."

"Perfect," I say. "We'll split up into pairs, hit up all the drugstores, stock up on as much as we can, then meet up near here to plan our next attack."

"Split up. Hit up. Stock up. Meet up," Yoo says. "Easy."

"True that," Smash says, giving him a little grin.

But it isn't easy.

Not even a little.

Pete and I make our way to our assignment, a CVS on Fulton Street. We race through the store, finally finding the section with all the hand products. There's nail polish and nail scissors and nail files but no nail polish remover.

"Am I missing it?" I say to Pete.

"I don't think so. But honestly, dude, I'm really bad at shopping."

I sprint to the front of the store, hearing the seconds tick away in my brain. "Do you have nail polish remover?" I shout at the teenage girl behind the counter.

"Should be with the hand stuff," she says, not seeming to gather the gravity of our situation.

"Can you show us?" The girl doesn't move. "Like, right now?"

She eyes me and Pete for a few long moments before sighing and walking out from behind the counter slower than any teenager has walked in the history of time. She snails back to the hand section and stares for a solid two minutes (which feel like two years), occasionally shifting some items around.

"Nope," she says finally. "Must be sold out."

"Of nail polish remover?" Pete asks. "Isn't that an important item?"

The girl looks down at our hands. "I think your nails will be okay," she says before turning and walking at a much faster pace back to the front of the store.

"No, it's not for that!" Pete shouts.

"Forget it," I tell him. "I'm sure the others are getting a bunch."

Right at that moment, Yoo texts the Monster Club thread: *Smash and I got nothin'*

Duane Reade out of stock

Got some blasters tho

Then Beanie: *Walgreens out too smh*

And Hollywood: *Whaaaaa?? Me and Keiko over at Fast Pharmacy, also sold out!!!!*

"What is it?" Pete says, shaking my shoulder. "What's happening? They get some?"

"No," I say. "It's, like, sold out everywhere. Must be some weird supply chain issues."

Nothing for us either, I send as we head back out to the sidewalk. *This is nuts.*

"Whoa," Pete says, looking at his phone. "It's even saying it's currently out of stock on Amazon."

"Oh geez. But that wouldn't matter anyway. We need it now."

"Right. Yeah," Pete says. "So what do we do? What's plan B?"

I have no idea until my eyes land on a small bit of graffiti on the side of a building.

Reconvene near Fulton Street, I text the thread. *Exact location TBD*

"Plan B is to get some extra help." I push record on my phone. "Uh, hey. Sorry to bother you, but, um . . . There's an emergency situation, and, uh, if you're down to access your negative space or whatever, we could really use your help."

I text the voice memo and pray that my new friend responds quickly.

32

BRICKMEN

Eric

"All right," Spooner says, pacing behind us like an army general or basketball coach. "Once you've outlined all your monsters, you'll pass them to me, and I'll cut them out with my X-ACTO knife."

We're all crouched over large pieces of poster board, sketching the outlines of our monsters with pens or pencils this time instead of the magic marker.

We ended up meeting at the cemetery in front of St. Paul's Chapel since it was only a couple of blocks away from the digging monsters. Another cemetery! Pretty random. But it's fairly secluded and much chiller than anywhere else right now. And we can use the flat grave-stones as hard surfaces to lean on as we draw. Maybe that's disrespectful. But if I'd been dead for over two hundred years, it would probably feel good to know I was actually being useful in some way.

"Done!" Yoo says, passing Spooner his poster board, upon which he's drawn six separate outlines of Belly-Beast.

"Sweet," Spooner says. "Good work." He lays the poster board on the grave of a man named Samuel who died in 1806 and gets to work with the X-ACTO knife. "I wanna be as precise as possible in order to capture all the details of your monster's physicality."

"Yo," Pete says, putting a hand on my shoulder as I sketch my fifth Brickman. "You sure there's not another piece of poster board?"

"Sorry, man, he only brought five sheets," I say. This was very intentional.

"Ah, okay." Pete's trying not to show how bummed he is. "I get it. Just thought StarPower could really contribute to the cause, you know?"

"Look," I say with a sigh. "If you wanna use my marker to draw a new StarPower on a piece of regular paper, you can. It's in my backpack over there." Six Star-Powers bouncing around would be insane, but a single one we can handle.

"Yes!" Pete says, bounding over to my bag. "Thanks, Sketch. You the man. I won't let you down."

I walk over to Spooner to pass him my sheet of

Brickmans—or Brickmen, I guess. He's already done cutting out all the BellyBeasts and is starting on Smash's six Skelegurls. "I'm finished," I say.

"Cool," Spooner says, brow furrowed in deep concentration, "just put it over here next to me."

"Thanks for doing this, man," I say as I place it down. "For coming here."

Spooner stops for a second and looks up. "Of course. My first instinct was to say no. But then I thought . . . What if saying yes is, somewhat paradoxically, a way of exploring my own negative space?"

"Huh. Yeah. Totally." I *almost* get what he means. "You should definitely make your own monster stencils if you want, by the way. Maybe a version of those incredible orange and yellow characters."

"Nah. I prefer any so-called magic connected to my art to result from the work itself, rather than from the medium used to create it. Thanks, though."

I shrug as Spooner goes back to work. "Okay, cool."

For a moment, I take in the scene around me: Spooner, wielding his X-ACTO knife like it's a baton he's using to conduct a symphony. Beanie finishing up her DecaSpyders with Lynsey holding down the poster board to keep it from slipping. Hollywood hamming it up for Keiko as she films him drawing RoboKillz. Yoo and Smash holding hands and whispering to each other several tombstones away. Pete smiling as he inks a brand-new StarPower. It's kind of amazing to see my new friends and my old friends and *their* new friends all here together, in a way that's a thousand times more harmonious and satisfying than that disastrous day when Yoo came into Manhattan to tag with us.

"So what happens next?" Hollywood asks, and I realize he and Beanie have handed Spooner their sheets of poster board. Once he's done cutting the stencils, we'll be good to go.

"Great question," I say. "Smash, all set with the cans?"

"Yup," she says, patting her backpack. When Spooner got here, he brought, along with all his stencil supplies, a bunch of cans of spray paint. (We couldn't get them because you have to be eighteen—not sure how Spooner got them because he's not eighteen either [probably just by being supercool].) Spooner handed them over to Smash, who used her brilliant YouTube-acquired knowledge to replace the paint with ink. It's the same technique we employed last summer to turn fire extinguishers into nail polish remover blasters and obliterate dozens of Noodle Monsters.

"Stencils are finito," Spooner announces.

"Incredible," I say. "Let's find a wall."

"Already found three," Keiko says, holding up her phone.

"Wow," Yoo says. "Did you, like, put 'Battery Park brick wall' into your maps app?"

"I asked my followers for recs on a graffiti-friendly wall in the area." She looks at her phone. "Oh, someone just mentioned another one."

Very glad she came today.

There's a loud *POP!* noise, and we all flinch before turning to see Pete jumping up and down in celebration next to a bouncing StarPower.

"StarPower lives!" Pete shouts.

"All right," I say as we all turn back to each other. "Lead the way, Keiko."

It is only once we've found a brick wall—Keiko led us to one that's down an alley, so we're less visible to passersby—and lined up with all our stencils pressed up against it that I realize we have no idea if the magical properties of the ink will work with this medium. We know it works on paper, and Isaac used it for tattoos, meaning it must have worked on skin (GROSS), so I'm assuming it'll work with brick.

Guess we'll find out in a matter of seconds.

"Three," Spooner shouts. "Two . . . one . . . spray!"

And we're off, a chorus of aerosol spray cans singing in perfect harmony. It reminds me of that game at Coney Island, water guns simultaneously blasting into clowns' mouths to see who can inflate and pop their balloon first. Except here we're hoping for many *POP!*s, not just one.

The ink is every bit as miraculous coming out of a spray can as it is out of a marker. Maybe even more so. I start by spraying across all six stencil cutouts, filling them in completely, and, as always, the ink knows exactly what shade of red to use for Brickman, what shade of black for his wrecking ball. Then, cutout by cutout, I quickly spray in details—Brickman's eyes, mouth, the interlocking bricks in his body—and the ink continues to adjust its color accordingly.

After I finish the sixth cutout, I keep holding the stencil to the wall, looking up and down the alley to see how the rest of Monster Club is doing. Everyone's almost done with their monsters, all of them looking as incredible as Brickman: the badass spray-painted version of themselves.

"So once you pull the stencils from the wall," Spooner says, "you seriously think these creatures will come to life?"

"I hope so. Everybody done?" I shout to the group.

"Hold on," Beanie says, still spraying. "Finishing touches."

"Ugh," Hollywood says. "We're gonna be here all day."

"Shut it, Ahmed," Beanie says. "Done!"

"All right," I say. "I'll count it off. Three . . . two . . . one . . . UNLEASH!"

We pull our stencils away from the wall, and it immediately begins to rumble.

"Uh, guys?" Yoo says, stepping toward the curb. "I feel like we shouldn't be standing this close to the wa—"

BOOM!

"Holy crapballs!" Yoo screams as we all start running out of the alley.

It's totally working! Probably should've realized it wouldn't be a *POP!* this time, what with it being a brick wall and not a piece of paper.

The first *BOOM!* is followed immediately by a series of twenty-nine more, many of them overlapping, creating a horrible cacophony, like a group of people walking through a field laid end to end with land mines. Pepper goes absolutely nuts, spinning in circles and barking her brain out.

"Are we about to accidentally demolish the building?" Smash says as Yoo grips her arm for dear life.

"I really, really hope not," I say. Small chunks of brick rain down onto the alley, narrowly missing Beanie and Lynsey, who are the last to run out of there.

Once the explosions stop and the brickstorm is over, we cluster around to peer down the alley. The building seems to be intact, though the wall is pocked with thirty one-by-one-foot holes, out of which more stuff starts falling.

It's not chunks of rubble this time, though.

It's our monsters.

They're all hopping down from the indentations where they were created, landing on the alley pavement.

"Wow, man, this is . . ." Spooner's in shock. His first monster sighting. "You were actually serious. Like, actual magic."

"Indeed."

The monsters greet each other in their usual way—fist bumps, headlocks, pounds on the back, grunts, screeches, electronic beeps, and so on—but since there are six of each of them, this includes greeting *themselves*. A group hug composed of three Brickmen is one of the more surreal things I've ever seen.

Then we all greet them, and they all greet us.

HEY, BRICKY!

I am in complete awe.

A Monster Club army.

Thirty-one of them in total. Six of each of our monsters, plus one StarPower.

Because we used spray paint and had to work so quickly, the specific details of each monster are a little fuzzier, less precise than usual. But, true to his word, Spooner's meticulous work cutting out each stencil means that the monsters' outlines are somehow more defined than they've ever been. The effect—along with the fact that there are just so dang many of them—is one of complete and total dopeness.

"Yo," Hollywood says. "I think our chances of destroying those freaky spinning hammer-tail monsters just shot way up."

"I agree," Keiko says, phone held out to film the congregation of newly born creatures.

"Is this a big enough army?" Spooner asks.

"I sure hope so," I say. "But you and those stencils are coming with us just in case. Now let's get outta here ASAP before we get arrested for trying to explode a building."

"True that," Smash says as more sirens blare our way.

We march back toward Fulton Street, new army in tow.

33

MANY MONSTERS

Eric

People stop in their tracks to gape and film our two-and-a-half-dozen dozen monsters the whole way to Fulton Street. Once we arrive, our army lines up in some kind of formation along the curb without us even telling them to.

The digging monsters have unfortunately made a lot of progress in our absence, moving even farther west down the street as they create some kind of underground network of tunnels. There's no way for us to undo this damage. But we can stop them from doing any more.

I shout "ATTACK!" and within seconds, it becomes very clear that Hollywood was right:

Our monsters are going to kick some serious butt.

Just like last time, the digging monsters are in the

middle of spinning down into fresh pavement when we arrive. And also like last time, they're startled by our arrival, allowing our monsters to get the upper hand.

Unlike last time, though, our monsters never lose that upper hand.

It's glorious. There are just too many of them.

A group of DecaSpyders immediately web up one of the digging monsters—within seconds, it's wrapped up in what seems like thirty layers of web—and RoboKillz again takes a buzz saw to its body. Once it's passed the webbing, sparks fly, and there's that same screeching noise, but with five other RoboKillz *also* aiming their buzz saws at that exact spot, they're finally able to break through the metal skin and—*POOF!*—the monster turns to black dust.

"Oh sweet god, this is incredible!" Hollywood yells. "Six RoboKillz from all over the multiverse, combining their powers! I am truly blessed!"

The second digging monster is being playfully tossed around like a volleyball from one BellyBeast to another. It's hilarious until one of the BellyBeasts gets careless and accidentally fumbles the digging monster, giving it a moment to lift up its tail into hammer mode and rapidly smash that BellyBeast into dust. This sobers up the surviving five BellyBeasts, who rush in and grab the digging monster, holding it in place so that all six

Skelegurls can attack with their swords.

The blades clang against its metal skin; no matter what angle the Skelegurls employ or how much force they use, they can't harm the monster.

"Give StarPower a crack at it!" Pete says, and in bounces his star-shaped monster, shrieking "Farfo jondy!" and shooting its yellow energy beams at the digging monster, still in the hands of the BellyBeasts. Unsurprisingly, the energy beams have absolutely no effect.

"Aw man, not fair!" Pete says, throwing his hands up.

But then one of the Skelegurls takes another swing with her blades—this time they slice cleanly through the digging monster, leaving the BellyBeasts holding a cloud of dust.

"StarPower's energy did that!" Pete says, nudging me four times in a row with his elbow. "Did you see that? His energy weakened the monster's defenses so that the pink-hair skeletons could kill it!"

"I saw," I say, laughing. "Great work, Pete."

"Thanks, Sketch. This might be the sickest day of my life."

I turn my attention back to the Brickmen, who have been working on the third digging monster this whole time. They had tackled it, but then it did that thing where it spins so fast that it burns you, and the Brickmen leapt away. The digging monster then lifted its tail into hammer mode, trying to smash each of the Brickmen as they circled, with their wrecking balls at the ready. The pattern has gone like this: monster hammers its tail down, one of the Brickmen dodges. Hammer, dodge, hammer, dodge.

But now one of the Brickmen mistimes his movements and gets smashed to dust.

"No!" I shout.

The digging monster roars, showing its fangs.

I'm confused to see three of the Brickmen run away, while two remain: one fires concrete at the monster, while the other swings at it with his wrecking ball. It's a valiant effort, but the digging monster keeps hammering at them with an increasing desperation—it knows it's the last one standing.

I feel Pepper's leash tighten. When I look down, I see the three Brickmen gripping her yellow fur as, one at a time, they each climb up her hind leg. They position themselves on her back, sitting one in front of the other, then grunt as they lightly kick into Pepper's sides like she's a horse. She takes off, the leash flying out of my hand.

"Whoa!" I shout. "Be careful, girl!"

Pepper charges toward the last digging monster as the Brickmen on her back all spin their wrecking balls in the air, precisely positioning them so they don't collide. As they pass by the creature—right as it's about to again hammer its tail down—they simultaneously wallop it, sending it soaring into the air.

The DecaSpyders shoot off webs to catch the digging monster and to reel it back down to the ground, where StarPower is waiting to douse it with yellow energy beams.

Finally, as if it's the climactic moment in a choreographed dance, the five BellyBeasts trudge side by side toward the webbed-up digging monster. They lift the hems of their AC/DC T-shirts a little higher and smack their bellies in unison, releasing their most powerful move: the sonic boom. Times FIVE.

The blast is epic, immediately disintegrating the digging monster to dust and sending any and all rubble in its path flying into the air. Various bystanders on the sidewalk are knocked to the ground. And, unfortunately, StarPower is in the sonic blast zone too.

"What the—?" Pete shouts. "Why did they kill Star-Power? He was *helping*!"

"Sorry, dude," Yoo says, putting an arm on his shoulder. "Friendly fire. It happens."

"I think you're gonna have to draw a new one," I say, passing him the marker. "StarPower was clutch. That energy stuff really worked."

"It really did, didn't it?" Pete says, nodding and grinning. "I'm telling you: sickest day of my life."

With the blast settled, we can take in the fact that we've won.

This battle, at least.

We cheer and hug and scream. I rub Pepper's head and tell her what a good job she did. People on the sidewalk applaud. Our monsters take bows.

"You really brought us to the next level," Beanie says to Spooner.

"True that," Smash agrees.

"Hey, thanks," Spooner says, and he actually smiles. "Can't believe what I just saw. All your monsters are incredible."

"Yup, well, couldn't have done it without you," Hollywood says, patting Spooner's shoulder. "You're part of Monster Club now."

I'm expecting Spooner to bristle at this, but, instead, he nods. Wow.

"And now," I announce triumphantly, "we press onward."

"Where is onward?" Yoo asks.

"To Neptune," I say.

"Where is Neptune?"

"I'm . . . not exactly sure. But the first sinkhole was in this direction." I point east. "Near City Hall. And the flooded subway stations are this way too. So if we head that way, I think we'll find him."

"Man," Hollywood says. "You are the king of vague, barely formed plans."

"Hey, they've gotten us this far, haven't they?"

"I guess, but—"

"Hold on," Beanie says, cutting us off before this blossoms into a full-flung argument. "You said Ol' King Neptune is actually the CEO of Pluto Properties, right?"

"Yeah," I say.

"Pluto Properties' office is in the Woolworth Building," Lynsey says, looking at her phone. "Four blocks from here."

"Oh. Okay. Thanks." Glad Lynsey is here too. Seeing as apparently none of us in Monster Club are capable of using Google. "So I guess that's a good place to start."

On the short walk to the Woolworth Building, we encounter four more digging monsters, which the twenty-eight surviving members of our monster army—plus a new StarPower—easily destroy.

We are unstoppable.

Every subway station we pass is now closed and blocked off, and there continue to be EMTs, firefighters, and police swarming in every direction, trying to figure out how to stop the underground flooding. Our plan remains, as Hollywood so eloquently put it, vague and barely formed: we'll go to the Woolworth Building, sneak up to the Pluto Properties offices, find King Neptune—or if he's not there, find someone who knows where he is—and use our monsters to stop him from causing any more damage to the city.

If all else fails, we'll improvise.

But, as we approach the Woolworth Building—our army of monsters walking, rolling, skittering, and flying along with us—it becomes apparent that the *finding Neptune* part of our plan isn't going to be very hard at all.

Because King Neptune is standing out front.

He's in his full godlike regalia—toga, crown, holding a large gold trident—and, most disturbing of all: he's smiling.

"Good day, children!" the god of the sea says in a booming voice, raising his trident into the air. "Good day, young prince! And good day, monsters!"

It's almost like . . . he's been waiting for us.

Which is very unsettling.

"That's the old dude we're fighting?" Pete says, confused and possibly on the verge of laughter.

"I'm so glad you're all here," King Neptune continues, "so you can witness my most exciting groundbreaking ceremony yet. Welcome to my new home . . . Atlantis!"

I'm wondering why none of the cops are paying attention to King Neptune, or trying to arrest him, when I realize there's no reason any of them would have a clue that this mentally unwell elderly man is the cause of all this chaos. In that way, the King Neptune disguise is sort of brilliant.

But, too bad for him, we're not falling for it.

"We're not here to witness anything, Neptune!" I shout. "Our monsters have taken out a bunch of your spinning creatures, and now we're here to stop you."

The monsters ready themselves for battle. The Belly-Beasts and Brickmen crack their knuckles. The Skele-gurls unsheathe their swords. The DecaSpyders tap their metallic legs. The RoboKillzes whir their buzz saws.

But King Neptune lets out a laugh so huge, it makes his white beard shake. "That's very cute. And, while I am considerably impressed that you seem to have had a backup supply of ink that I was not aware of, I'm not all that concerned. GO!"

At first I think he's commanding us to leave. But no, it was a signal.

Giant hoses blast at our legs, pummeling our army with a pungent-smelling liquid that instantly disintegrates most of our monsters into nothing.

"Noooooo!" I scream, surrounded by plumes of black dust.

It's Beard and Mustache yet again, in all their Vulture glory, each of them holding a hose attached to trucks on the street. I fumble blindly downward for whoever I can, grabbing two Brickmen and cradling them in my arms just in time to shield them from the attack.

"Acetone!" King Neptune shouts with glee. "Or, should I say: nail polish remover. Learned that one from you children. I guess you can teach an old god new tricks!"

34

UP

Eric

This is not how I hoped this would go.

Most of our monsters have been murdered, and we're surrounded by the odor of gross nail polish remover. Spooner's poster board stencils got soaked too, leaving them completely unusable. Suddenly, everything we've done to get to this point—the stencils, the ink spray paint, the triumphant battles—means nothing.

"It's funny," King Neptune says. "I bought up all the acetone I could so that you wouldn't be able to use it against my monsters. Little did I know I'd get to use it against YOU. What a joy!"

"Why are you doing this?" I shout, my voice shaking, the two Brickmen I protected still in my arms.

"I'm finally going to have a home, that's why!" King

Neptune is no longer smiling. "Do you know how long I've waited for this moment?"

"No, dude," Pete shouts, "and honestly, we don't care! You're a grown man wearing a crown!"

King Neptune narrows his eyes, and I'm wishing Pete hadn't spoken.

"I wish you and your hooligan friends had minded your own business, young prince," King Neptune says, as if he's trying to keep steam from blowing out of his ears. "This doesn't concern you. So my advice is: get off the premises forthright. I would hate to see the authorities take you away for trespassing."

He turns as if he's about to head back into the building, but then pauses and speaks over his shoulder.

"Also worth mentioning," he says. "Thanks to the magnificent power of that ink you gave me, it's about to get quite wet in a matter of moments. Dangerously wet. If I were occupying your skin, I would get myself back to the dry lands of Brooklyn. And don't look up. Godspeed!"

King Neptune strides back into the building.

"Wow," Smash says. "Ominous much?"

"I didn't like when he said 'occupying your skin,'" Yoo says with a shudder.

"Yeah," Beanie says, "that guy gives me immense heebie-jeebies."

I look down at the two surviving Brickmen in my hands.

They both give me stoic nods, and I make a decision.

"Take Pepper," I tell Yoo, handing over the leash as I run toward the entrance.

My friends follow.

But Beard and Mustache step in front of us to block our way.

"Did you not hear what the man said?" Beard asks. "Get out of here. Scram."

"No," I say, and I make a move to run around them. Beard reaches out a hand to grab at my jacket, but he misses.

I've only run a few steps past them, though, before another suited goon appears—a short, deceptively strong woman with an unsettling amount of ear hair—and she does not miss. She grabs my arm at the bicep and holds it tight.

"You are not going in there," Ear Hair says in a scratchy voice, leading me back to my friends as an abrasive alarm rings out from the building's lobby and a stream of people begin to emerge. "Whole place is being evacuated."

I look to Yoo, to Smash, to Beanie, to Hollywood, to see if any of them has a solution to our current conundrum, if any of them feel more hopeful than I do.

"What music you guys like?" Pete says to Beard and Mustache and Ear Hair.

"What the hell you talking about, kid?" Mustache says. I'm wondering that as well.

"I can get you VIP passes to the concert of your dreams," Pete says. "Who do you like? Lil Nas X? The 1975? Bad Bunny? My dad is superconnected in the business."

The effort is appreciated, but he may as well have offered them a bag of rocks. Neptune's goons have no idea who any of these people are.

"Springsteen?" Pete says casually, like it's an afterthought. "You like Springsteen?"

Beard's eyes light up. "You can't get us VIP passes to Springsteen."

"I absolutely can," Pete says. "You're interested?"

"Yeah right you can," Mustache says. "Springsteen my butt."

"OW!" Ear Hair says, and I feel her hand release my arm.

A quick glance downward, and I understand that one of the Brickmen has just used Pete's distraction as an opportunity to slam his wrecking ball into Ear Hair's wrist.

I make a break for it.

"Get the hell back here!" Ear Hair shouts from behind me as she gives chase.

I rocket into the lobby through the revolving door, still

holding my concrete buddies, moving against the tide of humans heading for the exit. I realize I don't know what floor Pluto Properties is on, so I look around for some kind of floor directory, the buzzy screech of the alarms reverberating off the walls. It's then when I see none other than my mother walking straight toward me.

Of course she's here; her office is in the Woolworth Building! I feel like a bad son for not remembering that. She's in the middle of a pack, a concerned look on her face as she talks to a woman she probably works with. Before she notices me, I dash over to the lobby desk and crouch next to it. Mom will definitely not approve of what I'm doing, and I will definitely be lectured about it later.

Assuming there is a later. . . .

Ear Hair runs past the lobby desk on the other side, still looking for me.

So now what? What do I do? Where do I go?

King Neptune's voice pops into my head:

And don't look up.

Up. I need to go up.

I sprint toward the elevator bank, making sure to avoid Ear Hair. A bunch of the elevators are out of order (something I vaguely remember Mom and Terry talking about), but, as the doors of a working one open, I slide in past the fifteen or so folks exiting. Still holding both Brickmen, I use my elbow to push the button marked

PH followed by the CLOSE DOOR button so I can speed the process along before Ear Hair or some other security guard can stop me.

The doors close, and I exhale.

"All right, Brickies," I say, looking down at my last two monsters, each of them held in one of my hands. "Are you ready for battle?"

They grunt and nod, but I can tell their hearts aren't totally in it.

"I'm sorry about all your friends. That was rough."

They nod.

"I just lost someone too," I say. "My aunt Betty. She died suddenly, and it sucked. Because she was a really amazing person. And I loved her."

One of the Brickmen pats my forearm.

"Thanks, buddy," I say, blinking away my tears. "Want to hear something really weird? This guy we're looking for? Neptune? *He* knew Aunt Betty too. He pretended to love her so he could try and get the ink. But he never actually got it till—"

The elevator doors open. Fast elevator.

"Okay," I whisper. "Our goal is to find that Neptune guy who killed your friends and try to stop him from hurting more people, okay? We don't need to hurt him, we just need to *stop* him."

We walk down a hallway to a door, behind which is stairs.

We go up and step through a pair of glass doors that lead to the roof. It feels colder up there. Wind whistles over the sound of the still-blaring building alarm.

I take cautious steps forward, and discover that, again, King Neptune is incredibly easy to find.

He's about thirty feet away across the roof, his hands on a large blue tarp. "Young prince, you made it!" he says, and I freeze. "I was hoping you would get to see this."

I'm confused. "You . . . told me to go away."

"Well, I couldn't have all your pesky friends up here. And it would be rude to invite just you, wouldn't it?" King Neptune steps backward, pulling the cloth tarp away to reveal a piece of art. "UNLEASH THE PUMP MONSTER!"

I walk closer. The artwork is drawn on a huge piece of paper. And by huge, I mean *huge*. It's the size of a living room rug, at least ten feet long and nearly as wide, with a blueprint-style drawing of a water tower printed upon it. The water tower is cylindrical, with a pointed roof above and six hoses extending from its sides.

It also has an eye, protruding from the roof.

And large teeth below that.

I've only gotten a glance at it when it begins to crumple up.

I take several large steps backward.

This doesn't bode well.

When it's fully balled up, it's roughly the size of a fridge. I place the Brickmen on the ground so I can cover my ears, seconds before experiencing the most mammoth *POP!* of all time. It gusts my hair back, knocks both Brickmen onto their butts, and sends King Neptune staggering as arm-length shreds of paper rain down around us.

And there, where the drawing was a minute ago, is a huge ten-foot-tall water tower monster.

"My goodness," King Neptune says, staring up at it. "Isn't it beautiful?"

Giant metal legs suddenly extend from the bottom of the monster, almost like scaffolding, jerkily lifting the tower higher and higher into the sky.

"Yes!" King Neptune shouts, raising his trident as if to mirror the monster's ascent. "Rise! Yes!" He runs toward the monster, stopping immediately in front of it to open up some kind of large hatch in the roof. As soon as he does, a massive hose emerges from below the monster's eye, almost like an elephant's trunk, getting longer and longer as it's lowered down through the hatch.

"This is my Pump Monster," King Neptune announces as he gleefully watches the trunk hose continue to extend. "Down, down, down through the elevator shaft it goes, down through the basement, until . . ."

The Pump Monster's pointed roof hat abruptly flips open, and a powerful geyser erupts from its head.

"Up, up, up comes the water!" King Neptune shouts.

The geyser is blasting out a ridiculous amount of liquid, some of which is flooding the roof, most of which is flooding the city below, like a torrential downpour times ten. The six hose arms start spewing water as well, wildly waving in the air around and above us, like out-of-control fire hoses.

"It's happening!" Neptune is hopping from foot to foot, a little celebratory dance. "It's all happening! Finally. My home! Thanks to you, young prince!"

"Oh man," I whisper.

35

SPLIT IN TWO

Eric

Before I can say a word to them, Brickman and Brickman start sprinting toward the Pump Monster. I have no idea how they'll be able to take on a beast so much larger than they are, but maybe their size will be an asset. Maybe they'll be able to climb up its legs and find some weakness on its body, some hidden vulnerability they can use their smallness to exploit.

POP! POP!

My stomach drops as both Brickmen turn to black dust, stabbed in quick succession by King Neptune's trident.

"It's wired up with acetone," he says with a grin. "Comes out of these tubes attached to the tips. Wasn't taking any chances."

And now it's just me up here, fifty-eight stories above the city. Me, Eric "Doodles" "Sketch" King, facing off against the god of the sea and his gigantic, crazed Pump Monster.

I don't want to be pessimistic, but *hopeless* is the only word that's coming to mind.

"You must take in the view, young prince!" King Neptune calls. He's looking out over the front edge of the roof. "See what you've helped make happen! My whole life I've worked for this. And I'd almost given up until you put the answer directly into the palm of my hand!"

One of the Pump Monster's hoses whips past me, and I dive to the ground just in time to dodge it. I army-crawl through a couple of inches of water toward the edge of the roof, a little ways down from where King Neptune is. I slowly and carefully get to my feet to peek over the five-foot-high ledge at the world below.

The view is dizzying. Broadway is flooded, the water level rising by the second.

I step away from the ledge.

I helped make this happen.

I need to stop it.

But what can I possibly do?

I have the marker and one more jar of ink left in my backpack, but I just saw how effective Brickman or any other monster is going to be in this particular situation.

I have no other weapons to speak of.

My vague, half-formed plan has finally hit a wall.

The only thing I have left . . . is me. So I start talking.

"I understand what you mean about wanting a home," I shout at King Neptune. With the Pump Monster blasting out seven separate streams, and the fire alarm ironically still blaring, it's like trying to speak over a malfunctioning waterfall.

I say it again, and I can tell from the way Neptune's shoulders rise that this time he's heard me. "Until last summer," I go on, shouting every word, "my home was Coney Island. With my mom and dad. I loved it there so much. But now our home is split in two, and I'm mostly here in Manhattan." I have no idea where I'm going with this, but suddenly I find myself getting choked up. "It doesn't feel like my home at all. It's been really hard."

King Neptune turns toward me. "You know nothing of what I've been through, young prince! Nothing!"

He's shouting. He's angry. He's listening. So I keep going.

"Back in Coney, everyone called me Doodles. But then here I became Sketch." I crouch to barely avoid another hose blast. It's like a sprinkler system on steroids. "And it's hard to know which one of those is the real me, you know?"

"I know who I am!" King Neptune bellows, taking

several terrifying steps toward me. "I am King Neptune, god of the sea!"

An idea comes to me, and I start frantically digging around in my backpack.

"You are!" I shout. "But you're also him!" I pull out a couple of photos from the front pocket and thrust them into the air. "Oscar!"

"I am not—" He stops in mid-sentence as he recognizes what's in my hand. Him and Aunt Betty at Coney Island. He is visibly thrown, and he slowly walks the rest of the way down the ledge until he's right next to me. "How did you— How did you obtain these?"

"These were Betty's," I say. "She saved them."

Neptune opens and closes his mouth, but no words come out.

"Yeah. All these years later. Because even though you hurt her, she loved you once. And once you've loved someone, that love might shrink or change, but it never fully goes away. It becomes one of your layers."

King Neptune takes the photos from me. In spite of all the chaos continuing around us, I'm surprised to see his eyes well up as he stares at them.

And suddenly I understand.

He didn't come to the cemetery to intimidate me.

He came for Betty.

He loved her. He really loved her.

Sure, maybe he was also scamming her all those years

back, but deep down, he cared too.

She was a home to him.

"No!" Neptune abruptly shouts, flinging the photos to the ground. They float on the surface of the now-ankle-deep water. "Who cares if she kept the photos? Lots of people keep lots of things! I've been working for this my entire life! I am a god!"

"But you don't have to do this!" I retrieve the photos from the ground, flapping them back and forth to try to dry them. "A flooded New York City isn't Atlantis, man. It won't be a home. Not really. And you're gonna do so much damage and harm to so many people. There's another way. You know there has to be!"

"And what is it?!" King Neptune throws his arms to his sides, still holding his trident, his eyes burning into my soul like he's genuinely asking. "What is the other way?!"

"I . . . I don't know," I admit, slipping the photos into my pocket. "But I do know that Oscar wouldn't want you to destroy the magic of this city the same way you accidentally destroyed the magic of Isaac's sideshow."

"It wasn't my fault!" King Neptune's voice cracks and quavers, and he starts sobbing, almost like a child. It's actually scarier than when he was screaming at me. "It wasn't my fault!"

"I know," I say, taking a step toward him, not at all sure what to do.

"No one knows!" he shouts, and he starts pacing in a circle, almost like he's lost all awareness of his surroundings. "Not my father, not my mother, not—"

"Neptune, watch out!" He walks straight into the path of one of Pump Monster's arm streams, and the force of the blast knocks him to his knees. "Aaagh!" he shouts as he drops his trident, right at my feet.

"Are you okay?" I ask.

He just sobs.

"Neptune, are you hurt?"

He holds his head in his hands and rocks back and forth, completely unreachable.

There's no more time to waste.

But now, at least, I have a weapon.

I pick up King Neptune's trident and, seeing no other options, charge toward the Pump Monster.

36

OUT OF MY DEPTH

Eric

It takes approximately fourteen seconds before I realize how profoundly out of my depth I am.

Yes, I have a gold trident.

Yes, it's wired up to pump out acetone, the one sure-fire weapon against the magical ink.

But also: yes, the Pump Monster is absolutely huge.

Its arms seem to be getting more wildly erratic by the second, and they are gushing explosive water in every direction, impossibly unpredictable in their movements. I'm dodging and weaving and jumping like I'm on *American Ninja Warrior*.

My stabs at the Pump Monster's long metallic legs do seem to burn some small holes in its skin, but to think that's going to destroy it is a joke. It's like trying to vacuum up an ocean a few drops at a time.

Speaking of which, the roof water is now at least four inches deep. My clothes are soaked. I have no doubt the city below us, receiving the massive volume of water still erupting from the Pump Monster's head, is doing far worse.

Like I said, I am so out of my depth.

Not so different from when I stood on top of the Parachute Jump facing off against the humongous Crumple Noodle.

I defeated that thing.

Maybe I can defeat this thing too.

I leap forward and drive Neptune's trident into another one of the Pump Monster's legs. I hear a sizzling sound as tiny wisps of black dust rise from the spots where I've made contact. Far above me, the monster lets out a bubbly roar, its arms whipping around.

I bend low and hop out of the way, first to one side, then quickly to the other. I need to keep fighting, but my stabs don't seem to be slowing Pump Monster, and I won't be able to keep this up much longer. I need a better strategy.

The trunk.

That mammoth monster trunk, pulling up all the water from underground. If I can destroy it, I would cut off the water supply and prevent any more flooding. It probably wouldn't kill the monster, but it will stop it from submerging the city.

The problem is, to get to the trunk, I need to pass through the Pump Monster's arms, which have formed a gauntlet in front of it.

If I'm fast, though—

I've taken just a few steps toward the trunk when two of the arms blast me directly, the spray so powerful that I drop the trident and am thrown to the edge of the roof.

I'm lying on top of the stone ledge, hugging it for dear life, however many stories over the street below.

I slowly rise up to a sitting position, intentionally not looking down, but while I'm lowering one leg to the roof, another blast connects with my right shoulder, propelling me backward again.

I frantically wave my arms, like I'm trying to swim my way back to the surface.

But it's air, not water, so it doesn't work.

I feel myself slip and fall off the ledge.

37

TWELVE YEARS OLD

Neptune

It wasn't his fault.

It wasn't his fault.

Sure, King Neptune knows that his presence at King's Sideshow set off a chain of events that created the fire that burned the place down, but that doesn't mean it was his *fault*.

He was just twelve years old. A child!

He is sitting on the roof of his building, arms wrapped around his knees, sobbing, a position not dissimilar to one he used to assume in his childhood bedroom.

This is unsightly, inappropriate behavior for a god, he knows, but he cannot help himself.

The King kid is still on the roof with his monstrous creation. He has his fallen trident, but Neptune cannot bring himself to care.

He is in too much pain as it is.

Betty kept the photos of him.

All these years later.

She truly cared about him.

And he cared about her. He did.

His search for the ink may have been how it started, but he'd felt something with Betty. Something real. And though the aquarium had indeed felt like home all those years, the best moment he had there wasn't with his creatures.

It was with Betty.

To connect with someone in that way was—

Neptune suddenly notices what is happening across the roof.

The King boy is battling the Pump Monster.

Dodging. Weaving. Striking.

It stirs something within him, though it takes him a long moment to figure out what that is.

Of course.

It transports him back to that same moment, when he was twelve, before everything fell apart, when he'd stood in the darkness backstage at the King's Sideshow Extraordinaire warehouse, secretly watching the King Neptune crab monster tattoo battle Leo the lion monster.

It was glorious.

Here, again, a battle unfolds before his eyes: the young prince, with his trident, doing all he can to stop his powerful adversary, in spite of the immense odds against him.

But why would the boy risk so much? Put himself directly in harm's way?

All at once, King Neptune understands.

The boy feels responsible. He's taking it upon himself to right his wrongs.

It is *this* type of courage and accountability and selfless sacrifice that makes a hero, much less a god.

King Neptune has truly lost himself.

Because the young prince was right:

He is King Neptune, but he is also still Oscar.

He is both of them.

Perhaps transforming Manhattan into his home was never the answer. The beauty of the magic he first witnessed when he was a boy was its ability to create, not *destroy*.

King Neptune wipes off his face, inhales snot, tries to center himself.

He looks up, experiencing a jolt as he watches the young prince get blasted so hard by his monster that the boy is flung twenty feet, right toward the edge of the roof, where he clings to the ledge for dear life.

King Neptune is stunned for a moment by the reality of what he's done, the danger he's put the boy in, the damage he's inflicting all around on such an epic scale.

Because, unlike when he was twelve, it is unquestionably his fault.

38

REGRET IN WATERWORLD

Eric

Time has slowed down.

Mere seconds are passing, yet, as I flail and then fall off the ledge of the Woolworth Building, my brain cycles through thousands of thoughts and images, like it has all the time in the world. Thoughts like:

Can I grab on to something? Can I save myself?

If I land in the floodwater fifty-eight stories below, will that allow me to survive?

This is the end, isn't it?

Yes. Yes it is.

And images like:

Mom kissing me on the forehead. Dad fixing a ride at Wonderland. Pepper nuzzling my leg. Yoo laughing as he holds up that strongman outfit. Monster Club standing together on the beach. Jenni holding my hand. Bobo calling me hard-core. Beanie stirring Swedish licorice in a water bottle. Pete bringing me up to light a candle.

Somehow even Terry makes the cut, giving me his special D&D—

Time freezes.

Or maybe it's not time. Maybe it's me.

Whatever the culprit is, I have stopped falling.

Oh—

There is a hand.

Gripping my forearm.

"Gotcha, kid."

It is King Neptune, his face turning red with the strain of holding on to me. He starts pulling me up, his other hand braced on the ledge. It's like every muscle in his body is tensed, veins bulging, tendons about to pop.

Slowly but surely, he pulls me back to safety, and we collapse onto the roof, lying in the still-rising pond that has formed.

"You saved me." I am shocked.

"Young prince," King Neptune says, breathing hard. "You were right. I lost myself. I am a god. But I am also Oscar. I am all of it. And this is not the path I intended to go down. Gods are courageous. So let us be courageous and destroy this beast."

We look over at the Pump Monster, steadily terrifying as it continues pushing out gallon upon gallon of water. My whole body is shaking, my heart is thumping in my ears, and I can't quite process this turnaround. If King Neptune hadn't just saved my life, I would definitely think this was another trap.

Is it possible that my words actually . . . worked?

"Are you well enough to take this on with me, young prince?" King Neptune asks, getting to his feet and putting a hand on my shoulder. "I'll go alone if need be."

"No, no." I am slowly coming back to myself. "Let's stop this thing. When I got hit, I was trying to attack the trunk with your trident. Like, thinking maybe that would cut off the water supply."

"Very wise," Neptune says. "That's exactly right."

"But the monster wasn't having it," I say, pushing up from the water to stand. "As soon as I made a move toward the trunk, those arms attacked me."

"Unfortunately that's what I designed the monster to do, kid. So that it would be unstoppable."

"Oh."

"Yes. I'm having some second thoughts about that now."

The water around us seems to be rising faster. It's up to our calves.

"But if we do cut off the water supply," King Neptune goes on, "the spigots will dry up, and the arms won't have anything to spray at us. We'll have a clear path to attack."

"When I stabbed at the monster's metal legs, though," I say, "the trident did pretty much nothing."

"Ah, yes. The legs are its strongest parts because they don't need to carry water. The arms and trunk, however, will be much more vulnerable. That's why I made them so difficult to get to."

"So, let me get this straight. . . . We won't be able to attack the trunk until we cut off the water supply and stop the arms. But the only way to cut off the water supply and stop the arms is to attack the trunk?"

"That's right."

"We're screwed," I say.

"Perhaps." As King Neptune stares at his creation, wheels in his brain spinning, I cautiously approach the ledge of the roof again. I stare down, wondering if all my friends are still out there, whether they've gone home. It's like I'm staring down at a lake. I don't see them.

"Wait," I shout to Neptune over the perpetually aggressive white noise of the gushing water. "The monster's trunk goes down to the basement, right? That's where it's accessing the water supply?"

"Yes. . . ."

"What if we attack it down there?"

King Neptune sighs, shakes his head. "Won't do much, I'm afraid. You may destroy some of the trunk, but it will simply extend the healthier parts of itself to continue pumping up water."

"Okay, okay," I say, pacing along the ledge, timing my steps to avoid the gush of the arms. "Oh! What if we clog it?"

"Clog it?"

"Yeah, the trunk. Put stuff in the trunk hole, or whatever it's called. Block the water from coming all the way up here."

King Neptune runs a hand through his beard. "Not a bad idea, young prince. However, I worry that, once we clog it, by the time we've made our way from the basement to the roof, the monster will have spit out the offending object."

"I may have a solution for that," I say.

"Oh thank god, you're alive!" Yoo shouts into the screen as soon as he answers his phone. Water is pouring down all around him. "You weren't responding to our texts. We were freaking the hell out!"

"I'm sorry!" I say. "I'm okay, just been a little busy up here."

"Are you on the roof?! With that gigantic monster water tower thing that's flooding the crap out of us?"

"I am. Are you all still down there?"

"We are." Yoo aims his phone down and around to reveal that he's thigh-deep in water, surrounded by the rest of Monster Club and the new friends, all of them soaked from the Pump Monster's unceasing output. Everyone has stayed, which is touching, but also makes me scared for their safety.

"We're living in *Waterworld*, yo!" Hollywood says. Yoo pans away, but Hollywood pulls the camera back. "I didn't just make that name up. It's a movie. Kevin Costner. 1995."

"Anyway," Yoo says, on-screen again. "We're here. In case you needed us."

"Yeah, here for you, bro!" Pete says, leaning into the frame.

"Okay, amazing," I say. "Because we do need you. We think we have a plan."

"'We'?" Yoo asks. "Who is 'we'? You and the Brick-men?"

"Oh, no, they died almost immediately after I got up

324

here. But King Neptune and I teamed up." I aim my phone at Neptune. He nods self-consciously and says hello.

"Wait, what?" Yoo's eyebrows are raised almost to his scalp. "Teamed up with King Neptune? Isn't he the one causing this? The one we're trying to stop?"

"Well, he was, but now he regrets it, and that water monster he created was designed to be unstoppable, even by him, but we're working together to try and stop it."

"Okey-dokey, then," Yoo says. "So what do you need us to do?"

I quickly explain how the Pump Monster works, the giant trunk descending down to the Woolworth basement that we need to clog.

"Okay, we can do that," Yoo says, looking around. "How big is this trunk? Like, should we try to clog it with a car?"

"A car?" I ask. "How would you even do that?"

Yoo turns his phone to show me various automobiles floating through the water about twenty feet away. "We could probably push one of those into the building, I don't know."

"That's too big," I say. "And be careful down there! Don't anybody get hit by a floating car. That would be horrible and weird."

"So, then what size are we talking here?" Yoo says.

"Like a sneaker? A gallon of milk?"

"Would my skateboard work?" Smash asks, her pink hair popping into frame before her face.

"No, bigger than those things." I look to King Neptune. "What size do you think to clog it? Approximately?"

"Hmm." He looks down at his hands, moving them different widths apart, finally settling on a distance about a foot out from his body on either side. "About this wide," he says as I train the phone on him. "And maybe this tall." One hand is at his neck, and the other is at his knees.

"Did you get that?" I ask Yoo and Smash.

"I don't know," Yoo says. "I mean kinda, but what exists that's that si—"

I'm distracted by something that appears behind Yoo, floating down the street-river toward him and Monster Club.

It's a huge yellow-and-red umbrella, the kind that attaches to a hot dog cart.

"That!" I shout.

"Dude, how are we going to get this into the trunk hole," Yoo says, holding the red-and-yellow umbrella.

He and Monster Club have made it into the flooded basement of the Woolworth Building, sneaking past the police barricade out front. Keiko, with her top-notch camera skills, has taken over Yoo's phone, holding it to his face so we can talk while he's holding the umbrella.

"Any and all thoughts or guidance would be greatly appreciated," Yoo says, standing in waist-deep water.

They're about ten feet from the Pump Monster's trunk, which extends down the elevator shaft through a large hole in the floor created by one of the Digging Monsters. It's pulsing. It looks like a gigantic vein.

"The entryway to the trunk," King Neptune says, "shouldn't be too far down that hole. Probably six feet or so."

"Six feet?" Yoo says, walking toward the trunk and looking down through the water. "Meaning I would have to, like, swim six feet down into that hole? While holding an open umbrella?"

"Indeed," King Neptune says. "Put the umbrella up to the opening in the trunk, and it should get pulled in, not unlike a vacuum cleaner. A very powerful vacuum cleaner."

"Wow. Okay." Yoo takes a deep breath.

"You can do this," I say. "I know it's scary, but it's the only way to stop the Pump Monster."

"What if it sucks me in too?"

"Do it carefully," King Neptune says, "and hopefully that will not happen."

Not the most reassuring words.

"Let me be the one to do it," Smash says, Keiko panning the camera over to her.

"What?" Yoo says. "But—"

"I'm smaller. I can do it. Trust me."

"Oh," Yoo says, seeming both grateful and anxious. "Only if you—"

"Hold up," Beanie says. "Lynsey wants to do it."

The camera shifts to Beanie and Lynsey, standing just to the left of Yoo and Smash.

"I mean, I don't have to," Lynsey says, looking a little sheepish. "Only if you all are okay with that."

"She's literally a swim champion," Beanie says.

"Well," Lynsey says. "I've won a few meets here and there. But yeah. I'm pretty comfortable in the water. I can do this."

Keiko turns the camera back to Yoo, who looks at Smash, then at Hollywood, then at Beanie and Lynsey. "All right," Yoo says. "If you're sure."

"I am." Lynsey nods.

"We can tie this around her ankle," Beanie says, holding a length of rope she must have found floating in the basement. "In case of emergency."

"Sounds like a plan, I guess." Yoo passes her the umbrella before looking back into the camera like: *Is this messed up? Are we gonna get this girl killed?*

"Okay," I say. "Thanks, Lynsey. Let's give this a shot."

39

ATTACK!

Eric

We are ready to strike.

King Neptune and I are still huddled near the ledge of the roof, occasionally dodging the Pump Monster's arms as we stare at my phone, waiting to see if Monster Club is successful. The trident is back in Neptune's hands, retrieved from where I dropped it earlier.

"What's going on?" I ask, staring at Yoo in my phone. "Did Lynsey do it yet?"

"No," Yoo says. "She's trying, but it turns out it's hard to carry an open umbrella through water. Wait, Smash is going too."

"Both of them?"

"Lynsey's diving down first, then Smash is gonna push the umbrella downward to pass it to her. Something

Beanie figured out with angles or something."

"Okay." King Neptune is looking out over the ledge, then back at me with eyes wide. "They figured something out with angles," I say.

"Young prince," he says. "The flooding is catastrophic. If your friends cannot pull this off, I may have to take matters into my own hands."

"What do you mean?" I ask.

"I must take accountability for my actions. I must—

"It got sucked in!" Yoo shouts from the phone. "At least we think it did . . . ?"

"It's too dark to really see!" Smash shouts from off camera.

King Neptune and I stare at the Pump Monster, looking for any slight shift.

It seems like nothing is happening.

But then the trunk stops pulsing.

The geyser vanishes.

"Good lord," King Neptune says, gripping his trident. "It's stopping."

The streams from all six arms get thinner and thinner, tapering down to drops and then nothing until finally the arms hang slack at the monster's sides.

"Now!" King Neptune shouts, wading forward through the water, me right beside him. "We must attack now!"

For a moment, the Pump Monster is still.

But then its entire body jerks violently, accompanied by a loud crunching rumble. It jerks again. And again. It's like someone trying to start a stalled car's engine.

"We don't have much time," King Neptune says. We're almost to the trunk. "It's attempting to clear the foreign object."

There's another jerk and crunch, the largest yet.

As we reach the trunk, King Neptune lifts the trident high in the air, almost as if he's trying to be as dramatic as possible.

The trunk begins to pulse.

"It pushed out the clog!" I say.

The arms start spraying water again.

But before the Pump Monster has time to blast us away, King Neptune grunts and stabs the trident diagonally downward into the trunk.

"BE GONE!" he shouts.

The Pump Monster lets out a sound way worse than the crunching rumble, a massive gurgling shriek.

The trunk turns to black dust, starting from the trident holes and rippling up and down in either direction. When the ripples reach the monster's water tower head, that explodes into particles too, followed closely by its metal legs.

All of it. Gone.

"We did it!" I shout to King Neptune, who seems

stunned, staring down at his trident. "You did it!"

"We all did it!" Yoo shouts from the phone in my pocket.

"Woo!" I shout to the screen. "Tell Lynsey and Smash they killed it! Literally!"

"Young prince," King Neptune says, still looking at his trident. "I must apologize for putting you through that. Through all this. It was never my . . ." He raises his head, noticing something, and then I notice it too.

The water on the roof seems to be spinning around us. Churning.

"It's all going down the elevator shaft," King Neptune says, seeming genuinely terrified. "Like it's a drain. It will create a whirlpool. Quick, we must hold on to somethi—"

But it's too late.

He's swept off his feet.

So am I.

As the water carries us faster and faster around, I try to keep my head above water, try to reach out for something. Anything.

There's nothing.

We're both sucked down the elevator shaft.

40

FLUSHED

Eric

Water.

Everywhere.

I can't breathe.

It's like we've been flushed down a giant toilet.

And now:

We're falling.

And falling.

I think I feel other limbs bumping into mine.

Arms. Or legs.

Neptune.

Or maybe it was nothing.

I can't breathe.

So much water.

All. Goes. Black.

41

FAMILY

Eric

"You should eat something," Aunt Betty says.

"Huh?" I say.

She gestures to a table. "There are some fresh bagels, lots of spreads. Have whatever you like."

We're sitting on a small couch in a room that looks a lot like where she used to live without being exactly the place where she used to live. I'm surprised that she's alive, but in a way, I guess it makes sense. We thought she was dead, but she wasn't. It's great news.

"So, Eric, my sweet boy, how are you?"

Aunt Betty smiles at me, and it's so good to see her.

"I'm fine," I say, though I suddenly realize that's a lie: I have no idea how I am. I feel stressed for some reason, panicked over something I can't quite place. "Or, I don't know. I'm okay."

"Well, I'm happy to see you," Aunt Betty says. "And I have a surprise for you. I think you'll like it. If you don't, well, I'm sorry, but it's happening, okay?" She laughs in that familiar, bouncy way.

"Uh, okay," I say. "What is the surprise?"

"Ta-da!" Aunt Betty gestures to the front door, and in walks a man in his fifties in a black top hat and suspenders.

"Hello, Eric. It is such a pleasure to meet you."

I shake his hand, and when I realize he's my great-great-grandfather, I feel like I'm meeting a celebrity.

"You're Isaac," I say, like an idiot.

"I am."

"I can't believe you're alive."

"I'm not," Isaac says with a sly smile. "Not in the way you are thinking, anyway. I live in here." He points to my head. "And here." He points to my chest.

"Oh," I say.

"Eric is an artist, Zayde," Aunt Betty says. "Like you."

"I know," Isaac says. "I am a great admirer of yours."

"Really?"

"Of course. I very much enjoy that Brickman. Strange and beautiful, like all my favorite art. Though your latest work inspires as well."

"Thank you," I say. "That really means a lot."

"You carry forward my legacy." Isaac tips his hat and bows his head. "I am grateful."

"See, I told you it would be a good surprise," Aunt Betty says with a wink.

Isaac walks to the table and holds up an everything bagel. "Can I get this toasted?"

"Did you two ever feel lost?" I suddenly blurt out. "When you were alive?" I'm not even sure why I've asked it.

"All the time," Isaac says with a chuckle before taking a crunchy bite of his bagel, now topped with cream cheese and lox.

"To be human is to often feel lost," Aunt Betty says, also chuckling. "That's part of the whole deal, I'm afraid."

"Did you not think I felt lost when I arrived in America alone?" Isaac asks. "I was just a kid, like you. I was terrified. But do you know what I realized?"

I shake my head no.

"Home is always with you. Do you know where?"

I think I do, but I shake my head anyway.

"It lives in here." He points to my head. "And here." As he points to my chest, I start spitting up water. I hear a deafening whoosh, and he and Aunt Betty swirl away into nothing.

My eyes open.

42

HER

Eric

It is only after I cough and splutter and vomit up water for a solid three minutes that I realize I have no idea where I am.

I'm lying on a hard surface.

Water is all around me.

I feel like crap.

I flinch as a couple of rats swim by.

I roll to the other side.

And that's when I see her.

Floating in the water next to me.

The mermaid.

She has long red hair and dazzlingly green eyes that are peering at me with concern. It's the same mermaid who was watching me from the ocean, first in the

Hamptons, then at Coney. Maybe the same mermaid who Isaac saved all those years ago.

"You saved me," I say.

She nods.

"Thank you." I realize I'm lying on a desk. The front desk of the Woolworth Building lobby, only a few inches of which are above water. The lobby is now more like a lake.

I look around, suddenly feeling panicked. "Neptune!" I shout with the little energy I can muster. "Are you here? Are you okay?"

There's a soft groan from farther back near the elevator bank.

The mermaid dives down into the water and torpedoes herself in that direction.

Ignoring how sore my body feels, I lower myself into the water and slowly wade after her.

King Neptune is floating on his back in the water, eyes open and occasionally blinking. The mermaid hefts him onto her back with a surprising amount of strength and swims over to the large desk where I was just lying, gingerly placing him down.

He's not coughing or sputtering like I did, and I see that, on either side of his neck, there are three pulsing slits. Gills. He has gills. But, even so, he doesn't seem well. He looks disoriented and scared and weak, like he can barely move. I guess even if you have gills, falling down an elevator shaft takes its toll. Especially if you're old.

It is only when King Neptune's eyes land on the mermaid that he seems, for the first time, somewhat calm. "You," he says, a note of awe in his quiet voice.

She nods.

"Oscar," I say, wading closer so that I'm right next to the mermaid. "We need to get you to a hospital."

He coughs and shakes his head. "No," he says. "No point. I'm dying."

"You can't know that!" I practically shout. It's weird. This man manipulated me, did so much damage to the city, almost got me killed, and yet, I can't help but feel bad for him.

"Young prince," King Neptune says, looking right at me. "I've spent much of my life as an immortal god. So I know. It's my time."

I nod as my eyes get as wet as the rest of my body.

"But I have to tell you," he continues. "Watching you . . . Up there, but also before this. You inspire me, kid. That spark came down the family line. Don't lose it."

I nod again and reach into my pocket. Somehow the photos of him and Betty are still in there. Floppy and on the verge of disintegrating, but there nevertheless.

I hand them to King Neptune, who receives them,

hands shaking, like the precious cargo they are.

He stares down at the photos, then closes his eyes and holds them to his chest.

I don't know what to do next.

"Um, Neptune," I say. "Do you have any requests for . . . Like, do you have any family or people we should call . . . ?"

Neptune, eyes still closed, shakes his head.

Someone touches my shoulder. It's the mermaid. She puts a hand to her chest and nods, as if to say, *Let me take him.*

"Oh," I say. Is it okay to send King Neptune off like this?

I lean in closer to him and whisper, "Uh, Oscar. King Neptune. The mermaid would like to take you with her to . . . Well, I'm not sure where, but she—"

King Neptune's eyes flick open. "Home," he says, his voice the opposite of booming. "She's taking me home."

The mermaid looks into my eyes: *Do not worry. This is what he wants.*

I nod and watch as she extends a hand toward King Neptune.

He slowly takes it, and I help him off the desk, easing him toward the mermaid, who's still floating there even as the water in the lobby is receding. She gets him into another impressive carry-hold, this one with her arm wrapped around his torso.

"Thank you," I say to the mermaid.

She nods and grips my foot with her free hand, like she's demanding my full attention. As I again stare into her green eyes, she removes the hand and points to her head.

Then she points to her chest.

I nod, stunned that she knows what happened in my dream, as she fully submerges with Neptune, aka Oscar Weissberger, and swims toward the front entrance.

I'm watching them go when there's a shout behind me.

"Eric!" Yoo and Monster Club wade toward me from a door near the elevator bank. "You're alive! Oh man, thank the sweet universe you're alive!"

"Dude is like Tom Cruise in *Edge of Tomorrow*," Hollywood says. "Endless amount of lives."

"Truly the most hard-core person I've ever met," Pete says.

"I'd like to put in a request for Eric to never stand on the top of a high building or structure ever again," Beanie says. "Because I believe next time I will for sure have a heart attack."

"True that," Smash says.

"Hey, everybody." My voice sounds small and tired. "You all killed it. We couldn't have stopped the Pump Monster without—"

"Whoa," Yoo says, catching a glimpse of Neptune and the mermaid as they cross the threshold, out of the building and out of sight. "Is that . . . ?"

"It is," I say.

I'm pretty sure I see Neptune's hand stick up from the water right before they disappear—one final goodbye— but I might just be imagining it.

43

ATLANTIS: FINAL PHASE

Neptune

King Neptune is swimming the streets of Manhattan.

Not fully, of course—he's being carried along—but the effect is more or less the same.

The mermaid guides them out the door of the Woolworth Building, gliding down the river that as recently as this morning was a street known as Broadway. She turns them onto the waterway that has overtaken John Street, taking it all the way to the South Street Seaport. They pass over submerged piers en route to the East River. Once they're past the Statue of Liberty, they move into the Upper New York Bay, then the Narrows, then Lower New York Bay before, finally, the Atlantic Ocean.

King Neptune doesn't know any of this, drifting in and out of consciousness, feeling life trickling away from his body, in a way that isn't entirely unpleasant. He keeps seeing his mother, on that long-ago beach, holding his small hand.

"What a beautiful shell, Oscar! You're so good at finding the best ones."

He'd loved her so much.

And though she'd thrown him out of the house and stopped speaking to him, she'd also left him the family business in her will.

Part of her had never stopped loving him.

He is comforted to remember this.

Once Neptune and the mermaid reach the ocean, he somehow senses the change, becomes more alert. Though he is dying—or, perhaps, *because* he is dying— he is able to experience the wonder and beauty of the ocean kingdom in a way that feels almost spiritual. A school of blue-green fish slide by. Down below, a manta ray.

Oh! A seahorse, hovering briefly ahead of him before dipping away.

To be here, amid the creatures, *his* creatures. His friends.

It's all he ever wanted.

And then, oh my goodness.

There, ahead of Neptune and the mermaid:

The glowing, wondrous magic of Atlantis!

Buildings. Throughways. Castles.

Shimmering.

Like a city of giant shells.

King Neptune cries salty tears that dissolve, invisible,
in the salty sea.

He is finally home.

Everything goes dark.

44

IT LIVES IN HERE. AND HERE.

Eric

I'm back at Mom's condo, shivering on the couch with a mug of hot cocoa, three blankets wrapped around me. Pepper's curled at my feet with three blankets of her own.

Shortly after King Neptune swam away with the mermaid, Mom and Terry rowed into the Woolworth Building in a red kayak. It was one of the more surreal moments of my life, but I was beyond happy to see her. I'm not even sure how she knew where we were, since I'd stopped responding to texts or calls sometime around when Spooner showed up, but if I had to guess, she'd probably been in touch with Yoo's mom.

Mom and Terry made a bunch of trips, rowing everyone west to dry land. Or, at least, *drier* land. The flooding made it all the way to Mom's building, but only a couple of inches deep. Which, compared to twelve *feet*, is really nothing.

The damage to lower Manhattan in general is extensive. I mean, it didn't turn into Atlantis like Neptune originally wanted, but the news is saying that the area is way more devastated than it was after Hurricane Zadie. Which means, yeah, it's bad.

The West Side Highway is still drivable, so Mom paid for all my friends to get rides back to Brooklyn. Seeing as it's currently the only real route open between the boroughs, Yoo keeps texting (on my mom's phone since mine is totally messed up; it's waterproof, but not *that* waterproof) that they're moving about half a mile an hour. But they'll get back eventually. Pete's family sent their driver down to pick him up, and Pete's taking Spooner up to dry land that way too.

I sort of can't believe all of it happened.

Love you too, I text Dad. We've been going back and forth for a while. He was terrified something happened to me, and again angry that I put myself in so much danger, but also proud of me.

I'm proud of me too. And similarly happy that I'm still alive.

"Are you sure you don't want to go to the hospital, sweetie?" Mom says, sitting down on the couch and wrapping her arm around me.

"I'm sure," I say. "I feel okay. And it would be kind of impossible to get to one right now, anyway."

"We could make it happen," Terry says from the kitchen, where he's making me a stir-fry.

"It's really okay. Thanks, Terry."

He nods. I've decided I officially like him. He's a good dude.

"Well," Mom says, "if you change your mind, let us know. I'm really sorry this happened to you today. I don't even fully understand what happened, but it seems like it's connected to those monsters that attacked Dad's park last summer, which means it was probably terrifying. You're very brave, Eric. Too brave."

"I know," I say.

"You're my baby." Mom hugs me tighter. "And my baby shouldn't be putting his life in peril every six months, okay?"

"Don't worry, I won't have to be that brave again anytime soon," I say. "Because it's over now. For real."

Me and Monster Club are going to see to that.

"We have to stop meeting like this," Yoo says as we congregate outside the main gate of Greenwood Cemetery.

"Hey, at least we don't have to use my dang back as a stepstool this time," Hollywood says. "Gonna feel nice just walking in, like normal humans do."

It's a cold, sunny Saturday afternoon, five days since

everything went down. Everyone's arrived: me, Yoo, Smash, Beanie, Lynsey, Hollywood, Keiko, Pete, and even Spooner.

We're here to finish this.

"Hey, man," Pete says, pulling me aside before we walk in. "Bobo wanted me to tell you how badass she thinks you are for what you did and is wondering why you're not returning her texts."

"Uh," I say, trying not to laugh. "You can tell her to keep wondering and maybe she'll figure it out someday."

"Word," Pete says, grinning.

Someone whose texts I *did* return was Jenni's. She reached out a few days ago to say she really appreciated my apology text and she's glad I'm okay after my latest monster encounter. We even ended up talking on the phone for a bit. She's seeing this new guy Andre who's math talent. He sounds pretty cool. I can't help feeling a little jealous, but not really. Truth is, I'm happy for her.

I gather everyone on the sidewalk. "Okay, so this is a two-step process. Step one happens out here. Follow me." I walk down the curb to the nearest sewer grate, pulling out the only remaining mason jar of ink from my bag. Since I now understand King Neptune was lying when he said only he knew how to destroy the ink, I know we can dispose of it the old-fashioned way: down the drain.

Everyone gathers around me as I pull off the lid and hold the ink high. I haven't really thought about what I'm going to say.

"So, uh," I start, "we thank you, magical mermaid blood ink, for bringing us real-life versions of our monsters. And adventure. And for bringing us all together. But we recognize that your power is too great to—"

"Wait, wait, I'm sorry," Hollywood says, "are we sure we want to get rid of this stuff?"

"Yeah," Keiko says. "Not sure if you've seen, but all the videos of our monsters posted by random people have gone beyond viral. The content possibilities are truly endless."

"Could be just the boost Dollywood Studios needs to really establish itself," Hollywood says, giving a flick of his eyebrows. "Dope new name, right? It's like Hollywood plus sweet, sweet dollars."

Yoo sighs. "You know Dollywood is the name of a theme park, right? Started by Dolly Parton?"

"Aw man, what?" Hollywood says. "Dang. Point is, we should at least consider keeping the ink."

We all stare at him and Keiko.

"Ahmed," Beanie says, giving him laser eyes.

"Seriously, dude," Smash adds.

"No, no, you're right," Hollywood says, looking at Keiko. "They're right."

"Okay." Keiko shrugs.

"So, yeah," I continue, "your inky power is too great to mess around with anymore. So we thank you and, um, goodbye."

I turn the mason jar over and the ink ever so slowly sludges out of it.

It's taking forever so I move it closer to the sewer grate and give it some hard shakes. It finally glops out of the jar, down through the gaps into the shadowy darkness below.

I take out my water bottle and pour some into the jar, slosh it around, and pour that down the sewer too. Need to account for every last drop.

"It's the right thing," Spooner says.

"Yeah, for sure," Pete agrees.

"On to step two, then," I say. "Beanie, you have the concrete?"

We're back at Isaac's grave, Beanie's concrete at the ready to patch up the magical snail shell, make sure the ink will never again flow out of it.

I have the idea that, just like the Jewish tradition of everyone shoveling in dirt at the burial, we should each take a turn spreading some concrete over the magical snail shell's opening. Because this is, in a way, the death of something. Or, at the very least, a definitive end.

I also like that it's concrete as a final tribute to Brickman. Feels right.

So, one by one, we take the plastic spreader, dip it into the bucket of concrete patch Beanie and Lynsey got from C&D Hardware, and spread it over the shell jutting out of the side of my great-great-grandfather's tombstone.

As I stare at the engraved name "Isaac King," he suddenly flashes into my mind:

Home is always with you. Do you know where?

And he pointed to my head and to my chest.

And so did the mermaid.

I get it.

So many places can be home.

So many people can be home.

People we see every day.

People who are gone.

I know Aunt Betty will always be a part of me.

So will Isaac, even though I've never actually met the guy.

And Brooklyn and Coney Island will too, even if I'm in Manhattan.

Even if I *stay* in Manhattan.

I don't have to run away from who I was.

I don't have to run away from who I'm becoming.

I can hold Monster Club in my heart along with my new friends. My new life.

All of it is me.

"I think that's everyone," Yoo says, holding up the concrete spreader.

"Yeah," I say, taking in all my friends. "I think so."

EPILOGUE

By the time he gets back home to his family's West Village brownstone, Pete is buzzing with excitement. He's pretty much been buzzing the entire week, still in disbelief about what he saw on Monday, what they all went through.

But he's also amped about this new bond he's formed, with Sketch and all of Sketch's friends. Even that Spooner kid, who's always seemed to despise him, has been friendly. It's sort of amazing. As new as these friendships are, they somehow already feel *realer* than what he has with Bobo and Knapp. That's why Pete went down to Brooklyn to seal up the gravestone. He feels like he's a part of something.

These are not the only reasons for his excitement, though.

Dad is finally home from his weeklong trip to LA.

And Pete has something to show him.

He runs to his room, crouches down to the titanium safe in his closet that his aunt and uncle gave him for his bar mitzvah. He types in the code, and the door opens.

Pete pulls out a water bottle.

It's one-third full with a sludgy, black, terrible-smelling substance.

When Sketch gave Pete permission to make a new StarPower on that insane day earlier this week, Pete went into Sketch's backpack for the marker, and, well . . . he'd spotted the last mason jar of ink.

So he'd taken some.

How could he not? He'd seen what it could do! The possibilities!

He knows they all just agreed to get rid of the ink for good, and he understands the thinking behind that. But in the hands of someone as smart as his father, it seems like an exception could be made.

Dad will be so impressed. And so grateful. He'll probably have a zillion ideas for how to use this stuff to help all his high-profile talent. Pete has already been imagining real-life monsters onstage with The 1975 at one of their concerts.

The crowd would go absolutely nuts.

"Hey, Dad," Pete says, knocking on the door to his office. "I'm so glad you're home. I, uh, know you don't like to be interrupted, but I have something you really gotta see. . . ."

ACKNOWLEDGMENTS

Big thanks from the bottom of our monstrous hearts to David Linker, Cait Hoyt, Cat Hobbs, Ronald Kurniawan, Jim Rugg, Matt Furie, and the entire team at HarperCollins. Thanks also to Mark Twain Intermediate School, Books are Magic, Vroman's, and all the other booksellers, librarians, and educators who do such an incredible job of getting books into the hands of young readers.